Mary Francis Cusack

The Lives of Saint Columba and Saint Brigit

Mary Francis Cusack

The Lives of Saint Columba and Saint Brigit

ISBN/EAN: 9783337340940

Printed in Europe, USA, Canada, Australia, Japan

Cover: Foto ©Raphael Reischuk / pixelio.de

More available books at **www.hansebooks.com**

THE LIVES

OF

SAINT COLUMBA

AND

SAINT BRIGIT.

𝔅𝔞𝔩𝔩𝔞𝔫𝔱𝔶𝔫𝔢 ℜ𝔯𝔢𝔰𝔰
BALLANTYNE, HANSON AND CO.
EDINBURGH AND LONDON

THE LIVES

OF

SAINT COLUMBA

AND

SAINT BRIGIT.

BY

M. F. CUSACK,

AUTHOR OF "THE LIFE OF ST. PATRICK, APOSTLE OF IRELAND,"
"JESUS AND JERUSALEM," ETC. ETC.

*" Death is better in reproachless Erinn,
Than perpetual life in Alba."*

KENMARE SERIES.
LIVES OF IRISH SAINTS.

LONDON:
BURNS & OATES, 17 PORTMAN STREET.
DUBLIN: H. GILL, AND KENMARE PUBLICATION OFFICE.
1877.

Emprimatur.

✠ D. MORIARTY, *Epis. Ker.*

Contents.

CHAPTER V.

CHAPTER VI.

The Life of St. Brigit.

THE LIFE OF SAINT COLUMBA.

CHAPTER I.

INTRODUCTION.

THE Church never dies. How, indeed, can it, since its founder is Divine and ever living? Human systems are perishable because they are human. Had the Church of God been of human origin, it would never have withstood the shocks of centuries, the relentless persecution of tyrants, the yet more dangerous assault of temporal prosperity, for there have been moments—supreme moments—in which the Church has had to govern, if it did not rule, the world.

Again and again the cry has gone up from the evil one in the abodes of darkness through his instruments on earth, The Church shall perish. When this Pontiff dies there will be no one to succeed him. When a Pius departs we shall have a new ruler, with more liberal voice, who shall overthrow the ark of

A

God by laying impious hands on the works and edicts of his predecessors. When this revolution has been accomplished we shall hear no more of Popery. When these cruel persecutors have done their work there will be no more of the faithful left to receive or to administer Sacraments.

Quare fremuerunt gentes. Why do the heathen rage? Why do they meditate such folly? Are they not yet wearied with defeat? are they not yet dispirited by repeated failure of their predictions? It would seem not. Ever and again we hear them repeated anew, reasserted with fresh confidence, reiterated with new assurance; yet even as the echo of the false prophecy dies away, the Church comes forth brighter and stronger, and yet more firmly established, through the very storm which was to have caused its ruin.

It would seem time for the enemies of God to have learned their impotence, yet we know that these things shall be until the end.

And everywhere in the bitter strife between the world and the Church, the Irish people have taken a foremost rank in the battle. When Europe was over-run with barbarous hordes, the Irish monk went forth to evangelise and to civilise its people. That this is no idle boast, no vaunting of a mere national vanity, we have already shown,* and that this is admitted by English writers at the present day, we have given

* In our *History of the Irish Nation.*

sufficient proof. Montalembert, the glory of France, and the faithful son of the Catholic Church, has poured forth his ardent tribute of praise to the zeal and devotion of the Irish Celt in the early ages of the Church. The credit of this great historian has never been impeached, and if his eloquence makes truth more beautiful, it is none the less true. He says :—

" A characteristic still more distinctive of the [Irish] monks, as of all their nation, was the imperious necessity of spreading themselves without, of seeking or carrying knowledge and faith afar, and of penetrating into the most distant regions to watch or combat paganism. This monastic nation, therefore, became the missionary nation *par excellence.* While some came to Ireland to procure religious instruction, the Irish missionaries launched forth from their island. They covered the land and seas of the West. Unwearied navigators, they landed on the most desert islands ; they overflowed the Continent with their successive immigrations. They saw in incessant visions a world known and unknown to be conquered for Christ. The Poem of the Pilgrimage of St. Brandon, that monkish Odyssey so celebrated in the Middle Ages, that popular prelude of the *Divina Commedia,* shows us the Irish monks in close contact with all the dreams and wonders of the Celtic ideal. Hereafter we shall see them struggling against the reality ; we shall speak of their metropolis upon the rock of Iona, in the Hebrides ; we shall tell what they did for the conversion of Great Britain. But we must follow them first into Gaul, that country from which the Gospel had been carried to them by Patrick. Several had already reached Armorica with that invasion of Celtic refugees which we have described in the preceding Book. But it was only in the end of the sixth century that the action of Ireland upon the countries directly subjected to Frank dominion became decisive. She thus generously repaid her debt to Gaul. She had received Patrick from Gaul ; in return, she sent Columbanus."

For a few centuries the cruel hand of persecution
proved a grievous hindrance to Irish missionary work.
But patient suffering of undeserved and cruel wrongs
prepared the ground for a yet richer harvest.　Truly
the Irish priest is everywhere.　In the burning sun
of India, on the arid wastes of Africa, in the desolate
lands around the northern Pole; in America, on the
Continent, and in the islands of the sea, the Irish
priest does his Master's work, and evangelises as truly
as Columbcille or Columbanus.　Yes, and even to
ungrateful England he repays the debt of vengeance,
as his Divine Lord repaid His enemies, by suffering
and working for her.　Truly, he takes a new revenge
upon his ancient foe.　Let the priests of Irish birth,
or of Irish descent, be taken from the English mission ; let the congregations of native Irish, or their
descendants, be taken from "Saxon-land," and it will
be left to a few of the rich and great ones of this world
to stand alone for the faith against an overwhelming
multitude.

But our principal object in these introductory
remarks is not so much to show what the Irish priest
has done, as what he has taught.　It is a subject of
grave importance.　Efforts have been made again and
again to undermine the faith of the Irish people by a
fanatical zeal, sometimes respectable for its earnestness
and honesty, but too often contemptible for the means
used.　And the grand, the crowning argument of such
fanaticism, has been that the faith taught by the Irish

priests of to-day is very different from the faith taught by Patrick and Columba, and practised by St. Brigit and St. Ita. Nothing could be more false; and honest Protestant clergymen have been themselves the very first to disprove it. If the Rev. Dr. Todd, in his Life of St. Patrick, has done his best to make the Saint a Protestant, the Rev., and not less gifted, Dr. Reeves has put together a mass of evidence which, though he does not intend it for such a purpose, proves beyond cavil, beyond question, that Ireland was Catholic, and, if you will, Roman, at the very same period.

And the facts which go to prove this assertion, an assertion which is of so much importance and interest to us all, are equally available, and valuable as proofs that our religion has not changed with the lapse of ages. What Christ taught to His Apostles, St. Patrick taught to us; and what St. Patrick taught to us, his successor, the Primate of all Ireland, teaches to-day. Not in one word is there a change, not in one iota is there a difference. Nor do we ask the reader to take this assertion on mere *ipse dixit*. The Life of St. Columba and St. Brigit will give ample proof; but as it is most desirable that we should all have accurate and perfectly reliable information on this important subject, we proceed now to draw attention to some special points.

And first, one of the greatest charges against the Catholic Church has been that she is Roman. It has been asserted, again and again, that the Irish were not originally subject to the Roman See, as they are now—that there was a time when they were "independent," as if any tree could have living "branches" which did not belong to itself.

Long ages before the name Protestant was ever heard, the Holy Scriptures were the special care of our Irish saints—they copied them, they preserved them, they taught from them, and in these Scriptures they learned, as we also learn, that there is but one Lord, one FAITH, one Baptism. Two Gods there could not be; nor could there be two different faiths, or forms of belief, equally true.

If, indeed, there were many Gods, there might be many religions, but the one God could only teach the one Faith, and ordain the one Baptism.

The Bible also tells us how our Lord made Peter chief and head of His Church. To all His Apostles He gave authority to teach, and to baptize, and to offer, as priests, the Adorable Sacrifice ; to Peter only He said, "On this rock will I build My Church." For nineteen hundred years the gates of hell and the powers of darkness have been in vain dashing themselves against this rock. But it stands unmoved; and to-day Pius teaches in Rome what Peter taught in Rome at the close of the first century of the Christian era. To-day Pius is persecuted because he teaches this faith,—then Peter was martyred because he taught it.

Christ said, " On this rock will I build My Church," and this is what Patrick and Columba taught. The proofs are simple and undeniable. We have still, thank God, some most ancient Irish manuscripts, of the authenticity of which there is no question. One of these manuscripts is called the Tripartite Life of St. Patrick, and is translated in full in the quarto edition of the present work. The copies which still exist of this work are very ancient. Jocelyn, who wrote in 1185, mentions it, and says it was written by *St. Eimhin* [Evin]; this is unquestionable authority. St. Evin lived about the year 500-520, and was the founder of the Church of Monasterevin.

In this Life he says :—

" When Patrick heard this thing [*i.e.*, the failure of the mission of St. Palladius], and knew that it was for him God designed the Apostleship of Erinn, he went subsequently to Rome to receive *grade ;* and it was Celestinus, Abbot of Rome [*i.e.*, Pope], who read *Grada* [conferred orders] over him, Germanus and Amatho, king of the Romans, being present."

Another extract on the same subject can scarcely fail to interest the reader, and to satisfy the most sceptical :—

" Patrick having set out for Rome after visiting the shrines of the Apostles with devout veneration, found favour with Pope Celestine, who was the forty-fifth from St. Peter. This Pope, as the conversion of nations belongs by right to the successors of St. Peter (cum successori Petri jure incumbat conversio gentium), had already sent the illustrious Deacon Palladius, with the apostolic number of twelve companions, to preach and announce the Word of God to the Irish."

In the annotations of Tirechan, contained in that part of the Book of Armagh which, as Dr. Graves has remarked, was evidently becoming illegible when the present copy was made from it more than a thousand years ago, we find the following express testimony to the Roman mission of our Saint :—

"In the thirteenth year of the Emperor Theodosius, the Bishop Patrick was sent by Celestine, Bishop and Pope of Rome, to instruct the Irish. Bishop Palladius was first sent, who was also called Patrick by a second name, and he was martyred among the Scots, as the old saints have said. Then the second Patrick was sent by the angel of God, Victor, and by Pope Celestine. All Ireland believed, and nearly all were baptized by him."

In the Vita Quarta, attributed to St. Eileran the Wise, who died A.D. 664, the Roman mission of St. Patrick is also attested thus :—

"St. Germanus sent the blessed Patrick to Rome, that thus he might receive the sanction (licentia) of the Bishop of the Apostolic See to go forth and preach, for so order requireth (sic enim ordo exigebat); and Patrick having come to Rome, was honourably received by the holy Pope Celestine; and relics of the Saints being given to him, he was sent into Ireland by the same Pope."

Perhaps the simplest and best evidence on this subject is that of the Saint himself. In the Life of St. Patrick by Probus, he records the following prayer of St. Patrick :—

"O Lord Jesus Christ . . . conduct me now, I beseech Thee, to the See of the Holy Roman Church, that receiving there the mission to preach with confidence, the Irish tribes may become Christian through me."

In truth, St. Patrick could not have undertaken such a mission without the express sanction of the See of Rome, and without obtaining jurisdiction from the then reigning Pontiff, so that even if the various writers of his Life had not alluded to the subject, there could be no question raised about it by those who were even cursorily acquainted with the ecclesiastical history of the period. Happily, however, as the subject is one of great interest, and which, for controversial reasons, it is important to prove beyond cavil, we can give extraneous evidence that the accounts of the early Irish biographers of St. Patrick were substantially correct. St. Eric, or Hericus, of Auxerre, the biographer of St. Germanus, is an independent and credible authority. He writes thus of the connection between St. Germanus and St. Patrick, and the Roman mission of the latter :—

" And as Germanus saw him magnanimous in religion, eminent for virtue, strenuous in the sacred ministry, and thinking it unfit that so strong a husbandman (robustissimum agricolam) should be inactive in the culture of the harvest of the Lord, he sent him to holy Celestine, the Pope of the city of Rome, accompanied by his own priest, Segetius, who might bear testimony to his ecclesiastical probity at the Apostolic See. Being thus approved by its judgment, supported by its authority, and strengthened by its blessing, he journeyed to Ireland, and, being given to that people as their chosen apostle, he enlightened the whole nation then by his preaching and miracles, as he continues to do at the present day, and will so for ever continue to do, by the wonderful privileges of his apostolate."

But the evidence on this all-important subject can

be obtained from other than Irish sources. An English
writer, who had ample opportunities of obtaining correct information, gives his evidence in the year 882.
In his *Historia Brittonum*, Bishop Marcus says :—

"Under divine guidance, Patrick was instructed in the Sacred
Scriptures, and then he went to Rome, and remained there a long
time studying, and, being filled with the Holy Ghost, learning the
Holy Scriptures and the Sacred Mysteries. And whilst he was
there applying himself to these pursuits, Palladius was sent by
Pope Celestine as first bishop to convert the Irish to Christ; but
God, by some storms and signs, prevented his success, and no one
can receive aught on earth unless it be given to him from above.
This Palladius, returning from Ireland to Britain, died there in the
land of the Picts. The death of Bishop Palladius being known, the
patricians, Theodosius and Valentinian, being the Roman rulers,
Patrick was sent by Pope Celestine, the angel of God, Victor,
accompanying, guiding, and assisting him, and by Bishop Germanus,
to convert the Irish to the belief in the Holy Trinity."

As the Life of St. Patrick, which we have already written, and the Life of St. Columba afford ample evidence
on this subject, we pass to another point, our only object
here being to give a compendium which can be easily
retained and used when it is necessary to give proofs
to those who differ from us. Now we have not only
evidence of the veneration of our Irish Saints for the
See of Rome, and their acknowledgment of the primacy
of Peter, but we have also the not less important
evidence of what doctrine was taught by the Popes of
Rome when St. Patrick and our Irish Saints went
thither to reverence the relics of St. Peter. It was
then that St. Leo, Pope, spoke to those who had

assembled from all parts of the world in the fourth and fifth centuries of the Christian era, even as they do at the present day. St. Leo's sermons are still happily preserved. In one of these he says :—

"The presence of my venerable brethren and fellow-bishops (consacerdotum), in itself desirable and so highly appreciated by me, becomes more sacred and more religious, if in the celebration of this feast they intend principally to honour him (St. Peter) whom they know to be the bishop, not of this see alone, but the primate of all bishops.

"St. Peter was chosen among the whole human race, and placed over the vocation of all nations, and over all the apostles and all the fathers of the Church, so that, though there are many priests and many bishops over the people of God, all are really governed by Peter who are under the sovereign government of Christ."

St. Patrick having obtained his mission or authority from Rome, we next proceed to note what doctrines were taught by him, and by St. Columba and the saints who followed him ; what St. Bridget believed, and what she taught to those who were under her guidance. We begin with the Sacrifice of the Mass. Certainly there was no doubtful teaching about this stupendous mystery. Happily ample and authentic evidence remains as to the teaching of the Holy Catholic Church on this subject from the earliest ages.

It could not be otherwise. The Adorable Sacrifice is the central doctrine of the Holy Catholic Church. All heretics have seen this, all schismatics have known it. The very foremost accusation against the Church, that it is a religion of "priestcraft," proves it. Yet those who make this rash assertion forget to examine that very Bible for which they profess so much veneration; and if we point to the simple and sublime teaching contained there on the Sacred Mysteries, they turn away with an evasion or indifference.

And we may here add, perhaps, one of the most extraordinary and marvellous anticipations of the Protestant heresy that could have been supposed possible.

We have briefly shown the deep reverence which the Irish entertained for the Holy See as the chair of Peter from the first year of their conversion to Christianity.

In the year 630 there had been a discussion in the Synod of Maghlene, into which it is not necessary to enter here. The subject was the time of keeping Easter. St. Cummian was one of the most noteworthy prelates who assisted there, and this is what he says :—

"What can be deemed more injurious to Mother Church than to say, Rome errs, Jerusalem errs, Alexandria errs, Antioch errs, the whole world is in error, only the Scots and the Britons know what is right ?"

And thus he shows how the Irish Church had always retained what was taught to them "from the successors of the apostles of the Lord." The question was only one of discipline, not one of faith ; and the Irish Church, as it has always done, submitted to the See of Peter, not only in faith, but in practice.

Hundreds of years passed away.

The Irish were asked to change their faith, or rather

to deny it, at the beck of a licentious tyrant; and what did these new teachers say? what did they publicly declare? They said "that Rome had erred, that Jerusalem had erred, that Antioch had erred, not only in matters of practice, but in matters of FAITH;" and this amazing statement is still on record, word for word, as we have given it here, and is printed in every Protestant prayer-book, and every Protestant clergyman is obliged to sign and attest his belief in thirty-nine articles, one of which containing this statement was prophetically condemned a thousand years before it was written.

So that the very words of this Protestant article was actually condemned ages before it was written by an Irish saint.

If this strange fact were put before intelligent and educated Protestants, it might tend to very serious reflections as to the advisability of belonging to a Church which, in its own articles, declares that it is liable to err in matters of faith. Certainly educated and intelligent Protestants would think very differently of the persecution to which Irish Catholics were subjected, when they were asked to forsake an infallible Church for one which, while it cruelly persecuted them for not accepting its form of belief, declared at the same time that the same form of belief was quite as likely to be false as true.

On the subject of the Mass we have the most positive and undeniable evidence. There is a manuscript still in existence called the Stowe Missal. This manuscript is written in peculiar writing, and its value and antiquity is maintained by an eminent Irish Protestant scholar, the late Dr. Todd, of Trinity College, Dublin.

He says, "The original manuscript was written in an ancient Lombardic character, which may well be deemed older than the sixth century." And he also states, "It is by no means impossible that the MS. may have been the original missal of St. Ruadhan himself, the founder of the Monastery of Lothra, who died A.D. 584."

The learned Bishop of Ossory thus describes this most precious manuscript :—

"The Mass begins with the Litanies of the Saints, which are preceded by the Antiphon Peccavimus. Then follows the Gloria in Excelsis Deo, with Collect or Prayer, and the Lesson from the First Epistle to the Corinthians, chapter xi., relating to the blessed Eucharist. In the versicle which follows, the blessing of salvation is asked for 'those who are present at the sacrifice.' The Gospel is that of St. John, in the sixth chapter. The Creed, too, forms part of the Mass, which is a remarkable peculiarity of the missal at so early a period, for the use of the Creed did not become general in the Church until many years later. What, however, is most important for our present purpose, not only are the words of consecration given as used at the present day, but also the subsequent prayers, 'agreeing literally with the Roman Canon down to the memento for the dead,' and thus, as of the nineteenth century, so in the Church of our sainted fathers of the sixth century, was used that beautiful prayer—'Humbly we beseech Thee, O Almighty God, command this offering to be carried by the hands of Thy holy angel unto Thy heavenly altar in the presence of Thy divine Majesty, that all of us who receive through the participation of this altar the most holy Body and Blood of Thy Son, may be filled with every heavenly blessing and grace, through the same Christ our Lord.'"

Such is the language of this venerable manuscript, whose writing, to use the words of Dr. Todd, is of itself a sufficient guarantee that "it is certainly not later than the sixth century."

In addition to the everyday Mass, the Missa Justotidiana, this missal presents to us a "Missa Apostolorum," a "Missa Martyrum," a "Missa Sanctorum et Sanctarum Virginum," also a Mass "pro pœnitentibus vivis," and, in fine, a "Missa pro mortuis." Surely this must be confessed to be a very un-Protestant-looking record of the faith of our fathers in the sixth century.

We have not space here to go more fully into this subject, and must turn with reluctance from a mass of evidence of a similar kind. There is, however, one other proof we may not leave unmentioned.

A written tradition, as ancient as the time of St. Patrick, records that a hymn, which commences with the *Sancti venite, Christi corpus,* was sung by angels when St. Patrick arrived at the Church of St. Sechnall during the Offertory. It is at least certain that this hymn was sung for centuries at the Offertory and during the Elevation in all the churches of Ireland, and it is also admitted on all sides that the original manuscript of this hymn, which is still extant, dates

back to very near the time of St. Patrick. We give
a translation of the hymn here in full :—

" Approach you who are holy,
  Receive the body of Christ,
  Drinking the sacred blood
  By which you are redeemed.

" Saved by the body
  And blood of Christ,
  Now nourished by it
  Let us sing praises unto God.

" By this sacrament
  Of the body and blood,
  All are rescued
  From the power of hell.

" The Giver of salvation,
  Christ, the Son of God,
  Redeemed the world
  By His cross and blood.

" For the whole world
  The Lord is offered up ;
  He is at the same time
  High priest and victim.

" In the law it is commanded
  To immolate victims :
  By it were foreshadowed
  These sacred mysteries.

" The Giver of all light,
  And the Saviour of all,
  Now bestows upon the holy
  An exceeding great grace.

" Let all approach,
  In the pure simplicity of faith ;
  Let them receive the eternal
  Preserver of their souls :

> "The Guardian of the Saints,
>   The Supreme Ruler and Lord,
>   The Bestower of eternal life
>   On those who believe in Him.
>
> "To the hungry He gives to eat
>   Of the heavenly food ;
>   To the thirsty He gives to drink
>   From the living fountain.
>
> "The Alpha and Omega,
>   Our Lord Christ Himself
>   Now comes ; He who shall one day come
>   To judge all mankind."

It is worth noting that a Protestant German writer, who had more love for archæology than Catholicity, left out the third verse of this hymn when he published it in his collection, and honourably gave his reason for doing so.

Of the Sacrament of Penance a brief notice must suffice. In a Penitential, or rule for the public and other penances which were so rigorously exacted in the early Church, we find the following :—

"When Christ commanded the girl that was dead to arise, He directed that food should be brought to her ; that is, when she was perfectly restored to health, and no longer detained in her infirmities, for she was healed by the Redeemer in the presence of Peter, James, and John, and also of her father and mother ; so, too, each one of us having confessed his sins, and eradicated them from his soul, and being enriched with the grace of God in the presence of his heavenly Father and of the Church, may, when strengthened by good works, receive the sacrifice."

And in the Penitential of St. Columbanus we find the following canon :—

C

"Special diligence must be used in confessing our sins and imperfections before the celebration of Mass, lest with an unclean heart we should approach the holy altar.   It is better to delay a little, and wait till our hearts be free from scandal and envy, than audaciously to approach to the judgment-seat; for the altar is the *tribunal of Christ, and His body, present there with His blood, judges those who unworthily approach.*   It is, therefore, not only from heinous crimes that we must be free before approaching to communicate, but also from the lesser faults and the infirmities of our sinful soul, that thus we may be possessors of true peace and sharers of eternal blessedness." [1]

We have elsewhere given very full details of the Brehon Laws, the most famous Code in existence. This work contains also a treatise on the Rights and Duties of the Church and Churchmen.   The following extract shows the deep reverence with which the priest was treated in Ireland from the very time of St. Patrick :—

"Every one who does not respect the rule of the spiritual director who is placed over him is not obedient to God or man; he is not entitled to have communion administered to him, neither should his requiem be chanted nor his burial be allowed in the Church of God, because it was he that refused to be obedient to God in the churches of the land Erin.   For the manner in which those who are in holy orders ought to be respected, and their directions

---

[1] "Essays on the Early Irish Church," by the Right Reverend Monsignor Moran.   We may note, too, as an eminent example of the custom by which the priest only receives in one kind when he is communicated by another priest, that when St. Patrick was dying we are told how he "received the Body of Christ." It is, of course, quite unnecessary to enter into such subjects as far as Catholics are concerned, for we know that the faith and teaching of the Catholic Church has never altered; but it is well, indeed, for Catholics to be able to give proof of this to others, and proof that cannot be contradicted.

followed, is the same as if they were the angels of God among men ; because it is through them the kingdom of heaven is gained—*by baptism and communion and chanting of prayers, and the sacrifice of the body of Christ and of His blood,* and the preaching of the Gospel, and the building of the churches of God."

But there is no subject in connection with our holy religion which has been treated with such opposition as the power which God has given to His Saints to work miracles, and the supernatural manifestations with which, by His Divine promise, they have been favoured. It is strange that it should be so, since the Bible, from Genesis to Revelation, is full of such subjects, since in the New Testament we are told that our Divine Lord Himself assured His disciples that miracles should continue. But they were to continue only in the one true Church, because, being worked by the power of God, such favours could not be granted to those who were outside His fold.

We are told in the Bible that the very "shadow" of St. Peter cured those who had diseases, and that this was so well known that the people brought their sick out into the streets and places where he passed. We are told how an angel was sent to free him from his chains, and to release him from prison. Now it is quite clear that all this was done by the power of God, that it was not by the power of St. Peter himself ; and it is equally clear that God could allow any other Saint to have similar power if it so pleased His Divine Majesty. And so we find when our Irish

Saints went to convert heathen nations, where great miracles were necessary to prove their mission, that they also were gifted with most marvellous power. On this subject we shall say no more, as the Life of St. Columba will amply prove it.

The Life of St. Brigit, too, has a very special lesson for us, and one of the deepest interest. Although we cannot say that she was the first Irish nun, yet she was certainly one of the first of that long line of saintly Irish maidens who have left all to follow their Spouse Jesus. Her life, too, is full of miracles of Divine love, and may well be the subject of our constant meditation and our thankful praise.

CHAPTER II.

ADAMNAN, the Irish monk and writer to whom we are indebted for the biography of St. Columba, was almost a contemporary of that Saint. He tells us that he conversed with those who had known St. Columba, and that he took the most accurate pains to be correctly informed on every subject on which he wrote. It is important that this assertion of the Saint should be well noted. It is contained in the preface which he wrote to St. Columba's Life, and these are his words :—

"In relating the life and character of our Columba [nostri Columbæ], I shall, in the first place, and with few words, give a brief summary, and place before the eyes of my reader his holy life.

"I will also briefly record his miracles for the purpose of exciting a desire for the full details which shall be given in the three last books. Of these books the first shall contain his prophetical revelations; the second, his Divine miracles; the third shall contain the angelic apparitions, and the celestial favours and lights granted to this man of God. Let no one suppose that I wrote of this great man what is false, or what I consider doubtful, or uncertain." [1]

And then he goes on to assure his readers, if possible yet more earnestly, that what he has written is founded on what he has heard from trustworthy men, or obtained from written authority, or from what he has heard himself from the more ancient monks, who had ample opportunity of knowing the truth of all they said.

Now, there are several points of very special importance to be noted here. First, we must observe the brief space of time which elapsed between the death of St. Columba and the writing of his Life by St. Adamnan.

St. Columba was born about the year 520. He established his monastery at Hy about the year 560, and he died, according to the annals of the Four Masters, A.D. 592. The date of St. Adamnan's birth is uncertain, but it must have occurred about the year 624. One date, however, is ascertained beyond question. In the year 679 he was elected Abbot of the very monastery of Hy which St. Columba founded. It will, therefore, be at once evident that though St. Adamnan was not contemporary with St. Columba, nor his successor in office, there was yet quite a

---

[1] Nemo itaque me de hoc tam prædicabili viro aut mentitum æstimet, etc.

sufficient nearness in the time at which they flourished to afford every opportunity for accurate knowledge.

There were many monks in that famous monastery who had received from their immediate predecessors ample details of this wonderful and saintly life, and, as St. Adamnan tells us so expressly, many of these details had been committed to writing.

But there is another point to be carefully observed also.

St. Adamnan has written two prefaces to the Life of St. Columba. He commences each preface thus : "In the Name of Jesus Christ." In the first preface he tells us that he wrote at the request of his brethren; in the second preface we have the passage above quoted. Now, it is evident that he anticipated some doubts as to the truth of the miracles which he has recorded, and he has therefore taken pains to make such doubts utterly untenable.

He tells us, especially and carefully, that he would not state a falsehood, and, not only so, but that he would not record anything "doubtful or uncertain," and, furthermore, he points out the plain and undeniable fact, that he had the best possible opportunities for ascertaining the truth. He lived so soon after the death of the Saint of whom he writes. He governed the very monastery the Saint had founded ; and he was surrounded by holy men who had heard all these things from those who preceded them, and who had been St. Columba's companions.

Granted, no Catholic can deny this, that miracles
are not only possible but probable ; that they not
only may happen, but that they are quite certain to
happen from time to time in God's Church.   There
is, then, no reason why we should question any of the
circumstances which St. Adamnan tells, as he has
had such opportunities of knowing, and has been at
such pains to verify.   We might almost think that
he had anticipated and prepared for coming ages of
unbelief.

We have said St. Adamnan was born about the
year 624.   There is no record of the place of his
birth, but it is supposed to have been in the barony
of Tirhugh, in the present county of Donegal.

Adamnan himself has left us a clue to the place of
his nativity in a few touching lines concerning the
marvels which were seen by holy persons at the death
of St. Columba.   He says that he himself saw a holy
old man, "a servant of Christ" (as truly all our Irish
fathers were), who told him he was fishing with others
on the night on which St. Columba made his blessed
migration from earth to heaven.   Suddenly he saw
the whole atmosphere illuminated, and then he saw a
pillar of fire as it were rising up, and giving forth such
brilliant light that the whole earth was illuminated
as a summer day at noon.   The light was seen also
by other parties of fishermen, who beheld it with
equal awe.

It was in the river Finn that this monk (St. Ernan)

was fishing, and it was at Drumhone the old Saint had lived.[1] Hence it is a fair inference that Adamnan lived there in his youth. It is certain, also, that his clan lived in this part of Ireland. His father, Ronan, was sixth in descent from Conall Gulban, the head of one of the two great branches of the northern Hy Nial. He was related also to St. Columba, and to many of the Irish monarchs. His mother, Ronnat, has the honour of being noted in the Book of Lecan in the catalogue (*De Matribus Sanctorum Hiberniæ*) of the mother of the Saints of Ireland. She was also descended from the royal race of the *Cinel Enna*, whose patrimony lay between the Foyle and the Swilly in the modern barony of Raphoe.

But one brief anecdote remains of St. Adamnan's early life. It would appear that, like other Irish students, he went from one monastic house to another to obtain the educational advantages which were then so abundant in Ireland. St. Columba had studied at Clonard, in Meath, and it was at least in this neighbourhood that Adamnan must have been when he met Finnachta the festive, a chief of the Southern Hy Nial, and afterwards monarch of Ireland. As the Prince came up with a numerous retinue, Adamnan, then a youth, was carrying a jar of milk which he had

---

[1] The river Finn, where this miracle was witnessed, rises at Lough Finn, county Donegal. The valley of the Finn, where these holy men were fishing, is a picturesque glen in the parish of Kilteevoge. Drumhone parish is between the town of Donegal and Ballyshannon.

begged for the support of some of his fellow-students. In escaping from the crowd he stumbled, and the jar fell and was broken. But the Prince begged him not to concern himself, and promised him his protection. The narrative then goes on to state that Adamnan informed Finnachta that he was one of the five attendants on "three godly students," for whom they took it in turn to provide.

St. Columba also prophesied St. Adamnan's birth and future fame.

There is incidental evidence that this Saint was distinguished even amongst the distinguished Irish students of his day. He had a critical acquaintance with Greek and Hebrew, and he cites Josephus and several of the Latin poets. An old poem states that Adamnan subsequently became "soul-friend" or spiritual director to Finnachta.

The learned English writer, Bede, gives high testimony to the virtues and learning of the Irish Saint, and the Four Masters say :—

"Adamnan was a good man, according to the teaching of St. Bede, for he was tearful, patient, given to prayer, diligent, ascetic, temperate ; he never used to eat except on Sunday and Thursday ; he made a slave of himself to those virtues ; and, moreover, he was wise and learned in the clear understandings of the Holy Scriptures of God."

One of the most noteworthy undertakings of St. Adamnan's life was the promulgation of the *Cáin-Adamnan* (Law of Adamnan), by which women were forbidden to assist at faction fights. The *Leabhar Breac* and the Book of Lecan give an interesting account of the origin of this Law.

It is said that Adamnan was carrying his mother over the plain of Bregia, where they encountered two armies fighting. Ronnat, the mother of Adamnan, perceived that one of the women was dragging another off the field of combat by a reaping-hook which she had fastened into her breast. Ronnat sat down and declared that she would not rise until her son had promised her that he would exempt the women of Erin for ever from excursions and host-ings. This he readily agreed to do, and took the very first opportunity of fulfilling his promise. It is on record that Adamnan assisted at several Synods.[1] At one of these, it is not certain which, several Laws or Canons were enacted at his desire, and one of them was the desired prohibition.

Adamnan was elected to the Abbacy of Hy in the year 679, about the fifty-fifth year of his age. Here the Saint was able soon to do a great temporal service to his country. Aldfrid, a Northumberland prince, known in Ireland as Flann Fina, had been an intimate friend of the new Abbot while the former was an exile in Ireland. On his restoration to his kingdom, the

---

[1] Adamnan assisted at a Synod held at Derry or Raphoe, and con-vened by Flann Felhla, Abbot of Armagh. This Synod was held about A.D. 695. At Tara there are still traces of an enclosure called the "Rath of the Synods," within which is noted the site of the tent of Adamnan.

Abbot of Hy visited his court to obtain the release of
some Irish men and women who had been carried off
to "Saxon-land" when the English plundered Magh
Breagh.

The account is thus fully given in the Irish
annals :—

"The North Saxons went to Erin and plundered Magh Breagh,
as far as Bealach-duin, and they carried off with them a great prey
of men and women. The men of Erin besought Adamnan to go in
quest of the captives to Saxon-land. Adamnan went to demand
the prisoners, and put in at Tracht-Romra. The strand is long and
the flood rapid—so rapid that if the best steed in Saxon-land,
ridden by the best horseman, were to start from the edge of the
tide, when the tide begins to flow, he could only bring his rider
ashore by swimming, so extensive is the strand and so impetuous is
the tide. The Saxons now were unwilling to permit Adamnan to
land upon the shore. 'Push your curachs on the shore,' said
Adamnan to his people, 'for both their land and their sea are
obedient to God, and nothing can be done without God's permission.' The clerics did as they were told. Adamnan drew a
circle with his crozier around the curachs, and he formed a high
wall of the sea about them, so that the place where they were was an
island, and the sea went to her limits past it, and did them no
injury. When the Saxons had observed this very great miracle,
they trembled for fear of Adamnan, and they gave him his full
demand. Adamnan's demand was that a complete restoration of the
captives should be made to him, and that no Saxon should ever
again go upon a predatory excursion to Erin; and Adamnan
brought back all the captives."

The result was that "Adamnan conducted sixty
captives to Ireland."

It would appear from the account given by Bede

that he was employed to conduct some political negotiations also.[1]

But the most important public event of the Saint's life was the part he took in the famous Paschal controversy, and this very subject is not one of the least interesting or least important evidences of the close connection between Ireland and Rome at this early age. We can only treat briefly on the subject here.

A controversy had arisen as to the exact time at which the great feast of Easter should be celebrated. The dispute ran high, and it needed the good offices of St. Irenæus to remind the disputants that there was no question of faith involved, but only one of practice. The General Council of Nice, A.D. 325, decided that the Roman observance should be followed. But Ireland and distant nations had yet to be converted, and it need scarcely be observed that intercourse with other

---

[1] We cannot help here noting and commenting on the miserable fatuity by which such support is given in Ireland towards English publications which are totally and often bitterly opposed, not only to our religion, but actually to the best proved incidents in our national history. We have the ample testimony of an English writer, Bede, who lived so near the time of Adamnan, to his culture and his learning. Yet a modern Englishman has done his best to discredit that for which there is as much and as strong historical evidence as for the existence of Julius Cæsar. We have elsewhere shown other grave faults in the same work, Wright's " History of Ireland." Bede prized very highly the writings of St. Adamnan, though, if we are to take Mr. Wright's opinion, it is doubtful if he ever existed. We fear it is only in the writing of Irish history or on the Catholic religion that men allow themselves to dilate on subjects of which they are utterly ignorant, on which, it is to be feared, they take no pains to be informed. Happily we have Protestant literary men and clergymen in Ireland of a very different spirit.

countries was not then what it is now. Hence local customs were likely to be observed and preferred until it was plainly shown that they were contrary to the usage of the universal Church. An Irish saint and monk was found to draw the attention of his country-men to the very important question of unity of custom as well as of faith.

This Saint was Cummain, of whom we have already spoken. It was he who anticipated and condemned beforehand the article of the Protestant Church which teaches heresy even in the very words which he used to condemn it.[1]

St. Cummain's argument turned more on the necessity of unity with the Church than on the justice of the decision.

"I turn me," he says, "to the words of the Bishop of Rome, Pope Gregory, whose authority is acknowledged in common by us, and who is gifted with the appellation of the Golden Mouth, and who, though writing last of all the Fathers, is deservedly preferred to all; and I find him writing on the passage of Job, 'Gold hath a place wherein it is melted,' that the gold is the great body of the saints; the place of melting is the unity of the Church; the fire is the offering of martyrdom; and he who is tried by fire out of the unity of the Church may be melted, indeed, but cannot be cleansed."

Then he exclaims :—

"Can anything more pernicious and injurious to Mother Church

---

[1] We cannot help calling attention again to this most curious fact. It is no wonder that the "Reformation" did not take root in Ireland when the chief articles of the new faith teaching the *"fallibility"* of the Church was condemned, we might say prophetically, nearly a thousand years before it was written.

be conceived, than to say Rome errs, Jerusalem errs, Antioch errs, the whole world errs, the Irish and Britons alone are right ?"

And he that be resolved, he says, to "interrogate his fathers, that they might declare to him—and his elders that they might narrate to him." Those whom he interrogated were the neighbouring Bishops of Emly, Clonmacnois, Birr, Mungret, and Clonfertmolva; and these Bishops—

"Having met together in Magh-lene, some being personally present, others sending their legates to represent them, they decreed and said : *Our predecessors, as we know from meet witnesses, of whom some are still living, others now sleep in peace, enacted that we should, humbly and without scruple, receive whatever things were better and more to be esteemed when they were sanctioned by the source of our baptism and faith, and brought to us from the successors of the Lord's Apostles.*

"After this, in accordance with the commandment : if a difference arise between cause and cause, and if judgment shall vary between leprosy and leprosy, they shall go up to the place which the Lord hath chosen ; and with the synodical decree, that *when causes were of great moment, they should be referred to the head of cities* (si causæ fuerint majores), juxta decretum synodicum ad caput urbium sint referendæ), our seniors judged it proper to send wise and humble men as children to their mother (velut natos ad matrem), and, by God's will, some of them, having had a prosperous journey, reached Rome in safety, and returned to us the third year, and saw that all things had been done precisely as had been told to us ; and they were the more convinced of these things, seeing them, than if they merely heard of them ; for, abiding together with Greek, and Oriental, and Scythian, and Egyptian, they found all celebrating together in St. Peter's Church at Easter, and before the Holy of Holies, they attested to us, saying : *Throughout the whole earth, Easter is, as we know, thus kept.* And in the relics, and the Scriptures which they brought with them, we found that there was the blessing of God; for, with our own eyes, we saw a young girl who was blind restored to her sight at these relics; and we saw a paralytic walk, and many wicked spirits cast out." [1]

But Adamnan, though he took the right side warmly, was not as successful with his monks as could have been desired. They did not receive the rule of the universal Church till 696—a few years before his blessed end.

St. Adamnan was the author of a considerable number of works, some of which are still extant. At that period of the world's history, religious were the great and chief promoters of literature, and even nuns were found in the ranks of authors, as well as being the generous supporters of their literary labours.

To be employed in this way was considered a duty and an honour. St. Columba was so devoted to literary pursuits that he was actually occupied in writing

---

[1] This was too plain spoken "Popery" for a Protestant clergyman of the name of King, who wrote a "History" of the Church of Ireland for the avowed purpose of proving that the Irish had always been Protestants. But, like Mr. Wright, who wrote a "History of Ireland," and could not well leave out all that gave honour to our early annals, he felt he had no resource but to omit or to "doctor." Mr. King "doctored," and Mr. Wright omitted; to omit was certainly the more honourable course. Mr. King inserted some sentences of his own in the above paragraph, which he had so printed as to make these appear as if they were part of the original, and so to alter the whole force of the passage. It is a poor religion which must prop itself on such subterfuges.

on the very day of his death. Cassiodorus writes thus to his monks :—

> "I confess that of all the works of manual labour in which you can be engaged, none pleases me more than that of the accurate antiquarian, because his employment instructs by the frequent perusal of Sacred Scriptures, and because it spreads the commandments of God far and wide by transcribing them. Happy thought, industry worthy of all praise, to preach to men with the hand, to open the tongue with the finger, to give mortals this silent means of salvation, and to fight against the evil suggestions of the enemy with pen and ink!"

And Peter, the abbot of the world-renowned Cluni, says :—

> "Shrubs cannot, perhaps, be planted, nor seeds watered, nor any other rural occupation undertaken, on account of monastic retirement. But, what is of greater interest, let the hand be applied to the pen in place of the plough ; let the page be sown with divine letters instead of cultivating the field ; let the seeds of the Word of God be sown on paper, which, when ripe, that is when the books are finished, may fill the hungry reader with manifold fruit, and appease the longing after heavenly bread,—thus truly shall you become a silent preacher of the Word of God ; and though your tongue be silent, your hand shall sound in the ear of many nations with a loud voice. The reward of your labours shall increase after death, as long as the life of your book continues."

Even Hallam, with all his prejudice, observes that "we certainly owe to the Church every spark of learning which then glimmered [in the "Dark" Ages], and which were preserved through that darkness to rekindle the light of a happier age."

The Book of Kells, the rarest and most beautiful of our ancient manuscripts, was written by St. Columba. Of this work O'Curry says :—

"The Book of Kells is no doubt ecclesiastical and scriptural, but this circumstance does not in the least invalidate our claim to originality in the production and combination of the colours used in the vestments there portrayed. On the contrary, the fact of finding them in illuminations such as these, still preserving all their brilliancy, in a book written, perhaps, about A.D. 590, only bears the stronger evidence to the truthfulness of the use of brilliant dyes in the colouring of costumes, to which attention has been directed in the course of these lectures. The purity and brilliancy of the green, the blue, the crimson, the scarlet, the yellow, and the purple of the book, like its penmanship, stand, perhaps, unrivalled, and can only be realised by an actual examination of this very beautiful manuscript itself."

This book, it has been always believed, was written by the hand of St. Columb-Cille himself, the original founder of the church of Ceanannus, now called Kells, in the county of Meath; and the following passage, from the "Annals of the Four-Masters," will show the esteem and veneration in which, from its antiquity and splendour, it was held even at the beginning of the eleventh century :—

"The great gospel of (St.) Columb-Cille was sacrilegiously stolen at night out of the western sacristy of the great stone church at Ceanannus [or Kells]. It was the chief relic of the Western world even as regards its shrine of human workmanship; and it was found in twenty nights and two months, after all its [ornamentation of] gold had been stolen off it, with sods turned over it."[1]

---

[1] Irish ladies were also famous for their skill in Church work. St. Patrick kept three embroideresses constantly occupied; his sister Lupait, Erc, the daughter of King Daire, and Cruunthores of Cenngoen. St. Columba had also his special embroideress, whose name was Coca, from whom Cille Choca, now Kilcock, in the county of Kildare, is named. This pious lady is mentioned in a note to the *Feilire Aenghuis* or *Fes-*

Before concluding this brief notice of the biographers of St. Columba, we can scarcely fail to observe the curious ignorance which English writers display when they write on such subjects.

Prejudice has plainly been the cause. The well-known " Ecclesiastical History of Bede " was re-edited some years since by a Doctor Giles.

He offers the gratuitous remark that he has " strong doubts " of the genuineness of Adamnan's Life of St. Columba, which is well known to be one of the best authenticated of our Irish manuscripts. He showed his capability for criticism by such absurd mistakes of his own that he was called to account by an English writer.

In the beginning of the eighteenth century a presbyterian writer, who did not like the " Romish " views of the Irish saints, also pronounced the history fabulous. Happily we have in our own day Irish Protestant clergymen with less prejudice and more learning.[1]

The churches in Ireland, of which St. Adamnan is patron, or which are dedicated to him, are *Rathbort,*

---

tology of *Aengus,* the *Ceile Dé* or Culdee, at her festival day, the 8th of January. This note is as follows :—" *Ercnat,* the virgin nun, was cook and robemaker to *St. Columb-Cille,* and her Church is Cille Choca [or Kilcock], in *Cairbre na Cairdha* [now Carbury, in the county of Kildare]. *Ercnat* was her true name, which means an embroideress, because *Ercadh* in the ancient Gaedhelic was the same as drawing and embroidering now ; for it was that virgin who was the embroideress, cutter, and sewer of clothes to St. *Columb-Cille* and his disciples."

[1] The Rev. Dr. Reeves, who has written an admirable notice of the Life of St. Columba, and enriched Adamnan's narrative with copious notes. We are indebted to his work for the list of Irish and other churches dedicated to this saint.

now Raphoe, where St. Adamnan's "bed" used to be
shown ; Skreen, in the diocese of Killala, co. Sligo.
Here the chief of Hy Fiachrach bestowed "three
pleasant portions of ground" on St. Columba and his
monks.   St. Adamnan is called here *Awnaun,* and
his well is shown ; indeed, the townland Toberawnaun
takes its name from it.   The bridge of Adamnan is
shown here also.   It is a flag nine feet long, and rests
on two stones in the bed of the river Dunmoran.

The church contained formerly the shrine of St.
Adamnan.   By some this shrine was believed to have
contained his own remains, which were brought to
Ireland in 727.   But Brother Michael O'Cleary gives
a different account, which he says he took from "an
old black and difficult manuscript of parchment."   It
commences thus :—

"Illustrious was this Adamnan.   By him was gathered the great
collection of the relics of the saints into one shrine, and that was
the shrine which Cilline Droictbech, son of Dicolla, brought to Erin
to make peace and friendship between the Cinel Conaill and Cinel
Eoghain."

This *Cilline Droicthech* was fourteenth abbot of Hy.
The shrine contained copies of the Gospels, articles
of clothing belonging to the Irish saints, kept as relics
like the garments which had touched the person of
St. Peter, and which we are told in the Acts of the
Apostles worked so many and such wonderful
miracles.

There were also some relics of St. Paul and of the

Blessed Virgin, to whom the Irish were singularly devout.

Drumhome, in the diocese of Raphoe, of which we have already written ; *Errigal*, in the diocese of Derry, once called *Airecal Adhamhnain* or the habitation of Adamnan ; *Dunbo*, in the same diocese, near Downhill ; *Boveogh*, also in the same county and barony of Keenaght ; *Greallach*, now Templemoyle, diocese of Derry, where traces of his church remain ; *Ballindrat*, in the parish of Clonleigh, diocese of Derry ; *Syonan*, in the diocese of Meath, called "the seat of Adamnan," where it is said he preached to his relatives, the descendants of Fiacha, son of Niall; and *Killonan*, a townland in the parish of Derrygalvin, Co. Limerick.

In the "Breviary" of Aberdeen, Adamnan is commemorated as patron of Turvie, in the parish of Slains, on the east coast of Aberdeen. He is also patron of Forglen, in Banff; the ruins of this chapel still remain. St. Columba's Banner, called the *Breac Bannach*, was formerly kept here. *Aboyne*, in Aberdeenshire ; *Tannadia*, in Forfar, where a rock is shown, called St, Arnold's Seat, for thus has the name of Adamnan been corrupted, as is shown by documents dating back to 1527. The few other names are not noteworthy.

Giolla Adhamhnain, or servant of Adamnan, was early used in Ireland as a Christian name, the Celt ever loving to place his life under the protection of God's chosen ones.

CHAPTER III.

THE EARLY LIFE OF ST. COLUMBA.

THE name of Columba is dear to every Irish heart. The holy Triad—Patrick, Columba, and Briget—are still loved and venerated together.

In life they were not greatly divided. In death they lay in one common grave. The life of Columba, or Columcille, the Dove of the Churches, is characteristic of his name, as still and ever the "dove" of Christ. He had not need like Patrick to fight a spiritual warfare with a heathen people, to do the stern work of a first missionary, and so we find throughout his life that touch of almost fierce tenderness which is inseparable from the union of an ardent nature with mental culture and great sanctity. To him, as to the dear Francis of Assisi, bird and beast and flower told of his Lord's dear love, and he poured forth on them the torrent of a charity almost too great for earth.

One touching anecdote is told of his love for his spiritual children, and his love for God's lowest creatures. Saint-like he devises how to help both without hurt to either.

As he occupied himself, as usual, in writing, a monk named Molua came to him and asked him to bless a knife which he held in his hand. The dear Saint made the sign of the Cross on it, still holding the pen which he was using, and not looking at what he had blessed. His faithful Diarmind was ever near at hand, and to him St. Columba turned, and asked what kind of knife he had blessed. The monk replied it was a knife for killing oxen. "Then," said the Saint, "I trust in my Lord that the knife I have blessed will never wound man or beast." And his desire was fulfilled by Him who loves to accomplish the wishes of His faithful ones. In vain Molua tried the power of his knife, it would hurt nothing, it would not even graze the skin of an animal; and so the monks melted down the iron, and covered all their tools with a thin coating of the metal, and in all Hy neither man nor beast could be hurt again.

In the summer of the year in which he made his migration to the heavenly country, he went hither and thither to see the faces of his children for the last time, to look on the land which had been so dear to him, only, perhaps, less dear than heaven. As he spoke to some of his spiritual children who were engaged in manual labour in the centre of the island, he told them that they would never see him in that place again. And as they grieved for his words, knowing too well his gift of prophecy, he raised his holy hands and blessed the place, saying, " From this time no venomous reptiles shall be able to hurt man or beast in this island, so long as the commandments of Christ are observed."

And to this very day the Saint's benediction holds good. No snakes or vipers have ever been seen in Hy, though they abound on the opposite coast.

It was this wonderful tenderness, this Christ-like love, that made him defer his departure from this world until the Paschal joys were past, lest this gladdest solemnity should be turned into a season of sorrow for his monks.

The materials for the Life and Acts of St. Columba are abundant. Adamnan occupied himself chiefly with the incidents of monastic life, with a record of miracles and supernatural events; but there are other sources of information concerning his public career.

Cummene the Fair had already noted down some circumstances, and Adamnan tells us that he incorporated a considerable part of his manuscript into his own work. He alludes also to another chronicle. Such a life could not but be authentic, for nothing less than a deliberate determination to invent could have built up such a history. And even if any one person was so evilly-disposed as to write down a series of imaginary incidents and pass them for real, there were hundreds to attest the truth or falsehood of what was written.

It is quite true that the life of St. Columba is full of marvels ; and Protestant writers, while admitting its genuineness and antiquity, would fain have these discredited. But if we admit one part of the narrative, we must credit all. The same evidence holds good for all. The monastic chronicle, from which Adamnan copied, was there to be read by the hundred monks of the very monastery where its recorded events had occurred, and there was no haze of distant ages to throw a veil of fancy over a network of facts. Men who had known and conversed with Columba and his monks were still living under the good guidance of Adamnan, and it would, indeed, require a more than Protestant credulity to believe that so many persons would unite in supporting and assisting a series of fictitious narratives.

But there was, if we may say so, even material evidence. The Saint who loved so tenderly could not fail to evoke a tender affection in return ; and when he passed from the love of earth to the charity of heaven, his sorrowful children marked with crosses many sites where wonderful events had occurred. And so they had a cross where Gruan fell dead, and a prophecy of the Saint was fulfilled, that he should not see this holy man ; and they had the stone pillow on which he died.

There were also hymns or metrical compositions in honour of the Saint, of which we shall speak later. One of these was composed by Baithen Mor; another by St. Mura of Fathan, now Fahan, near Inishowen.[1]

The well-known Irish priest and writer, Thomas Messingham, published the life and gave an engraving of the Saint, with the motto, *Quis dabit mihi pennas sicut Columbæ, et volabo, et requiescam.* And, indeed, the wings of this Dove of the Churches ever bore him up and on towards the heavenly country until he took his final flight thither. Father White, a Jesuit, supplied Colgan with the life that he has published in his "Trias Thaumaturga" as the fourth life.[2]

Dr. Reeves, who has published the Latin text of Adamnan, has shown valuable research and care, not only in the republication of the original with various readings, but also in the valuable notes, which double the bulk and value of this volume, and are of interest to every antiquarian as well as to the hagiographer.

The first manuscript, which is, in fact, the basis of

---

[1] An English writer, by no means prejudiced in favour of Ireland or the Catholic faith, has declared the Life of St. Columba to be " the most complete piece of such biography that all Europe can boast of, not only at so early a period, but even through the whole Middle Ages."— *Pinkerton*, Enquiry, pre., vol. i. p. 48.

[2] *Quarta Vita S. Columbæ Abbatis, Scotorum et Pictorum Apostoli, et utriusque Scotiæ Patroni. Authore S. Adamnano Abbate, ex membranis Angliæ Divitis in Germania.*

We must here express our grateful thanks to the Very Rev. Father Guardian of the Franciscan Convent, Merchants' Quay, Dublin, for the loan of this scarce and valuable work.

the text, is a codex of the eighth century, the antiquity and authenticity of which is undeniable. It is signed, as is usual with such manuscripts, by the scribe who copied it. This scribe signs himself *Dorbenens*, and there is little doubt that he was the monk who was elected abbot of Hy in 713, and that this is indeed the very manuscript that he wrote.

Saint Columba was born at Gartan, in the county Donegal, on the 7th of December, on " Thursday of the week-days," probably in the year 521. The date matters little, except to critical scholarship, where such circumstances are justly noted with much controversy.

The author of the " Quinta Vita " tells us that it was towards the middle of the sixth century, making the date later ; he adds, it was " a time when Ireland, the island of saints, was the fruitful mother of as many holy men as there are stars in the firmament."[1] The death of one of old Erin's holy men is recorded on the same day as the birth of Columba—St. Bute, the founder of the glorious old monastery of Monasterboice, was passing to his eternal reward. He spoke of the birth of Columba. "To-day," he said, " a child is born, whose name is Columba, who shall be glorious in the sight of God and men." And in the old martyrologies his birthday is commemorated as the birthday of the immaculate and glorious Columba.

A quatrain commemorating him, and attributed to St. Mura, runs thus :—

[1] " Quinta Vita," Colgan, p. 389.

> " He was born at Gartan by his will,
>   And he was nursed at Cill-Mic-Neoin,
>   And the son of goodness was baptized
>   At Inlach-Dubhglaise of God."

The Latin lives of the Saints are more occupied with his virtues and his miracles than with his history. To the old monks the spiritual life was *the* life, though in truth the Irish religious were not always free from a touch of national or family vanity.

Tradition in Ireland, always so reliable because so coincident with our written and monumental history, long as that was hidden from our people, has pointed out for a thousand years and more the various sites connected with the early history of the Dove of the Churches, the most loving and not the least saintly of the glorious Triad. A group of ecclesiastical remains still exists in the townland of Churchtown, county Donegal, and here is the holy well, the carved cross, and the walls of St. Columba's Chapel. In the townland of Lecknacor, a flag is shown on which it is said the Saint was born, and the people here long held a tradition, that those who sleep thereon before leaving their native land will be free from that "home sickness," that thirst for fatherland, which everywhere characterises the Irish Celt. Strange and touching tradition of a people, ever persecuted in their native land, and yet ever clinging to it, even when wealth and honour might have made them content in exile.

The "grey eye" still looks back upon Erin, whether it travels to "Alba of the Ravens" in the sixth century, or to the Western world in the nineteenth.

> "'Large is the tear of my soft grey eye,
> When I look back upon Erin.'
>
> Melodious her clerics, melodious her birds,
> Gentle her youths, wise her seniors."

Still does the exile cry, "Take my blessing with thee to the West;" and still does he "break his heart for his great love of the gaedhil" of the dear land with its "crowds of white angels." May they assist our souls to-night.[1]

Columba came of a princely race. His father Feidhlimidh was directly descended from Niall of the nine hostages, and he was also closely allied to the Scotch chiefs of Dalriada. His mother Eithne was of a Leinster family, and is commemorated as of saintly life. Columba was baptized by a priest called Cruithnechan at *Inlach - Dubhglaise*, now Temple Douglas, a place about half way between Gartan and Letterkenny. The country people call the place Dooglass; it obtains its name from a little stream the *Dubh-glas* (Black Stream).

Cruithnechan is called "the illustrious priest," and there is a parish in the diocese of Derry now called Kilcronaghan, that is the church or cell of Cruch-

---

[1] The verses are from a poem attributed to St. Columba, which will bé given later on. We write on the evening of the Feast of the Guardian Angels.

nacan, which is probably connected with his memory.
The Saint was baptized by the name of Columb ; the
affix, by which he is distinguished from St. Columbanus, was given to him in a way singularly characteristic of his after life.　It is said he was called so by
the little children whom he used to come out of his
" cell " to meet.　No doubt his loving ways attracted
them, and as the Saint's life tells us, they would say
to each other, " Has our little Columb come to-day
from the cell ? "　So the name came to be given him
of Columb of the Cell—the cell place or church where
" he read his psalms."

Of his early days we have some touching records.
It is said that an angel appeared to his mother Eithne
one night before he was born, and brought her a
robe in which the rarest colours were blended like
flowers.　He then took the robe from her, and
spreading it out, let it fly through the air.　But
as she grieved for the loss of this rare garment, the
venerable man[1] told her that it was too great an
honour for her to be allowed to retain it longer,
and she saw it expand until it exceeded in size
plains and mountains and forests; and the angel said
to her, " Woman, do not be troubled, for you shall
bring forth a son who is destined by God to lead
innumerable souls to heaven, and will be counted as
one of the prophets of God."

The Saint was placed at an early age under the

---

[1] So called, as also " Angel," by Adamnan, and in Colgan.

care and instructions of the good priest who had baptized him. On one occasion when he returned home after celebrating the Divine Mystery in the church, he found the house illuminated with a supernatural light; this proceeded from a ball of fire which was suspended over the face of the child as he lay asleep. This remarkable sight filled the priest with holy fear, and he prostrated himself on the ground, knowing that it indicated the grace of the Holy Spirit which was poured forth so abundantly upon his charge.

St. Columba's boyhood was spent at *Doric Eithne,* afterwards called *Cillmac-nenain,* the Church of the Sons of Enan. Their mother Miucholeth was a sister of the Saint. Adamnan has not given us many records of his youth, but the "Quinta Vita" abounds with anecdotes, strangely like many that are related of more modern saints, whose biographers could certainly have never read one line of Irish hagiology; and in truth, the more we study this, the more we find a brother likeness in the ways and acts and words of God's holy ones.

Amongst the visions or apparitions of his youthful days, one is noted in which three beautiful virgins appeared to him. At first, not recognising their heavenly character, he was about to flee from them; but they recalled him, and inquired why he seemed so indifferent to their attractions? The young Saint wisely replied, "I know not who you are," fearing, no doubt, the temptation of demons which might come even in the form of angels. But they answered, "We are three sisters who have just been betrothed to thee by our Father." "And who is He," inquired the Saint. They replied, "God, and the Saviour and Lord of all mankind, Jesus Christ." Then Columba became joyful and answered, "Truly you are of a great Father; tell me your names." They replied, "Virginity, and Wisdom, and Prophecy, who are to be your companions for ever, and to fill you with a true and eternal love." And even as they spoke they vanished from his sight, and the young Saint thanked God that He had given so great a grace to one so unworthy.

On another occasion an angel came to him to give him "the choice of his death," when and where it should be, and how it should happen. And the Saint chose "a death natural and not violent, which should result from long fasting and voluntary penance and long mortification of his body; that it should be after his youth and before the decrepitude of old age; so that by not dying young, he might be better prepared; so that by not living to a troublesome old age, he might not need to relax his austerities; and for the place he chose a foreign land and not his own, and that he might die with tears in his eyes, and penitence; for those who are exiles from their early homes are wont to grieve, and to transfer their thoughts from the things of this world to those of the next."

Before he was favoured with the vision of the three virgins, an angel, probably his guardian angel, came to him to tell him, amongst other things, that our Lord had given him permission to choose whatever gifts and virtues he desired to have. And the angel warned him at the same time to choose carefully and wisely. The Saint did not need long consideration. He asked the gift of virginity, that gift so characteristic of the saints of Erin, so dear to celestial hosts, so honoured of God ; and he chose wisdom.

Then the angel told him that he had done well, and that as a reward for his holy choice, God would add to these gifts the gift of prophecy. One night as he lay in peaceful and holy slumber, this dear angel came to him. "clad in white and shining garments," and said to him, "The Lord be with thee! Play the man, and let thy heart trust in the Lord. Behold, I am with thee, by the command of the Lord, to be thy guardian and director, that I may help thee in all thy ways, lest thou shouldst dash thy foot against a stone."

Columba was amazed at the vision and the words of the angel, and asked what was his name? The angel replied that his name was Help,[1] and that he was so called because he would defend him from

---

[1] *Auxil Nomen.* Colgan, Quinta Vita, p. 394. In a note on this word, Colgan says, that as the angel of St. Patrick was properly called Victor, because he enabled him to get the victory over the magi, and so many foes, so the angel of Columba was justly named Help, because he constantly assisted him in so many difficulties.

D

the snares of perfidious foes, from the deceit of the world, and from the allurements of the flesh.

As the young Saint was meditating on this wonderful vision, and gazing in awe upon the beauty of the angelic form, he asked at last if all the holy angels were thus resplendent with beauty and thus glorified? But the angel told him that his beauty in the heavenly courts far outshone his beauty on earth, for no mortal eye could behold the glory and splendour of his heavenly appearance unless specially strengthened by Divine power.

And then he told his holy charge how he, too, might attain to that kingdom of eternal beauty, and that to do this he should keep his virginity undefiled to the end, when, as a reward, he should receive so glorious a garment that no words could describe its magnificence.

Then Columba begged his angel to sign his head and body with the holy sign of the Cross, so that he might attain this glory, and ever after he remained faithful to the instructions of his heavenly visitant.

Indeed Columba may well be called a "wonder-working Saint." It is said that he restored his own tutor to life while he was himself still a youth. One day as they were walking together on their return from a funeral, the aged ecclesiastic fell down dead. Columba thought that he was only wearied from his journey, and that he had lain down to sleep. Even then the tender nature of the great loving heart manifested itself. He took off his own mantle and covered the priest with it. He then began to learn his task; and it is said that as he recited aloud, his voice was heard in a convent of nuns which was more than half a mile distant.

The priest, like some of the early Irish saints, had lived in the married state before his vocation to serve at the altar. Several of his daughters had taken the veil in this convent, and hearing the voice of Columba they hastened to the place whence it proceeded, and found their father dead.[1]

The wonder-working fame of the holy boy was already well known, so the religious, seeing that he thought his tutor was sleeping, concealed the matter, and asked him urgently to try and arouse their aged father. But he did more than this, for he restored him to life in their presence; and when he found how great a miracle he had been enabled to perform, he gave thanks with them to God.

He was permitted to work another miracle for his tutor also, or, rather, he became himself the subject of a supernatural favour for his benefit. The boy and his tutor were asked to spend the great Christmas festival with the holy bishop Brugach, son of Deagadh of *Kath-enaigh*, now Kaymochy, in the barony of

---

[1] The original of his life says, "They were born before the priest had taken on him the service of Christ." Yet another evidence, if evidence were needed, that the celibacy of the priesthood was observed from the days of Patrick.

Raphoe. Here they chanted the office in choir, but when they came to the psalm *Misericordias Domini*, the voice of the old priest, Cruithnech, failed him, for, indeed, it was " worn out with use." [1] But the youth. though he had only learned his *abecedarium*, took the book from his master's hand and continued the chant without hesitation or mistake.

The old pagan customs lingered on for some years after the introduction of Christianity. One of our greatest, because one of our truest, modern poets has versified the conflict between the pagan and the Christian with rare poetic fire.

Some half believing, yet half doubting, half won to the beauty of the Faith, and perhaps more than half held in the chains of error, the conflict was, as should be expected, stern and rough. They were days when men's words were not nicely measured, and had a sledge-hammer power of their own, none the less effective because physical force was quite as likely to be used to sum up the argument.

The persuasive words of the gospel of peace and its angelic teaching did, indeed, appeal to the highly-gifted mind of the pre-Christian Celt, a mind not altogether devoid of the gentleness inseparable from keen appreciation of physical force. But the wisdom of those days held in honour what the apostle of Erin taught to be forbidden. King Laeghaire thought " it was better to believe than die "—

[1] Colgan, Quinta Vita, p. 394, xxxii.

" Then Patrick discoursed of the things to be,
  When time gives way to eternity ;
Of kingdoms that fall, which are dreams not things,
  And the Kingdom built by the King of kings ;
Of Him he spake who reigns from the Cross,
  Of the death which is life, and the life which is loss ;
How all things were made by the Infant Lord,
  And the small hand the Magian kings adored.
His voice sounded on like a throbbing flood
  That swells all night from some far-off wood,
And when it was ended—that wondrous strain—
  Invisible myriads breathed—' Amen !'
While he spake, men say that the refluent tide
  On the shore by Colpa ceased to sink ;
They say that the white deer by Mulla's side
  O'er the green marge bending forbore to drink ;
That the Brandon eagle forgot to soar ;
  That no leaf stirred in the wood by Lee.
Such stupor hung the Island o'er,
  For none might guess what the end would be."[1]

Yet though Laeghaire gave some kind of credence to the Faith at Tara, yet he could swear later—

" By the moon divine and the earth and air ;"

And he died without learning Patrick's

" Sweet new song,
Though hate is strong, yet love is stronger !"

St. Columba, it will be remembered, was of princely race. One of his ancestors, Conall Goulban, was head of one of the two great races of the northern Hy-Neill, and occupied the territory then called *Tir-aedha,* and now Tirhugh, in the present county Donegal.

[1] The Legend of St. Patrick ; *de Vere.*

Conall, according to the custom of the times, kept bards and druids in his retinue.[1]

According to the legend, Conall used to be attended by those persons when he went to hunt. But it was useless to expect sport in the neighbourhood of Gartan. The wild boar (*torc faidhain*), or the wolf (*un allaidh*), or the red deer (*faidh ruadh*), degenerate descendant of the famous Irish elk, might roam here at their own sweet pleasure. The dogs would not hunt them down, or if they captured them for a moment, would let them go gently. And then as Conall marvelled greatly, he inquired why this had happened, and was told a son of his race should be born in time to come who would turn that place into a peaceful asylum, and that the escape of the poor animals predicted the tranquillity which should abide there through him.

Oh! rare and blessed glimpses of a happy time, when men, in the full vigour of an undegenerate youth and manhood, knew how to believe—when doubt was not honoured as a proof of intellect, when unbelief was not worshipped as a god, when the conventionalities and pride of a modern age had not yet interposed a barrier between God and His creatures, when He spoke to them through Nature and they believed and adored!

---

[1] For a full account of the druidic customs and superstitions of the various races who peopled ancient Ireland, see "The History of the Irish Nation," by the present writer.

CHAPTER IV.

THE EDUCATION AND ORDINATION OF ST. COLUMBA.

T may seem strange even to some of our Irish readers to speak of the high culture which obtained in Ireland at this period, yet there is ample proof of it.

The saints of ancient Erin were not rude, uncultured men, converted from a half savage paganism to a half pagan Christianity. The early teachers of the Christian Faith were not always men of high birth, but they were men who had that special culture which Christianity alone can give, and which as a rule mere culture can never impart. We have no space here for historical details or proofs, and the most incontrovertible proofs are given in another

place.[1]   Here we can only call attention to the high
education given to ecclesiastical students.

On this subject we cannot do better than quote the
words of one of the distinguished Irish writers of our
day.   He says :—

"Saint Patrick found the country teeming with men distinguished for their acquirements in the native language and literature,
if not in other languages—philosophers, poets, druids, judges, &c.
On his first appearance at Tara, he found the poet *Dubhthach* in-
stalled there as the monarch's chief poet ; and we have seen already
that Vros and Fergus were also distinguished poets and scholars,
learned in the laws and history of the country, as well as Dubhthach.
We have also seen that Laeghaire had his druids, who contended
with Saint Patrick ; and it appears that he had entrusted the education of his two daughters to the druids Macl and Coplait, even at
such a distance from his court at Tara as his Palace of *Cruchain* (in
the present county of Roscommon).   From all our ancient records
we have abundant reason to believe that these, as well as all the
other druids with whom the country abounded at this time, were
men learned in the literature and poetry of the country, as well as
in druidism ; and we have reason to believe that their druidic
system was a more refined and a more philosophic one than that
of their neighbours the Britons and Gauls.   So as these men, as
well as the poets, were all active teachers to all comers, it is not to
be wondered at that Saint Patrick found before him on his arrival
many men among the people of Erin of cultivated mind, sharp-
ened by study, capable of appreciating new ideas, and thus quick
to recognise the sublime truths of Divine revelation in preference
to the unsatisfactory mysteries and secret ceremonies of their ancient
mythology, however venerable it had become in their eyes."

My object in dwelling so long on the learning and
cultivation of the period of our history before the
coming of St. Patrick is, to show upon authority that
we were, even at that remote period, a nation not

---

[1] "The History of the Irish Nation," in the early chapters.

entirely without a native literature and a national
cultivation sufficient to sustain a system of society,
and an internal political government so enlightened
that, as our history proves, Christianity did not seek
to subvert, but rather endeavoured to unite with it ;
a system, moreover, which had sufficient vitality to
remain in full force through all the vicissitudes of the
country, even till many ages after the intrusion of the
Anglo-Normans in the twelfth century, who themselves, indeed, found it so just and comprehensive
that they adopted it in preference to the laws of
the countries from which they came.

Having said so much on this important subject, let
me now, with as much brevity as possible, adduce
some proofs that although Erin adopted a new
creed, whose preachers introduced a new literature,
and one which was cultivated with a fervour not
often exceeded, still her own ancient language
was not abandoned or neglected, but rather even
cherished and cutivated with more ardour, if possible, than ever. For it is certain that the ancient
language and literature continued to be taught in
all the schools and colleges, both lay and ecclesiastical ; and that there was never a priest or bishop
educated in Erin, from Saint Patrick's time down to
the year 1600, who had not deeply studied Gaedhelic
literature and history, as part of his college course.
And thus it is that so many of the learned and wise
ecclesiastics who have adorned the Catholic Church

of Erin, or taught in its seminaries, have left us more memorials of their piety and wisdom in their native language, than even in the Latin itself; though the Latin tongue had in other countries so generally usurped the literature of the Christian world for many ages, and though our native clergy were educated in that language also, as many historical facts might be quoted to prove.

The introduction of Christianity, and with it of the classical languages, did not supersede the cultivation of the Gaedhelic tongue, but, on the contrary, it appears to have encouraged and promoted it; and this can be very clearly proved by the fact that several, if not all, of our most eminent classical scholars and divines were also the greatest Gaedhelic scholars of whom we have any reliable account. Of the great ecclesiastical schools O'Curry writes thus :—

"After the introduction of Christianity into Erin, the enthusiasm which marked its reception by the people, and more particularly by the more learned and better educated among them, gave to almost all the great schools a certain ecclesiastical character. The schools of the early Saints were, however, by no means exclusively of this kind ; but as the most learned men were precisely those who most actively applied themselves to the work of the gospel, and as it had always been the habit of students to surround the dwelling of the most learned, to dwell near the chosen master, and thus (somewhat as in Ancient Greece), to make for themselves a true academy wherever a great master was to be found, so did the laity also, as well as those intended for the sacred ministry, gather in great numbers round the early Saints, who were also the great teachers of history and general learning. And so, while from such academies naturally sprang hundreds of priests, saints, and religious, there also were the great bulk of the more comfortable portion of the lay population constantly educated. Every part of educated Europe has heard of the great University of Ardmacha, where so much as the third of the city was appropriated even to the exclusive use of foreign, but particularly of Saxon and British students, so great was the concourse to its schools from all the neighbouring nations. Who has not read of the great schools, with their hundreds and their thousands of scholars, of Beannchoir [Bangor, county Down], under Saint Comgall and his successors; of Clonard, under Saint Finen; of Lothrei, under Saint Ruadan; of Glas-Nasidhen [Glas-nevin, near Dublin], under Saint Mobi; of *Clonmacnois*, under Saint *Ciaran;* of Tallaght, under Saint *Maolruain* and the learned *Aengus Ceilé De; Birra* (Birr) and *Cluainferta* [Clonfert], under Saint *Brendan;* of Roscrea, under Saint *Cronan;* of *Iniscelltra*, under Saint *Caimin;* of Killaloe, under Saint *Flauvan;* of *Mungaret* [Mungret, near Limerick], under the holy deacon *Nessan;* of Emiligh (Emly), under Saint Ailbhi, where the students were so numerous in the reign of *Cathal Mac Finguiné* (about the year 740), that they were forced to live in huts in the neighbouring fields; of Saint Finnbar's in Cork; of the great lay school of *Colman Ua Cluasaigh*, in the same place; of the great school of *Cluain Umha* [Cloyne], under Saint *Colman MacLenin*, the converted poet; of *Ross Ailithri*, in the same county, under Saint Fachtna (I possess myself a copy of a most curious poem on Universal Geography, written, and of course taught in this great school, by *MacCoisé*, one of its professors, about the year 900); of *Glennda-locha*, under Saint Caeimhin [or Kevin]; of Tuam, under Saint *Jarlaithe;* of Swoards, under the successors of Saint *Colum Cille;* of Monasterboice, under the successors of Saint Buité; of *Tuaim Drecain*, under Saint Bricin; of Louth, under Saint *Mochta;* and of Kildare, under Saint Brigid, where Saint Finnen taught and preached before the foundation of Clonard by him." [1]

It was the custom then for young men who had obtained the grace of a vocation to the priesthood, to place themselves under famous masters, and not unfrequently to pass from one college or school to

[1] O'Curry's Lectures, vol. ii. p. 72.

another, according to their advancement, or the special qualifications of their tutors in particular branches of study.

St. Columba had now attained an age when it was necessary to make a more immediate preparation for the sacerdotal office. He selected St. Finnian for his master.

So great were the number of his pupils who became distinguished for sanctity, that he was called "The Tutor of the Saints of Ireland," and was known as "The wise."

The incidents of the life of the young student and Saint at this period have been narrated with more regard to devotion than to chronological sequence. But it was either here or at Clonard that the following miracle occurred. It is thus recorded :—

While the venerable man was yet a youth in Ireland, "learning the wisdom of the Holy Scriptures," the priest or bishop, who was about to celebrate mass, found that there was no wine for the sacrifice. Columba was at that time a deacon, and in the performance of his office went to the well to obtain pure water for the ministry of the Holy Eucharist. But as he returned he blessed the water, invoking the name of Jesus who had changed water into wine for the marriage feast at Cana in Galilee, and imploring Him to work yet again the same miracle for the great Feast of the Christian Church. The prayer of faith was heard. The water became wine, and the young deacon placed it near the altar, saying, "You have wine which the Lord Jesus has sent to celebrate the mystery."

The bishop and his attendants were filled with amazement, but Columba would not allow them to attribute the grace to him, saying that the miracle was performed for the sake of the bishop.

At Durrow it is said that he blessed an apple-tree which was laden with fruit in autumn, but the fruit, though so abundant, was unfit for use until he gave it the benediction which removed its bitterness.

Raising his holy hand, he blessed it, saying : " In the name of the Almighty God, O bitter tree, let all thy bitterness depart from thee : and let all thy fruit, hitherto so bitter, be changed into the sweetest."

After a short residence at Moville with St. Finnian, the Saint proceeded towards the great southern monasteries and schools, which were then so famous.

In Leinster he placed himself for a time under the instruction of an aged bard called Gemman.[1]

Possibly historical studies were perused under the Christian bards as a speciality. It is, at all events,

[1] Dr. Reeves has cleared up any doubt as to the identity of this individual.—*Adamnan*, p. 137. He shows how even Colgan supposed the name to be an error, and proposed *Gormanum* as an emendation. But a passage in the Life of St. Finnian of Clonard, shows him to have been a distinguished poet and a devout Christian. His name is given in Adamnan's life as Gemanus.

certain that the saints of the early Irish Church availed themselves of every opportunity for studying and cultivating their natural gifts.

Another St. Finnian presided over the famous monastic school of Clonard. Here St. Columba found a number of students, who afterwards were famous, and were counted as special fathers of the Irish Church.

We cannot doubt the warmth and enduring tenderness of the holy friendships which were formed in this place. St. Comgall, St. Ciaran, and St. Caimach were amongst his companions here, and later they were with him at Glasnevin.

It would appear from several circumstances that the number of pupils at these monastic schools was limited to fifty.

There is a poem still extant, written by Colman O'Cluasigh, who was head of a great school in Cork, "as a shield of protection" to himself and his pupils when a plague was desolating Ireland in 657–664.

The Preface states that Colman only wrote the first and last verses, and that the other twenty-five verses were written by his pupils, two lines by each, which would give the number of fifty.

This beautiful poem might be quoted, were such evidence needed, as proof that the faith of the Irish has known no change for a thousand years and more. Now as then we could use the very words of the Southern poet and his pupils :

THE HYMN OF ST. COLMAN FOR PROTECTION AGAINST PESTILENCE.

" May the Son of Mary shield us,
　　For the blessing of God we wait ;
　To-night may He protect us,
　　Be our numbers ever so great.

" Whether at rest or in motion,
　　Whether we sit or stand ;
　For Thy help is our supplication,
　　O King of the Heavenly Land.

" May the prayer of Adam's son Abel
　　And of Heli and Enoch aid ;
　In all parts of the world may they keep us,
　　And we shall be never afraid.

" Noe and Abraham and Isaac,
　　A wonderful son was he !
　May they come around and protect us,
　　So no harm shall come to me.

" I beseech the illustrious Joseph,
　　And Isaac, of twelve the sire ;
　May the King of angels save us
　　From pestilence, foe, and fire.

" May the good leader Moses aid us,
　　Who protected in crossing the Sea ;
　With Josue, Aaron, and David,
　　A brave, bold youth was he.

" Against the great plague poison
　　May Job assist with his pain,
　With the seven sons of Maccabæus,
　　And the prophets with God who reign.

" Great John the Baptist, we name him,
　　May he high protection yield,
　With Christ and His twelve Apostles,
　　To be our constant shield.

" May Mary and Joseph guard us,
　　And the spirit of Stephen pure ;
　We invoke the great Ignatius
　　To make our deliverance sure.

" Every martyr and every hermit,
　　And each saint of chastity,
　Be my constant shield and protection,
　　And drive the demons from me.

" O King of kings, we beseech Thee,
　　Our words on Thee still wait,
　Who saved Noe and his companions
　　In the time of the deluge great.

" Melchisedech, king of Salem,
　　Unknown his pedigree,
　May his prayers be my deliverance
　　From every misery.

" May Christ, who saved Lot from the burning,
　　Who liveth for evermore,
　Hear our prayer and our supplication—
　　This we fervently implore.

" May the Lord, who delivered Abram,
　　Be our deliverance too ;
　May He save us, who saved His people,
　　And streams from the hard rock drew.

" May He save us, who saved great David
　　From the hands of the giant dread,
　Who delivered the three youths faithful
　　From the fire of the furnace red.

" Thou noble Lord of bright Heaven,
　　Look down on us to-day :
　Who never hast left Thy prophets
　　To be the lions' prey.

" And like as He sent the angel
　　To free Peter from his chain,
　So may He send His mercy
　　To make our path smooth and plain.

" To Him we submit our willing,
  Our words, and our deeds to-day,
That we may be with Him in glory,
  And in Paradise live alway.

" As He delivered Jonas—
  Great deed—from the dreadful whale,
So may the good King protect us,
  May His blessing never fail.

" Amen, Amen, Lord Jesus,
  Protect Thy servant's school,
And put a bright guard of angels
  Around the place where I rule.

" Amen, Amen, Lord Jesus,
  May we all find the peace of the King,
And wherever we may be scattered,
  Each one to Thy kingdom bring.

" That we may live ever and ever
  With angels in life eternal ;
That we may find ever and ever
  The joys of the life supernal.

" Patriarchs, prophets, apostles,
  Angels a glorious host,
Come they with our Father in Heaven,
  And demons no more shall boast.

―――――

" A blessing on Patron Patrick,
  With the Saints of Erin around ;
A blessing on this good city,
  And on every one in it found.

" A blessing on Patron Brigit,
  With the virgins of Erin fair ;
All praise to the cloister pure ones,
  Who the portion of virgins bear.

" And a blessing on holy Colum-cille,
 And the Saints whom Alba saw,
On the soul of pure Adamnan,
 Who put on the claus a law.

" May the King, the great Creator,
 Take us all beneath His care,
With the Holy Spirit and Jesus,
 Whom Mary the Virgin bare.

————

" Pray for us, all ye holy ones in heaven, whom we commemorate on earth, that our sins may be blotted out by the mercy of the holy name of Jesus, who reigneth for ever and ever. Amen."

————

When the young student presented himself to his new master, he asked where he should place his hut. This was the general custom. The first monasteries were, in fact, little encampments, each student having his own hut near the church where the master generally gave instructions—the stately buildings of later times taking their place gradually.

The course of study was severe. O'Curry says :—
" It is to be remembered that the chief professor or master of every one of the divinity colleges was fully educated in the native as well as in the classical and foreign languages. For to be a Fer-Leighinn, Drum-chli, or chief master in a college, or great school, the candidate was obliged by law to be master of the whole course of Gaedhelic literature in prose and verse (besides that of the Scriptures, ' from the Ten Commandments up to the whole Bible '), as well as the

learned languages, as already said. The legal arrangement of these great public schools was as follows :—

"The college professors (according to law) included :

" 1. The *Coagdach*, or 'fifty man,' who was the lowest, having only to chant 150 Psalms.

" 2. The *Foghlantidh*, or school, who taught ten out of the twelve books of the college course of the Fochoire, or native education.

" 3. The *Staraidh*, or historian, who had also, besides history, thirty lessons of divinity in his course.

" 4. The *Foircetlaidh*, or lecturer, who professed grammar, orthography, criticism, enumeration, the course of the year, and the course of the sun and moon (*i.e.*, astronomy).

" 5. The *Saoi Canoine*, or professor of divinity, who taught 'the Canons and the Gospel of Jesus, that is, the Word of God, in the sacred place in which it is, that is, who taught the Catholic canonical wisdom.'

" 6. The *Drumchli*, or chief head, a master who knew the whole course of learning, ' from the greatest book, which is called *Cuilmen*, down to the smallest book, called the Ten Commandments, in which is properly arranged the good Testament which God prepared for Moses.'"

As a further proof that the native language and literature made no inconsiderable part of the divinity student's college course of education, there is scarcely one of our most eminent Irish ecclesiastics, from St. Patrick in the fifth century down to the eighteenth, that was not distinguished for his knowledge of the Gaedhelic language and history. I shall content myself by enumerating a short list of the names of those early ecclesiastics, whose verses are quoted in the notes and commentaries on a single work, the Fes-

tology of *Aengus Ceilé Dé* (or "the Culdee"), in the
Leabhar Mor Duna Doighré (or *Leabhar Breac*):—
St. Patrick himself in the fifth century ; St. Ciaran
of Saighir, of the same period ; St. Comgall of Benn-
chuir ; St. Colum-Cille ; St. Ité the Virgin (of Cill
Ite, in the county of Limerick) ; St. Caeimhghin of
Glenn-da-locha ; St. Ciaran of Cluainmacnois ; St.
Molaisé of Daimhinis in Loch Erne—all of the sixth
century ; St. Mochuda of Lismore ; St. Moling of
St. Mullins, in Carlow ; St. Fechin of Tabhar (now
Fare, in Westmeath) ; St. Aireran "the Wise," of
Clonard—all of the seventh century ; St. Macbruan
of Tamhlaght (or Tallaght) ; St. Adamnan of Rath
Boith (Raphoe) ; and I Colum Cillé (Iona) ; and St.
Aengus, "the Culdee," himself—of the eighth century.

It is to be recollected that these are but names
found among those quoted in the notes and commentaries on Aengus' work, which was written in the year
798. But if I were to swell the list from other available sources, it would occupy the greater part, if not
the whole, of the space occupied for this chapter. Now
these writers were all Irish scholars and literary
teachers as well as eminent divines, and we may be
certain that that which they were taught themselves,
and the language in which they continued to write
during their lives, they taught to their pupils again
in like manner."

St. Finnian directed the Saint to build his hut at
the church door, but when he went to look after his

pupil he found that his order was not obeyed. "You have not followed my directions," said the master, "that spot is not at the door." But Columba replied, "True, it is not, but the door will be at this place hereafter." And the prediction was fulfilled. The school soon became so famous that its boundaries extended on all sides, and no less than three hundred youths and adults are said to have been in it at one time.

As St. Columba studied under two Saints of the same name who were also contemporary, there has been some uncertainty as to the order of the events recorded. But of one or the other saint it is said that when Columba came to visit him before his departure for Tara, he saw him attended by an angel as he approached him.

St. Finnian of Clonard is commemorated on the 12th December. He had not received episcopal orders, and it is noted that few of his pupils were bishops. St. Columba had a very serious dispute with one of his old masters, illustrative of the customs of the times.

It has already been observed that St. Columba was devoted to literary pursuits. On one occasion, while visiting St. Finnian, he borrowed his copy of the Book of Psalms. But the Saint was not satisfied without having a copy of his own, and for some reason he believed that Finnian would refuse him permission to copy his manuscript.

St. Columba therefore remained in the church where the precious treasure was left, and occupied himself in copying it after the people had left. Some of St. Finnian's followers discovered how he was occupied, and reported the matter to their master; but he took no notice of what was going on until the book was copied. He then sent for Columba and demanded the copy, saying that, as the original was his, and as he gave no permission to have it copied, the transcript must be his also.

But Columba was not disposed to yield his treasure so easily, and he referred the question to the arbitration of Diarmiad, then monarch of Ireland. The Saint agreed, and both parties journeyed to Tara to obtain the royal decision.

But the king decided in favour of Finnian, and his royal decision remains a proverb in Ireland to this day. He said, " *Le goch boin a boinin*, to every cow belongeth her little cow [or calf], and in the same way to every book belongs its copy; accordingly, the book that you wrote, *O Colum-cille*, belongs by right to Finnian."

But though St. Columba had appealed to the royal decision, he was by no means content to abide by it when it went against himself, and he declared that it was an unjust decree, and that he would avenge it. "This is an unjust decision, O Diarmiad!" said *Colum-cille*, "and I will avenge it on you." It was the commencement of a serious war.

All parties were hot and prepared for an open rupture, and, as usual in such cases, the occasion was not far to seek.

A son of the King of Connaught was at this very time a hostage at Tara. He was at the moment occupied in a game of hurling with the son of one of Diarmiad's chief officers. They had a dispute about the game, during which the prince killed the youth with his hurley. He fled at once for sanctuary to St. Columba, who was still in the king's presence.

But the king, contrary to all precedent, refused to respect the undoubted right of the Saint to protect his client ; and he ordered the unhappy prince to be torn from his very arms and carried out to instant execution.

The king knew very well that he had acted most unjustly, and had many reasons to fear the consequence. He ordered a guard to watch the Saint, and to prevent him from leaving Tara, at least until his just indignation had been in some measure abated. But guards were of little use when a Saint of such miraculous power was in question ; and as the chronicle says, "The justice of God threw a veil of unrecognition around him," and he passed through all quite unmolested.

Having escaped from the immediate precincts of the court, he sent his attendants by the great northern road which led from Tara to Tirconnell, the present Donegal. He took a longer path over the mountains

himself, chanting a hymn, still preserved, and
which is one of the finest compositions of ancient
times.

ALONE I AM UPON THE MOUNTAIN.

Alone I am upon the mountain,
O God of Heaven! prosper my way;
So shall I pass more free and fearless
Than if six thousand were my stay.
My flesh, indeed, might be defended;
But when the time comes life is ended.
If by six thousand I was guarded,
Or placed in islet in a lake,
Or in a fortress strong protected,
Or in a church my refuge take,
Still God will guard His own with care,
And even in battle safe they fare:
No man can slay me till the day
When God shall take my life away;
And when my earthly time is ended,
I die, no matter how defended.
    My life!
Without His will no less can it be made;
As God shall please so let it be,
Nor can they add to it without His leave.
The lot which He has given that I shall see,
Nor prince upon his throne one hour can get
Of life beyond what God for him has set.
    A guard!
A guard, indeed, may guide a man full safe,
But never guard can keep a man from death;
For One alone has rule of every fate—
Alone can give or take our mortal breath.
Nor shall I fear though poverty may come—
The Son of Mary still shall give my share;
For all the Master portions out some dole of food,
And under His protection all shall safely fare.
What is well spent to bounteous hand returns,
What is denied the niggard keeper spurns.

O Living God, alas ! for evil-working men ;
That which they think not comes to mar their life,
That which they hope for vanishes away,
And leaves them lonely in a world of strife.
No augur's word can tell our future fate—
No bird, no omen, say how long our death shall wait.
I trust not in a bird, or twig, or dream,
But in the Lord of Heaven's eternal might ;
He who has made us all will help me now,
Nor leave me in this mountain lone to-night.
I have no love of earthly kin or kind,
The love of Christ, the Son of God, fills my mind.
The great King's Son, my Lord and abbot, rules ;
All that I have is in the great King's hands :
The houses of my order are at Kells and Moore—
He will protect my people and my lands.
Praise be for evermore, and endless merit,
Unto the Father, Son, and Holy Spirit.

Columba reached his old home and relatives in the North of Ireland in perfect safety.

But his relatives were not prepared to brook the insult which had been offered him, and speedy preparations were made for war. It was, indeed, one of the great misfortunes of Ireland that domestic dissensions were of perpetual recurrence ; that smouldering fires were ready at any moment to break out ; that an excitable and brave people, who had no foreign foe, should expend their energy and their best years in conflicts which should have been avoided at all cost.

The men of Tirconnell and the men of Tyrone took up the quarrel, and they were joined by *Eochaidh Tircharna*, the king of Connaught, whose son had been so cruelly slain.

A bloody battle was the result, in which the royal

army was defeated with great loss, and the king was obliged to withdraw to Tara.

The battle was fought at Cooldrevey, in the county Sligo, in 561. It must be added, however, that there are some reasonable doubts as to whether the Saint was the actual instigator of this battle, as the circumstance is not noted in the earlier lives. It was not, however, unfrequent for the clergy at that time, not only in Ireland, but on the Continent, to take a very active part in secular affairs; as there is historical evidence for the battle and the preceding events, it is more than probable that the share of St. Columba in the affair is also given correctly.[1]

---

[1] The clergy were exempted from taking any active share in battle, under the following circumstances :—

In the year 799, *Aedh Oirdnidhe*, the then monarch of Erin, raised a large army, with which he marched against the people of the province of Leinster, and proceeded as far as *Dun Cuar*, on the confines of that province, and Meath, where he encamped. The monarch, on this occasion, compelled the attendance of Connacht, the successor of St. Patrick and Primate of Armagh, with all his clergy, to attend this expedition. When the army rested, however, the clergy complained to the king of the hardship and inconsistency of their being called upon to attend on such occasions. The king listened to their complaint, and offered to lay it before his own poet, tutor, and adviser, the learned *Fothadh*, and abide by his decision, which was accordingly done. The poet's views were favourable to the clergy, and he gave his decision in a short poem of three quatrains, which are preserved in this preface, and of which the following may be taken as a literal translation (see original in Appendix, No. CXII.) :—

" The Church of the Living God,
    Touch her not, nor waste ;
    Let her rights be reserved,
    As best ever they were.
Every true monk who is
    Possessed of a pious conscience,

It is said that only one person was slain on St. Columba's side. Keating, a most trustworthy authority, who had access to ancient manuscripts now lost, gives the following account of the whole affair:—

" Now this is the cause why Molaise sentenced Colum-cille to go into Alba, because it came of him to occasion three battles in Erin, viz., the battle of Cul-Dreimhne, the battle of Rathan, and the battle of Cuil Feadha. The cause of the battle of Cuil Feadha, according to the old book called the Leabhar Uidhre of Ciaran, Diarmiad, son of Fergus Cerrbhoil, king of Ireland, made the Feast of Tara ; and a noble man was killed at that Feast by Curnan, son of Aodh, son of Eochuidh Tiorm-carna ; wherefore Diarmiad killed him in revenge for that, because he committed murder at the Feast of Tara, against law and the sanctuary of the feast ; and before Curnan was put to death he fled to the protection of Colum-cille, and notwithstanding the protection of Colum-cille, he was killed by Diarmiad. And from that it arose that Colum-cille mustered the Clanna Neills of the north, because his own protection and the protection of the sons of Earc was violated ; whereupon the battle of Cuile Dreimhne was gained over Diarmiad and over the Connaught-men, so that they were defeated through the prayer of Colum-cille."

The Black Book of Molaga assigns another cause why the battle of Cul Dreimhne was fought, viz., in consequence of the false judgment which Diarmiad

---

To the Church to which it is due
Let him act as any servant.
Every faithful subject from that out,
Who is not bound by vows of obedience,
Has liberty to join in the battles
Of Aedh the Great, son of Niall."

And by this decision the clergy were exempted for ever after from attending military expeditions. This decision obtained the name of a Canon, and its author has ever since been known in Irish history by the name of *Fothadh na Canoine*, or *Fothadh* " of the Canon."

gave against Colum-cille, when he wrote the Gospel out of the book of Finnian without his knowledge. Finnian said that it was to himself belonged the Son-book [copy] which was written from his book, and they both selected Diarmiad as judge between them. This is the decision that Diarmiad made: That to every book belongs its son-book [copy], as to every cow belongs her calf. So that this is one of the two causes why the battle of Cuile Drcimhne was fought.

"This was the cause which brought Colum-cille to be induced to fight the battle of Cuil Rathan, against the Dal-n-Araidhe and against the Ultonians, viz., in consequence of the controversy that took place between Colum and Comgall, because they took part against Colum in that controversy.

"This was the cause that occasioned the fighting of the battle of Cuil Feadha against Colman MacDear-mada, viz., in revenge for his having been outraged in the case of Baodan, son of Ninneadh (king of Erin), who was killed by Cuimin, son of Colman, at Leim-an-eich, in violation of the sanctuary of Colum."

The *Cathach* is one of the most authentic and interesting of our early remains. It is thus described by O'Donnell :—

"Now the *Cathach* is the name of the book on account of which the battle was fought, and it is the chief relic of Colum-cille in the territory of Cinell Conaill Gulban, and it is covered with silver under gold, and it is not lawful to open it ; and if it be sent thrice, rightwise, around the army of the Cinell Conaill, when they are going to battle, they will return safe with victory ; and it is on the breast of a coward or a cleric, who is to the best of his power free from mortal sin, that the Cathach should be, when brought round the army."

The Four Masters record the battle thus:—

" The seventeenth year of Diarmiad. The battle of Cul-Dreimhne was gained against Diarmiad, son of Cearbhall, by Fearghus and Domhnall, the two sons of Muircheartach, son of Earca ; by Aiumire, son of Sedna ; and by Nainnidh, son of Duach ; and by Aedh, son of Eochaidh Tirmacharna, king of Connaught. It was in revenge of the killing of Curnan, son of Aedh, son of Eochaidh Tirmacharna, while under the protection of Colum-cille that the Clanna Neill of the north and the Connaughtmen gave this battle of Cul-Dreimhne to King Diarmiad ; and also on account of the false sentence which Diarmiad passed against Colum-cille about a book of Finnian, Colum had transcribed without the knowledge of Finnian, when they left it to the award of Diarmiad, who pronounced the celebrated decision, ' *To every cow belongs its calf,*' &c."

It is to be observed that the Annals of Tighernach and Ulster attribute the success of the northerns to St. Columba's intercession : "Per orationem Coluim-celle dicentis," &c., while the Four Masters, with their usual caution, merely state that "Colum-cille said," adding, from Tighernach, the verses which were supposed to have produced so marvellous a result :—

"O God, wilt Thou not drive off the fog, which envelopes our
 number ?
The host which has deprived us of our livelihood,
The host which proceeds around the cairns !
He is a son of storm who betrays us.
My Druid,—He will not refuse me,—is the Son of God, and
 may He side with me ;

> How grandly he bears his course, the steed of Baedan before
> the host ;
> Power by Baedan of the yellow hair will be borne from Ireland
> on him [the steed]."

Traechan, son of Teninson, was he who made the Erbhe-Druadh for Diarmiad. Tuathan, son of Dimman, son of Saran, son of Carmac, son of Eoghan, was he who placed the Erbhe Druadh, over his head. Three thousand was the number that fell of Diarmiad's people. One man only fell on the other side, Mag Laim was his name, for it was he that passed beyond the Erbhe Druadh."[1]

There is some question as to whether the manuscript which still remains to us is in the handwriting of St. Columba or of some other scribe ; but there is fair probability that we have the original manuscript of the Saint. The name Cathach rendered *Prædiator* by O'Donnel means "battle," or the Book of the Battle.

The manuscript is a small quarto, and consists of fifty-eight leaves of fine vellum, written in small,

---

[1] In the account of this battle, which was mentioned in the *Leabhar Buidhe*, now preserved in the Library of Trinity College, Dublin, it is said that Fracchan, son of Teinsan, was King Diarmiad's Druid, and the person who made the druidical charm between the two armies. Dr. O'Donovan has a very unfair and, indeed, absurd note on this point in his Notes to the Annals of the Four Masters. He choses to think, without any authority whatsoever, that Colgan did not like to admit that there were Druids in Ireland so long after the arrival of St. Patrick, and therefore he suppresses a reference to them. This is a curious and not uninstructive evidence of the force of prejudice. Colgan quotes many passages elsewhere which show, what is perfectly true, that Druidism did not die at once. It would be crediting St. Patrick with more than apostolic power to suppose him capable of effecting such a task.

uniform hand, but apparently with some haste. There are some slight attempts at its illumination.[1]

The case, properly the Cathach, has been preserved for thirteen hundred years, and handed down through the O'Domhnaills (O'Donnells) as the heirloom of the great clan *Conaill.*

The relic is thus described by O'Curry :—

" This sacred relic appears at all times to have received the greatest veneration from the noble family of the O'Donnells of Donnegall, who for the last seven hundred years have been the most important branch of the line of the descendants of *Conall Gulban,* the remote ancestor of this and the other great families of Tirconnell. This Conall, who was the son of the monarch Niall the Great, was converted by St. Patrick. It has been stated, on the authority of a tradition in the O'Donnell family, that at the time of his conversion Conall had received the Saint's benediction, together with a special mark of favour, for that the Saint inscribed a cross with the spike or heel of his pastoral staff (the celebrated *Bachall Iosa* (or staff of Jesus) on his shield, and recommended him to adopt the motto of ' In hoc signo vinces,' which the O'Donnells accordingly retained down to the time of the dispersion of the clan in the seventeenth century. This was, in fact, the belief of the O'Donnells and old families of *Tir chonaill* from the close of the sixteenth century down at least. The belief was first put forth in a poem by *Eoghan Ruadh Mac-an-Bhaird,* who took it from the 138th chapter of Jocelyn's Life of St. Patrick. Jocelyn, however, does not apply the passage to Conall Gulban. The Tripartite Life of the Saint applies to the Conall the son of Amhalgaidh, king of Connacht, who at the same time received from the Saint the name

---

[1] Through the kindness of the Very Rev. Monsignor Woodlock, Rector of the Catholic University, Dublin, we are able to give a facsimile of part of this manuscript. It is placed at the head of this chapter in the illustrated edition.

of *Conall Sciath Bhachall,* or Conall of the Crozier Shield. This Conall's race is not now known."

This book of St. Colum-cille must have been encased in an ornamental shrine at some early period ; but we find that it was further cared for at the close of the eleventh century by Cathbharr O'Donnell, chief of Tirconnell, and Donnell O'Rafferty, abbot of Kells (in Meath), who was one of the O'Raffertys of Tirconnell, and thus eligible to succeed his family patron Saint, Colum-cille, in any of the many churches founded by him throughout Erin, one of which was the important church of Kells. This O'Rafferty died in the year 1098, and Cathbharr died in the year 1106, so that the magnificent silver-gilt and stone-set case which now surmounts the older cases of this most ancient and interesting relic must have been made some time before the year 1098, in which this abbot of Kells died. The authority for these dates is found on the shrine itself, in the following words :—

"A prayer for Cathbharr O'Donnell, by whom [that is, by whose desire and at whose expense] this shrine was made ; and for Sitric, the son of Mac Aedha [Mac Hugh], who made it ; and for *Domhnall Na Robhartnigh* [Donnell O'Rafferty], the *Comharba* [or successor] of Cerrannus [Kells], by whom it was made [that is, at whose joint expense, with that of O'Donnell, it was made]."

The last mark of devotion conferred on this relic was a solid silver rim or frame, into which the original shrine fits. This rim contains an inscription, from which it appears that it was made in the year 1723, by order of Daniel O'Donnell, who, there is reason to believe, fought at the battle of the Boyne, after which he retired to the Continent. At his death, or some time previously, it appears he deposited this important heirloom of his ancient family in a monastery in Belgium, with a written injunction that it should be kept until claimed by the true representative of the house of O'Donnell; and here it was discovered accidentally in or about the year 1816 by a Mrs. Molyneaux, an Irish lady, who had been travelling on the Continent, and who, upon her return home, reported the circumstance to Sir Neal O'Donnell of Westport. This gentleman had asserted his claim to the chieftainship of his name and race, under the authority of the late Sir William Betham, Ulster king at arms; and, thus prepared, he applied for the Cathach through his brother, the late Conall O'Donnell, then in Belgium, who succeeded in obtaining it accordingly.

From Sir Neal O'Donnell the Cathach descended to his son, the present Sir Richard O'Donnell of Newport, county Mayo, who, with characteristic liberality, has left it for exhibition among the many congenial objects of Christian, historical, and antiquarian reverence preserved in the Museum of the Royal Irish Academy. Dr. Reeves says :—

"Cathbarr O'Donnell, son of Gillachrist [ob. 1038], son of Cathbarr, son of Domhnall Mor, the progenitor of the O'Donnells, was chief of the Ceriel Luighdech, and died in 1106. Domhnall Mac Robhartaigh, successor of Columba at Kells, died, according to the

F

Four Masters, in 1098. His name occurs in the charters which are entered in the blank pages of the Book of Kells. Sitric was son of Mac Ædha, who was surnamed *Cerd*, that is, 'Artificer,' in the charters of Kells, where mention is made of *Flaud Mac Mic Ædha* also. The family of Mac Ædha seem to have been the hereditary mechanics of Kells. It is interesting to observe the relation here recorded, as subsisting through the Columbrian system between remote parts of Ireland ; O'Donnell being lord of a territory in the extreme north of the island, yet associated with the abbot of a midland monastery, and that abbot the member of a family which also was seated in the remote north, supplying hezenachs to two churches in St. Columba's region of Tirconnell, and occasionally appearing in the administration of St. Columba's church of Derry. In 1497 the *Cathach* was employed for military purposes, but failed of procuring victory for its possessors. Con O'Donnell led an army into Moylurg, in Connaught, to attack Mac Dermott, but was defeated at the battle of Bealach-buidhe. Mac Robhartaigh, the keeper of the Cathach of Colum-cille, was slain, and the Cathach taken from the Tirconallians. Two years after, it was restored (Four Masters). In the early part of the sixteenth century it was still the great reliquary of Tirconnell, and in the following century it continued to be in the custody of the family of Mac Robhartaigh, the official keepers under the Lord of Tirconnell. When it reappears in the next century, it is found in the possession of the head of the O'Donnell family, who recorded his guardianship in an inscription on the silver frame which he made for its preservation :—' Jacobo. 3. M. B. Rege Exulante, Daniel O'Donel in Etianiss⁰ Imp⁰ Præfectus Rei Bellicæ Hususce Hœraditarii Sancti Columbani Pignoris Vulgo Caah Dicti Tegmen Argenteum Vetustate consumptum Restaurauit Anno Salutis 1723.' This most remarkable reliquary, combining so many exciting associations, is the property of Sir Richard Annesley O'Donnell, Bart., a descendant of the Cathbarr Ua Domhnaill, whose name is engraved upon the case, between whom and the present possessor four and twenty generations of this illustrious house have passed by."[1]

---

[1] In the Notes to his publication of Adamnan's "Life of St. Columba," p. 320.

There are, indeed, few nations, and few families, who can boast the possession of such a treasure.

Another relic of St. Columba was called the *Cuilebath*. The legend connected with this is precisely one of those very early Celtic histories which have been so interwoven with a thread of poetic fiction as to throw doubt on its authenticity. It is not difficult to an unprejudiced mind to discover the underlying foundation of fact.

The narrative is thus given by O'Curry from original documents :—

" On the death of the monarch Domhnall, son of Aedh, son of Ainmire (A.D. 639), his eldest son Donuchadh (or Donach) became king of the *Cinel Conaill ;* and his younger son, Finacha, became king of the Fer Rois. Fiacha much oppressed his subjects, and his oppression was at length the cause of his death at their hands. It is stated that in the second year of his reign, he held a meeting of his people at the mouth of the river Boyne, and that, during the holding of that meeting, a wild deer, started by them, was followed by the king's guards ; whereupon the men of Ross, enraged at such an assertion of ' prerogative,' killed the king himself with his own weapons. *Fiacha's* brother, Donuchadh, came upon them in revenge ; but he stayed his vengeance until he should consult his Aumchara (literally, ' soul's friend '), the Comharba (successor) of Saint Columcille, to whom he sent a message to Iona to ask his advice on the case.

" The Comharba of St. Colum-cille sent over two of his confidential clerics, Snedhgus and MacRiaghla, with his advice, which was, that Donuchadh should send sixty couples of the men and women of Ross, in boats out upon the sea, and then leave them to the judgment of God. The exiles were accordingly put into small boats, launched upon the water, and watched, so that they should not land again.

"The priests, Snedhgus and Mac Riaghla, having discharged their own duties, set out upon their return to Iona. As they were passing along over the sea, they determined to go of their own will on a wandering pilgrimage, and leave to Providence the direction of their course; praying, at the same time, to be carried to wherever the sixty banished couples had found a resting-place. They then ceased to work or direct their boat; and the wind carried them north-westwards, into the ocean.

"The legend then proceeds with a fanciful account of how they were driven to several wonderful islands, some inhabited and some uninhabited. In some they were received with friendship, in others with hostility. After being carried to several of these islands, however, the wind at last blew them to one, in which there was an immense tree on which were perched a flock of beautiful white birds, with a chief bird having a golden head and silver wings. This great bird related to them the history of the world from its beginning; the Birth of Christ, of Mary the Virgin; His Baptism, Passion, and Resurrection; as well as His coming to the judgment. And when the great bird had concluded, all the rest lashed their sides with their wings until the blood gushed from them, out of terror of the day of judgment. And the great bird gave one of the leaves of the foliage of this great tree to the priests; and this leaf was as large as the hide of a great ox; and he ordered them to carry it away, and lay it on St. Colum-cille's altar. 'And it is St. Colum-cille's Cuilefadh at this day in Cennanas [or Kells].'

"'Sweet was the music of these birds,' continues the story, singing psalms and canticles in praise of the Lord, for they were birds of the psalms of Heaven; and the leaves, or body of the tree upon which they were, never decay. And the clerics left the island, and were driven by the wind to another island; and as they were approaching the land they heard the sweet voices of women singing; and immediately they recognised this music, and said, 'That is the *Seanan* [or sweet plaintive song] of the women of Erin;' and having come to land, they were joyfully received by the women of Erin, who spoke to them in their own language, and conducted them to the house of their chief, who told them he was the chief of the banished men of Erin. The clerics then returned safely home."

It is to be remarked that after every little prose article in this curious piece on the adventures of the clerics, the incidents are summed up in verse, from which it may be inferred, that the whole story was originally written in verse. The tale is preserved in the MS. H. 2 16 Library of T. C. D.

It is further to be remarked that in the short metrical summary of this legend, there is no mention that the great leaf, or Cuilefadh, was placed on the altar of St. Colum-cille at Kells; and from this circumstance we may fairly assume that the verse is older than the prose, and that what was originally a short narrative poem, was at a subsequent period broken up and interpolated with a prose commentary. That this was done some time after the year 1090, before which the Cuilefadh was not at Kells, will appear quite clear from the following curious entry in the continuation of the Annals of Tighernach at that year.

" 1090. The sacred relics of St. Colum-cille, namely, the *Clog-na-Righ* [or bell of the kings], and the Cuilebaigh, and the two gospels, were brought from Tirconnell, and seven score ounces of silver; and it was Aengus O'Domhnallain that brought them from the north."

It may be asked to what place they were brought? This, I think, is sufficiently shown to have been Kells, by the following entry which I take from the Annals of the Four Masters in the year 1109 :—

"Aengus O'Domhnaillain, chief spiritual director and chief elder of St. Colum-cille's people, died at Kells."

His name likewise appears as a witness to a charter of land in an entry in the Great Book of Kells in Trinity College.

The *Cuilefadh* of St. Patrick, or of Armagh, is alluded to in the Annals of the Four Masters, at the year 1128, where mention is made of a young priest, who had been carrying it, being killed by an assault of the O'Rourkes of *Briefné* on the Comharba or Primate of Armagh, when returning from Connaught with his offerings. A third *Cuilefadh* is spoken of in connection with another Saint—Saint Eimhin, from whom the modern town of Monaster-even takes its name. It is referred to in a vellum MS. of the year 1463, in the Royal Irish Academy.

But we must return to the interrupted narrative of St. Columba's monastic life in Ireland.

St. Adamnan relates an incident in the life of the Saint, which occurred while he was with Gemnan, and while he was yet a deacon.

The Saint and his master were one day occupied in reading, and seated on the plain in the part of Leinster where they lived. While they were thus employed, a young girl, who was pursued by a cruel persecutor, fled to Gemnan for refuge and protec-

tion. He called to Columba, who was but a little distance off, to assist in rescuing her ; but before they
could attain their object, the man had stabbed the girl,
though they had thrown their mantles over her, an
act which was equivalent to claiming sanctuary for
her. This right of an ecclesiastic to give sanctuary
was ever respected except by the utterly abandoned
and degraded. The old man cried out to St. Columba,
"How long will God, the great Judge, allow this
crime and sacrilegious injustice to go unpunished?"
Columba replied, "The soul of the murderer will
descend into hell the very instant that the soul of
this girl, whom he has murdered, ascends into heaven."
And even as he spoke, the murderer, "like Ananias
before Peter," fell dead at the feet of the Saint.

The news of this miracle was quickly spread
throughout Ireland, and the fame of St. Columba
became greatly increased.

As there is but little chronological sequence in the
narrative of St. Columba's miracles, we may record
here some others of a similar nature.

Once when the Saint was living in the island of
Hinba, a site which has not been identified, he found
it necessary to excommunicate the sons of Conall,
who were oppressing religious houses. One of the
associates of these men, "instigated by the devil,"
rushed on the Saint with a spear to kill him. But
one of his disciples, named Finlagan, put on the
Saint's mantle, and like Ordann, the charioteer of

Saint Patrick, was prepared to sacrifice his own life to save his master. But the mantle proved a protective case against the sharp spear which *Manus Dextra* used, and the good monk escaped unhurt.[1]

Exactly a year afterwards, when, in the island of Hy, he said:—"A year has passed to-day since Lamhders [Manus dextra] tried to kill Finlagan in my place, but he is himself amongst the slain this very hour."

Soon after, the news came to Hy that the Saint's persecutor was indeed killed in battle, on the very day and at the very time that the Saint had declared.

On another occasion the Saint asked and obtained hospitality for a certain Pict of noble family, from a rich man who lived in the island of Islay. This man was named Tarain, and the same name is found at a later date in the catalogue of the Pictish kings.

Teradach, a Celtic name, was the person to whom this chief was confided. For some reason which is not given, Tarain proved a traitor, and killed his guest.

When St. Columba heard of this fearful crime he said, "This unhappy man has not lied to me, but to God, and his name shall be blotted out of the Book of Life.

---

[1] The monk has been identified with Finnloga, the brother of St. Finton, of Down, in the county Tyrone. Finnloga was certainly contemporary with St. Columba, St. Finnian, and St. Comgall. His church is at Tamlaght, Finlagan, near Newtownlimavady. *Manus dextra* is the Latin translation of the Irish words, right hand.

"I speak now in summer time; but before autumn, before he can eat the flesh of the swine fattened by the fruit of the trees, he shall be seized by death suddenly, and shall be carried off to the infernal regions."

The prediction was fulfilled to the letter. The unhappy man had some food prepared for him at the earliest day possible when the swine had fattened on the autumn fruit, but even as he stretched out his hand to seize a morsel, he fell and expired. "And all who saw this, and all who heard of it, feared and marvelled greatly, and honoured Christ in His holy prophet."

The loving nature of the Saint led him to care tenderly for all those who were so happy as to enjoy his friendship. Amongst those who were thus honoured we find mention of several persons bearing the name of Columbanus. One of these persons, we are told, was a poor man who entertained the Saint hospitably for a night.

In the morning Columba inquired what worldly goods he possessed, and was informed that he had only five cows, poor and small, "but," he added, "if you bless them they will increase." The Saint desired him to bring them before him; and when this was done he said, "Your cattle will increase to one hundred and five, and you shall be blessed with many children and good children." And all fell out even as the Saint predicted, the number of cattle always remaining the same.

Some member of the race of Conell made prey several times upon the cattle and goods of Columbanus. On the third occasion he was reproved by St. Columba, who desired him to repent and restore his booty. But Joan only mocked at his words, and embarked with the stolen property.

He forgot that he had to do with a Saint. Columba went down into the water, and there raised up his hands to Heaven, and "prayed Christ, who glorified His elect, to glorify him." Then he went and sat on a hill with some of his disciples, and predicted that the vessel should never return to the port from which he had sailed, or reach the land whither he was going—that a cloud should arise from the earth bringing a storm which should destroy him and his companions.

The day was calm and serene, but in a few moments a cloud arose from the sea, and a hurricane began to blow. The ship was dashed to pieces between Mull and Colonsay, and the words of the Saint were verified, for none escaped, though the sea around was not disturbed.

There is an incident recorded of another Columbanus, which is evidence of the great veneration for the sign of the Cross and its power.

This youth, called Columbanus Briun, is conjectured by Colgan to have been St. Colman of Lindisfarne. He was carrying home a vessel of new milk, and he stopped at the door of the little cell where the Saint was writing as usual, and asked him to bless his burden.

But when the Saint made the sign of the Cross there appeared a strange commotion in the vessel, the lid was suddenly flung off, and the greater part of the milk was spilled. The youth laid down the vessel and began to pray. But the Saint desired him to rise, and said, "You have acted unwisely to-day, in that you did not make the sign of the Cross of our Lord on your vessel before you poured the milk into it. Therefore the demon has entered there, but being unable to bear the sign of the Cross, he has fled." Then he desired him to bring the vessel near to him that he might bless it, and when he had done so, "the benediction of his holy hand" so increased the little milk which remained that the pail was again completely filled. We may be assured that this was a lesson not easily forgotten, and that the all-powerful sign of our redemption would be used more devoutly and more frequently than ever.[1]

Another Columbanus, who is spoken of as a priest, was also favoured by our Saint with a miracle. And in recording this, Adamnan quotes the passage of Holy Scripture, "All things are possible to him that believeth." We may note here that if very wonderful

---

[1] Tertullian, one of the early fathers of the Church, relates that the Christians used this sign almost at every moment. That no action of the day was begun or ended without being placed under the protection of God by the devout use of the holy sign.

events are recorded by the one Saint of the other, it is no mere collection of idle tales or fanciful legends. We have already shown what ample opportunities Adamnan had for obtaining information on the subjects on which he writes. We have seen how solemnly he declares his belief that all that he relates is true, and what pains he took to be accurate and truthful; and we find here, as frequently through his writings, that he was well read and learned in Holy Scripture, as, indeed, were all the fathers of the early Irish Church. This fact, which cannot be denied, ought certainly to have weight with those who fancy that the supernatural is only believed by those who are ignorant of Scripture.

Probably no Protestant ever devoted half the time to the study of the Scriptures that was given to them by St. Columba and St. Adamnan. It was not because they were ignorant of Holy Scripture, or indifferent to it, but rather because they loved it, and believed it, that they thus wrote of the favours granted by our Lord to His Saints—favours which He himself had promised in these very Scriptures should be granted to those who believed in His name.

On one occasion Baitheneus and the "priest Columbanus" were both to depart from Hy in different directions, and both wanted a favourable wind—a matter of no small importance in those days, when steam was unknown, and a frail coracle the only sea-going craft.

This seemed hard to ask, certainly ; but then, what was the use of having a Saint for your friend if he could not do something for you—and a Saint, more-over, who was a *Thaumaturgus,* or wonder-worker ?

So Baitheneus and Columbanus asked, and "the Lord granted"—the Lord, the ruler of the waves and winds, and the lover of His Saints. And in truth those who disbelieve, or those who are so fearful, for the humility of God's chosen ones, for those to whom He grants many favours not given to others, need trouble themselves little. It is "the Lord" who gives, and none know it so well or recognise so truly that the favours or the gifts are not their own, as do those blessed ones to whom such graces are given.

Baitheneus set out in the morning, and crossed safely "the whole of the great sea as far as the land of Ethica !" At the third hour the Saint called Columbanus to him and said, "Baitheneus has now reached his port after a peaceful voyage, do you pre-pare to sail now, the Lord will soon change the wind to the north." After he had taken his departure, St. Columba uttered these prophetic words : "The holy man Columbanus, whom we have blessed on his departure to-day, will not again see my face in this world."

And this prophecy also was fulfilled, for in a year's

time St. Columba made his migration to the heavenly country.[1]

[1] This Columbanus has been identified with St. Colman Ela, sometimes called Colmanellus. He derived his name from Ela, a river which gives its name to his church of Iann-Ela, now Lynelly, near Tullamore, in King's County. He was born at Glenelly, in the county Tyrone, A.D. 555, and died at his monastery of Lynelly in 611. His festival is noted on September 26. He was a relative of St. Columba. His mother, Mar, was daughter of St. Columba's sister Fedblunidh, according to the calendar of Donegal.

CHAPTER V.

ST. COLUMBA IN IRELAND.

BUT we must return to Ireland. While St. Columba was at Clonard, he was sent by St. Finnian to receive episcopal consecration from a bishop called Etchen. The story as told in several accounts is undoubtedly a mistake, probably the result of some trifling error in transcription. Columba was not then ordained priest, and it is made to appear as if he was consecrated to the episcopacy though he had not yet received orders. This is simply impossible; no such occurrence is ever mentioned, inferred, or hinted in the annals of the Irish Church. Bishops were far more numerous then than now, but the reason is obvious. In an age when communication between one part of the country and another was difficult and often impossible for a considerable period of time, it was necessary that there should be bishops in every locality.[1]

It is at least certain that Etchen was a bishop, and that he ordained St. Columba priest. Etchen was Bishop of Clonfod, in the territory now called Farbill, in Westmeath.

St. Columba left St. Finnian then, or soon after, and went to the monastery of *Mobhi Clarainech* at *Glas-Naoidhen,* now Glasnevin, near Dublin.[2]

Many circumstances of interest are related in connection with St. Columba's residence at Glasnevin.

The students' huts were at the west side of the river Tolka, the church or oratory was at the other side. One night in winter time, the bell rang as usual for matins, but the river was frozen over. The Saint passed it fearlessly, and was saluted by Saint Mobhi with the exclamation, "Bravely hast thou acted, descendant of Niall." The Saint replied, "God is competent to relieve us of this difficulty." The office over, the students were about to get back to their huts as best they might, when each found his

---

[1] We do not go into the question here more fully, as it would occupy considerable space, and is not directly connected with our present subject.

[2] *Mobhi Clarainech.* The latter word signifying flat-faced. He is said to have been a fellow-student with St. Columba at Clonard. He is called also Berchan. He is noted as one of the twelve apostles of Eriu ; his festival is kept on the 12th October.

own on the east bank of the river, and close to the church.

A plague, which from time to time devastated Ireland, broke out when Columba was here, and Mobhi dismissed his pupils. Saints Congall, Ciaran, and Camieach were companions of St. Columba at this school.

As St. Columba journeyed north, he passed the little river Bior, now called the Moyola Water, which runs into Lough Neagh on the north-west, and he prayed that the fatal plague might not extend further northward. A somewhat similar incident is related by Adamnan. While the Saint was living at Iona, he saw a dense cloud rise from the sea, as he sat on a hill. He turned to one of his monks called Silman, and said, " This cloud will be very hurtful to man and cattle, and passing rapidly over Ireland from *Aithine* [the Delvin river, Co. Meath] to *Ath-cliath* [Dublin], it will discharge a pestilential rain. This will raise ulcers on men and cattle, and cause many to die. But we ought to give them relief with the Divine assistance. Do you, therefore, come down from this hill, and prepare for your voyage on to-morrow."

The following day Silman was ready to obey the commands of the Saint, who gave him bread which he had blessed, and which the monk was to dip in water, and then sprinkle the water on man and beast.

The monk set out and had a most favourable voyage, as the Saint had promised him. On his arrival in the district which is known at present as the Co. Louth,

G

he found six men in a house who were already in the agony of death, and these six men were at once cured by the application of the water in which the bread had been dipped.

They praised "Christ and St. Columba," for then, as now, Catholics knew by whose power such miracles were performed, and were very far from giving undue honour to creatures. The cure soon became known far and wide, the fame of the miracle was spread abroad, and as the sick were brought a few centuries before to the shadow of Peter for healing, so now did they flock to obtain the bread of the Thaumaturgus of Ireland.

And here, again, we have yet another instance of the careful accuracy of the Saint who records all these marvels. Not satisfied with the strong assurance of his veracity which he had already put on record, and the care he had taken to ascertain the truth of every record, he here adds, "Silman, a soldier of Christ, testified to the truth of this in every particular, in the presence of the abbot Sigienus and other seniors." Thus we see, that marvellous as the records are, they were taken from the lips of those who had witnessed them, and noted down with solemn accuracy by those who wrote them.[1]

While on this subject, though the narrative does not follow with chronological accuracy, we may nar-

---

[1] Sigienus, or *Seghine*, son of Fiachna, was the fifth abbot of Hy, and governed that monastery from A.D. 623 to 652. His festival is August 12. He is mentioned by Bede.

rate another miraculous event which shows how St. Columba's heart was still in the land of his birth.

During the time that he was abbot of Iona, he called one of the monks to him one morning after Prime, and told him to prepare for a quick voyage to Ireland. The holy virgin Maugina, daughter of Diamen, had fallen on her return home from the oratory after mass, and had broken her thigh in two places. "She is now," said the Saint, "calling on me earnestly, hoping that she may receive some consolation from the Lord." Then he gave a piece of blessed bread in a little casket of pine-wood to the monk Lugaidh, and ordered him to have it dipped in water, and let the water be poured on the injured limb.

Quid plura? What more! what shall we say more, exclaims Adamnan—saintly biographer of a Saint; to whom it seemed, if we may say so, but natural that the miracle should follow. All was done as Columba had commanded. The fractured bone was instantly made whole. And on the cover of the casket the Saint wrote the number of three-and-twenty years, which the holy virgin was to live after her cure, and this also was fulfilled as the Saint had predicted.[1]

[1] It must be remembered that all the persons mentioned in the Life of St. Columba, as having been the subjects of miraculous cures or assistance of any kind were well known and historical. Even those who deny or question the miracles of the Saint, cannot, and indeed do not wish to, deny the existence of the persons named. Indeed, it would be impossible to do so, for all these events occurred at a time when our annals were put on written and well-authorised records. Daimin, the father of this holy virgin, was king or chief of the district of *Air-*

The church of Derry was founded by St. Columba in 546, according to the annals of Ulster.

The various incidents connected with this foundation are deeply interesting, and characteristic of the times.

When Columba went to the North, after the breaking up of the school of St. Mobi, he passed a short time with his relatives, and then reached *Daire Calgaich*, now Londonderry.

The royal fort of Aedh, son of Aimmce, then king of Ireland, was here, and Aedh offered the fort to Columba to found a monastery. But Columba refused the gift, because, when he was leaving *Mobi* (Berchan, abbot of Glasnevin), he had forbidden him to receive anything of the world until he heard of his death. The next day, however, three of Mobi's disciples met him, and they told him of his death, and they showed him Mobi's girdle which they had with them.

The Saint to honour his master pronounced the following quatrain :—

> Mobi's girdle, Mobi's girdle,
> It closed not upon emptiness,
> It opened not upon satiety,
> Nor did it shut upon falsehood.

Columba then went to the king, and said, "The offering which thou gavest to me yesterday, give to me now." The king complied with his request, but that night the fort was burned. How this happened is not very clear.[1]

---

ghialla, where the See of Clogher was founded by St. Maccarthen, in the lifetime of St. Patrick.

[1] In the "Quinta Vita" of Colgan it is more than insinuated that

The king was exceedingly displeased, and said, "If the place had not been burned there would never have been any lack of food or raiment therein." But Columba replied, that "there never should be any want therein, and whoever might be in it they should never be a night without food."

St. Columba composed a hymn at this time, which has been happily preserved ; great store was set by it in the early Irish Church, and it was believed that the recital of it would be a protection against fire and thunderstorms.

That the fire was accidental, or, perhaps, it might be more correct to say providential, there can be little question. The Preface, which is admittedly of great antiquity, says :—"The fire, however, in consequence of its greatness, threatened to burn the whole *Daire*, so that it was to save it at that time that this hymn was composed." Now, it is certainly not likely that the Saint would have composed the hymn to save the *Daire*, if he had been in any way the means of setting it on fire. The opening verse of the hymn, too, seems to indicate that the place had been consumed by the effects of a thunderstorm.

In the following translation we have endeavoured to keep as close as possible to the original text in word and metre :—

Columba formed the plan himself, and that his object was to have it rebuilt by those who should do the work with holy hands. It is said also, that he removed all the inhabitants first. But the narrative is given elsewhere, as if the conflagration had been accidental.

NOLI, PATER, INDULGERE TONITRUI CUM FULGERE.

Noli, pater, indulgere	Father, keep under
Tonitrua cum fulgure,	The tempest and thunder,
Ac frangamur formidine	Lest we should be shattered
Hujus atque uridine.	By Thy lightning's shafts scattered.
Te timemus terribilem	Thy terrors while hearing,
Nullum credentes similem,	We listen still fearing
Te cuncta canunt carmina	The resonant song
Angelorum per agmina.	Of the bright angel throng,
Teque exultent culmina	As they wander and praise Thee,
Cœli vagi per fulmina,	Shouts of honour still raise Thee.
O Jehesu amantissime	To the King ruling right,
O rex regum rectissime.	Jesu, lover and light,
Benedictus in secula	As with wine and clear mead,
Recta regens regimina.	Filled with God's grace indeed,
Johannes coram domino	Precursor John Baptist's word,
Adhuc matris in utero.	Told of the coming Lord,
Repletus dei gratia pro	Whom, blessed for evermore,
Vino atque siccera.	All men should bow before.
Elizabeth et Zacharias	Zacharias, Elizabeth,
Verum magnum genuit,	This Saint begot.
Johannem baptizam	May the fire of Thy love live in my
Precursorem domini.	heart yet,
Manet in meo corde	As jewel of gold in a silver vase
Dei amoris flamma	set ![1]
Ut in argenti vase auri	
Ponitur gemma.	

We add the hymn *In te Christe* here, because it was also composed by St. Columba, though on a different occasion :—

In te Christe credentium	Thou who all men dost relieve,
Miserearis omnium,	Christ in Thee I do believe,
Tu es deus in secula	Come unto my aid, O Lord,
Seculorum in gloria.	While I labour for Thy word ;

---

[1] In Colgan's version of the Preface, he says, that two graces are believed to be granted to the recital of this hymn. First, that those

Deus in adjutorium
Intende laborantium,
Ad dolorum remedium
Festina in auxilium.
Deus pater credentium,
Deus vita viventium,
Deus deorum omnium,
Deus virtus virtutium.
Deus formator omnium,
Deus et judex judicum,
Deus et princeps principum
Elimentorum omnium.
Deus opis eximiæ
Celestis hierusolimæ,
Deus rex regni in gloria,
Deus ipse viventium.
Deus æterni luminis
Deus inenarrabilis,
Deus altus amabilis
Deus inestimabilis.
Deus largus longanimis
Deus doctor docibilis,
Deus qui facit omnia
Nova cuncta et vetera.
Dei patris in nomine
Filique sui prospere,
Sancti spiritus utique
Recto vado itenere.
Christus redemptor gentium
Christus amator virginium,
Christus fons sapientium,
Christus fides credentium.
Christus lorica militum,
Christus creator omnium,
Christus salus viventium
Et vita morientium.

Hasten to my help, I pray,
Bear my burden every day.
Of all mankind the maker Thou,
Before Thy throne our Judge we
bow.

O Lord of lords and King of kings !
To Thee all nature homage brings.
The angels all alone in state,
In the celestial city wait.

O God of gods, eternal Light,
O Lord most high, most sweet,
most bright ;
O God of patience, past all thought ;
O God, Thou teacher of the taught ;

O God, who hast made all that
was,
Of past and present Thou the cause.
O Father, for Thy Son's dear sake,
Prepare the way that I shall take,

And let Thy Holy Spirit guide
My soul through all my wandering
wide.

Christ, lover of the virgin choir,
Christ, man's Redeemer from hell-
fire,
Christ, fount of wisdom, pure and
clear,
Christ, in whose word we hope and
fear,

who recite it should be preserved from the effects of thunder and
lightning. Secondly, that those who recite it at night before going to
rest, and in the morning when they rise, shall be preserved from all
adversity.

Coronavit exercitum nostrum
Cum turba martirum,
Christus crucem ascenderat,
Christus mundum salvaverat.
Christus et nos redemeret,
Christus pro nobis passus est,
Christus infernum penetrat,
Christus cœlum ascenderat.
Christus cum deo sederat
Ubi nunquam defuerat.
Gloria hæc est altissimo
Deo patri ingenito,
Honor ac summo filio
Unico unigenito.
Spirituique obtimo
Sancto perfecto sedulo,
Amen fiat perpetua
In sempiterna secula.

Christ, breastplate in the hour of
fight,
Christ, who hast made the world
and light.

Christ, of the dead the living life,
Christ, of the living, strength in
strife.
Christ, crowner of each conquering
soul,
Who counts them in the martyrs'
roll.

Christ, Saviour of the world so wide,
Christ, on the Cross at Passion tide.
Christ, into depths of hell descends,
Christ, into heaven above ascends.

There is no doubt that Derry was the Saint's favourite country. In the beautiful poem given in full below we find ample evidence of this, as well as of the passionate love of the Saint for his native land. To have "the stern of his coracle turned upon Derry" was no slight addition to the pain of expatriation.

> Delightful to be on Benn-Edar,[1]
>   Before going o'er the white sea :
>   The dashing of the waves against its face,
>   The bareness of its shores and its borders.
>
> Delightful to be on Benn-Edar,
>   After coming o'er the white-bosomed sea,
>   To row one's little coracle,
>   Ochone ! on the surf-waved shore.

---

[1] Benn Edar, the highest part of the peninsula of Howth, near Dublin, was called Benn-Edar.

How rapid the speed of my coracle,
   And its stern turned upon Derry ;
   I grieve at my errand, o'er the noble sea
   Travelling to Alba of the ravens.

My fort is my sweet little coracle,
   My sad heart still bleeding :
   Weak is the man that cannot lead ;
   Totally blind are all the ignorant.

There is a grey eye
   That looks back upon Erin ;
   It shall not see, during life,
   The men of Erin, nor their wives.

My vision o'er the brine I stretch
   From the ample oaken planks ;
   Large is the tear of my soft grey eye,
   When I look back upon Erin.

Upon Erin my attention is fixed,
   Upon Loch Levin, upon Line,
   Upon the lands the Ultonians own,
   Upon smooth Munster, upon Meath.

Numerous in the East are all champions,
   Many the diseases and distempers there,
   Many they with scanty clothes,
   Many the hard and jealous hearts.

Plentiful in the West the apple fruit ;
   Many the kings and princes ;
   Plentiful its luxuriant sloes,
   Plentiful its noble acorn-bearing oaks.

Melodious her clerics, melodious her birds ;
   Gentle her youths, wise her seniors ;
   Illustrious her men, noble to behold ;
   Illustrious her women for fond espousal.

It is in the West sweet Brendan is,
 And Colum son of Crimthann ;
 And in the West fair Baithen shall be,
 And in the West shall Adamnan be.

Carry my inquiries after that
 Unto Comgall of eternal life ;
 Carry my inquiries after that
 To the bold king of fair Emania.

Carry with thee, thou noble youth,
 My blessing and my benediction,
 One half upon Erin, sevenfold ;
 And half on Alba at the same time.

Carry my benediction over the sea
 To the nobles of Island of the Gaedhil ;
 Let them not credit Molaisi's [1] words,
 Nor his threatened prosecution.

Were it not for Molaisi's words
 At the cross of Ath-Imlaisi,
 I should not now permit
 Disease or distemper in Ireland.

Take my blessing with thee to the West ;
 Broken is my heart in my breast :
 Should sudden death overtake me,
 It is for my great love of the Gaedhil.

Gaedhil, Gaedhil, beloved name !
 My only desire is to invoke it :
 Beloved is Cuimin of fair hair ;
 Beloved are Cainnech and Comghall.

---

[1] Molaisi's words. This is an allusion to the exile, said to have been enjoined on him as a penance by St. Molaise.

Were the tribute of all Alba mine,
　　From its centre to its border,
　　I would prefer the site of one house
　　In the middle of fair Derry.

The reason I love Derry is,
　　For its quietness, for its purity,
　　And for its crowds of white angels
　　From the one end to the other.

The reason why I love Derry is,
　　For its quietness, for its purity,
　　Crowded full of heaven's angels
　　Is every leaf of the oaks of Derry.

My Derry, my little oak-grove,
　　My dwelling and my little cell;
　　O eternal God, in heaven above,
　　Woe be to him who violates it !

Beloved are Durrow and Derry,
　　Beloved is Raphoe in purity,
　　Beloved Drumhome of rich fruits,
　　Beloved are Swords and Kells.

Beloved to my heart also in the West,
　　Drumcliff, at Culcinne's strand :
　　To behold the fair Loch Fewal,
　　The form of its shores is delightful.

Delightful is that, and delightful
　　The salt main on which the sea-gulls cry,
　　On my coming from Derry afar ;
　　It is quiet, and it is delightful.

Like many of the saints, his love of God expended
itself even on inanimate nature. The oak groves

were specially dear to him, and it is said, that when
a tree fell in his beloved wood he would not allow it
to be touched for nine days, and then a tenth part
was set aside for the poor, and a third for the use of
strangers, and the rest was distributed amongst all the
people of Derry.   Indeed, a love of benefactors, and a
desire to do them every possible service, has ever been
characteristic of God's greatest saints.

When his church was to be built he would not
allow the trees to be cut down, but preferred having
it placed in a less convenient site to avoid touching
them.   Yet, he had the holy altar placed at the
east end, that he might not depart from the custom
of the Church, and here he offered the adorable
sacrifice.

One of those rarely beautiful and instructive incidents, common to the lives of many saints, is recorded
as having happened at Derry.

The Saint fed a hundred poor men daily, but his
steward, or dispenser, did not quite appreciate the
liberality of his master.   He had a fixed time for
giving the dole of food, and any one who came late
was peremptorily dismissed.

A poor man came one day late, and was, as usual,
sent away.   The next day he came in time, but was
told there was nothing for him.   For many days he
came, but each time he met with some repulse.

He then sent a message to Columba, to tell him
that he advised him for the future to put no limit to

his charity while he had alms to give, except what God set on the number of those who came for it.

Columba was struck by the message, and came down to the gate of the monastery, not waiting even to put on his cloak. He hastened after the beggar; but when he had gone some distance he found not the poor man, but Christ, who had taken the form of a beggar. Then, as he fell down and adored his Lord, he obtained from him a royal alms—new lights, new graces, new and yet more wonderful powers of miracle and prophecy. In the precise language of the chronicle, "He saw both the secrets of Holy Scripture, things happening at a distant place or time, and even what was passing in a man's thoughts; and he came to know about beasts and birds, and their affections, and their language, and of what great value it was to have pity on the poor, when that virtue was joined on to other virtues." And so it came to pass that when St. Brendan came to visit him with a hundred men there was food for all, and the very lakes were filled with fish for his service.

St. Columba's first church at Derry was called *Dubh-regles*, the Black Church. In a quatrain quoted by the ancient annalist Tighernach, this church is thus mentioned:—

> "Three years, without light, was
> Colum in his Black Church;
> He passed to angels from his body,
> After seven years and seventy."

From this it would appear as if the Saint had spent some time here in penitential exercises. The remains of the church, which existed as late as 1520, show that it had been built north and south, thus giving another evidence of the strict accuracy of our chronicles, whether religious or secular. In the fourteenth century it was called *Cella Nigra de Deria*. The round tower remained until the seventeenth century.

Certainly a hundred years of Protestant iconoclasm did more to destroy the most ancient and venerable relics of this country than all burnings or drownings of Danes or Saxons.

But the Saint was by no means satisfied with the erection of one church and monastery. We are told that his heart burned to evangelise, and that he placed a relative of his own over his beloved house at Derry, and then passed to other parts of Ireland.

The monastery of Durrow was his chief foundation, and this is mentioned by the English, and almost contemporary historian, Bede. The Irish name is *Dair-Magh*, and sometimes abbey church. A sculptured cross still remains called St. Columkill's Cross, and a well dedicated to his honour. Durrow is situated in the present barony of Ballycowan, King's County; according to the annals of Tighernach Aedh, the son of Brendan, king of Tebhtha (Teffia), bestowed Darmach on Columkille. Aedh became chief of Teffia in 553.

A poem still remains which St. Columba is said to

have composed on leaving Durrow (the field of the apple-trees) for the last time.

> Beloved the excellent seven
>   Whom Christ has chosen to His kingdom,
>   To whom I leave for their purity
>   The constant care of this my church.
>
> Three of whom are here at this side :
>   Cormac, son of Dima and Angus,
>   And Collan of pure heart,
>   Who has joined himself to them.
>
> Libren, Senan, comely Conrach,
>   The son of Ua Chien, and his brother,
>   Are the four, besides the others
>   Who shall arrive at this place.
>
> They are the seven pillars,
>   And they are the seven chiefs,
>   Whom God has surely commanded
>   To dwell in the same abode.

Cormac, son of Dima, or Cormac Ua Laithain, was of a Munster family. He is mentioned by Adamnan in the first book of "St. Columba's Miracles" thus :—

"St. Columba," he says, "prophesied of Connar Ua Laithain, who went thrice to seek for 'the desert in the ocean,' but did not find it, that he was then embarking from that district which lies beyond the river Moig [Co. Sligo], and that he should not find what he sought, for no other fault than this, that he had taken with him a monk who had left his monastery without the leave of his superior."

From this it is evident how strictly monastic discipline was observed.

In Cormac's second voyage this incident is related. He had sailed far from the land over the "boundless ocean," when St. Columba thus secured protection for him on his return. He addressed the chief of the Orkney Isles in the presence of King Bende, and asked him to direct that chief whose hostages were in his hands to respect some of his brethren who should soon arrive in the Orkneys.

This prevision saved Cormac's life, as his companions having landed a few months later in the island were treated with respect.

A few months after the Saint had claimed hospitality and protection for Cormac, some of his monks were speaking of him, and wondering if his voyage had been successful. Columba replied, " You will see him arrive here to-day." In about one hour after, the prophetic words were fulfilled by the arrival of the traveller.

Cormac appears to have had a passion for the sea; for we hear of a third voyage, in which he also obtained miraculous assistance from his holy patron. Adverse winds and loathesome insects combined to place his vessel and his companions in danger; but they invoked the help of St. Columba, " who, though far distant in body, was near in spirit."

Then, by Divine interposition, the Saint knew of the peril in which the monks were placed, and calling all the brethren who were with him to the oratory, he began to pray fervently for a favourable wind, and soon rising from his knees, he declared that the favour had been granted. Cormac was then enabled to land safely, and proceeded at once to thank the Saint, to whose intercession he attributed his deliverance.

While the monastery of Durrow was building, St. Columba went to visit the monks who were living at Clonmacnoise, which had been founded by Ciaran (A.D. 548). As soon as his arrival was made known, all the monks assembled, together with their abbot, *Ailithir,* and went out "as one man" to meet and honour the Saint.[1]

As they met him they bowed down their heads in reverence to one so favoured by God, and embracing him warmly they led him to the church with hymns and canticles. A canopy was held over his head by four men, to prevent his being pressed on by the multitude.

As they passed along, a boy who had not been in much repute with the community, and whose dress and manners were not in his favour, stole behind the Saint and touched his garment. "The Saint saw with the eyes of his soul what he could not see with the eyes of his body," and at once turned round and seized the boy.

The lad was terrified when he found he was discovered, and all around called loudly to the Saint not to touch one so sinful. But the Saint begged them to

---

[1] It may, perhaps, be well to note that these incidents are all of historical accuracy. Ailithir was the fourth abbot of Clonmacnoise, the most famous of the ancient Irish monasteries. His death is recorded by Tighernach under the year 599.

allow him to carry out his designs. He took the boy, put out his tongue which he blessed, and then, turning to those around, he predicted that this contemptible and worthless youth should have a great future, and that from henceforth he should please the monks as much as he had hitherto displeased them.

This boy was known afterwards, and honoured as a Saint, his festival being kept on the 18th of August as Erinn or Ernenens, and a church was dedicated to him at Wicklow, and other places.

St. Columba is said to have predicted the disputes which should arise about the keeping of Easter on this occasion also.

It was during the Saint's residence at Durrow that he blessed an apple-tree which bore fruit, indeed, but of so sour a kind that it could not be used. "Quicker than the word," bitterness was changed to sweetness, and the tree henceforth bore only sweet fruit.

St. Columba founded a considerable number of religious houses in Ireland. Of these, Kells and Swords are the most noteworthy. The site of the monastery at Kells was known anciently as *Dunchuile-Sibrinne.* In the time of the Saint it was the *dun*, seat or royal fortress of *Diarmod Mac Cerbhail.*

The ancient lives of the Saint say that "Colum-cille marked out the extent of the city as it now is, and blessed it all; and said that it would become the most illustrious possession he should have in the land, although it would not be there his resurrection should be." In O'Donnell's Life of the Saint, he says, that Diarmiat granted it to Columba in amends for injuries which he had done him.

This foundation, however, did not become a place — of much monastic importance until the year 804, when the annals of Ulster say: "Kells was given without battle to Columkille, the harmonious, in this year." The attacks made on Hy on account of its exposed situation obliged the monks to look for a place of refuge in Ireland, and from this period Kells became the great seat of the monks of St. Columba. The round tower still remains, and the oratory called St. Columkille's house, with many other interesting relics of its past history.

It is said that Columba blessed a cowl for Aedh Slane, Diarmiat's son, in return for the donation of the monastic site at Kells, so that he should not be wounded while he wore it. But Aedh was guilty of fratricide, and four years after he went on a predatory expedition and forgot the cowl, and, as the annals pithily describe it, " he was slain that day."

The annals of Ulster have the following record under the year 1034 :—

" Marina Ua h Uchtain, Lecturer of Kells, was lost on his voyage from Scotland, and Colum-cille's *Culebadh* and three of St. Patrick's relics and thirty men with him."

The annals of Tighernach under the year 1090

have a reference to the same garment or to another
of the same kind :—

"The reliquaries of Columkille, namely the Bell of the
Kings, and the *Cuillebaigh,* came from Tirconnell with
120 ounces of silver, and Aongus O'Doumallain was the
one who brought them from the north to Kells."

In the Preface to the *Amhra Colum-cille,* the way
in which the Saint came to Ireland to attend the
convention of Drumceat is thus described, "And the
way that Colum-cille came was, with a cere-cloth over
his eyes, and his *culpart* over that, and the hood of
his cowl over that; so that he should neither behold
the men nor women of Erin."

Another life thus describes the same circumstance,
but omits the disputed word :—

"There was a sod of the earth of Alba under his feet ;
There was a cere-cloth over his eyes ;
There was his moblen-cap down on that ;
There was his hood, and his cowl, over that."

There is no doubt that the garment in question was
some kind of tunic, and the Irish in attributing virtue
or protection to any garment worn by a Saint, simply
followed the custom and opinion of the times of the
holy apostles, whose garments were permitted by God
to work miracles, according to the record of Holy
Scripture.

Adamnan records one very interesting miracle, as
having occurred in connection with the devout use
of the Saint's tunic. He says that the Island of Hy

was afflicted with a great drought about fourteen
years before the time at which he wrote. He feared
the most serious consequence, and took counsel with
his monks as to what means should be taken to avert
the threatened calamity.

After consultation, it was agreed that the senior
monks of the community should walk round the fields
which had been ploughed and sown, taking with them
the white tunic of St. Columba, and some book written
in his own hand. They were then directed to raise the
book in the air, a touching appeal to the dear father
above, and to shake the tunic which the Saint had
worn at his death. Then they were to open and to
read the book on "the little hill of the angels," on
which the inhabitants of heaven had been so often
seen to descend at the bidding of the Saint.

Can we not picture to ourselves the scene. Can we
not imagine the wrapt and fervent countenances of the
monks, some of whom had known, all of whom loved,
the dear one who had taken his flight to the land
where no summer sun can parch or blight. In the
Eternal sunlight of the Summer Land, he would not
forget his own. All scriptures, all the tradition of
God's Holy Church and of His chosen ones, goes to
show that we can help, and be helped by, those who
are gone from us where we also may hope one day to
go. The Communion of Saints is as true a part of the
Catholic creed as the Life Everlasting.

No tie is broken by death, though links of love are

severed for a little while ; the blessed are gone from
our sight, but we know that they may still see us,
and we know certainly that they can help us by their
prayers. The dead, indeed, rest from life's cares and
trials, but they love still, and loving, how can they
choose but aid.

The step is not far for men to take from the
denial of the Communion of Saints to the denial
of Life Everlasting. Let us take care lest the foul
vapours of a noisome infidelity should infect our
faith, should dull our hope, or cool the fervour of our
charity.

And so the monks, knowing that God had given
power to His Saints, and that He loved to honour
them in heaven, as He had loved to honour them
on earth, by giving them a share of His Divine power
and authority, were worthy to obtain that which they
had worthily entreated.

Soon refreshing rain fell day and night, and the
parched earth produced an abundant harvest through
the intercession of the Saint.

Nor was this the only occasion on which miracles
were worked by the relics of the Saint. Adamnan has
observed with a simple candour, which should carry
conviction to all, that he could well believe in the
miracles which he did not see because of the miracles
of which he was an eye-witness. Even then, as now,
there were unbelievers and sceptics, and it is noteworthy, yet once more, how carefully and accurately

every statement is made, so that doubters might be left without an excuse. Either they must say they will not believe in a miracle under any circumstance, or that they would not believe in these particular miracles.

The choice lies pretty much on either ground. If they would not believe in miracles they should deny the holy gospels, and the promise of Christ Himself, that His disciples should be permitted to exercise supernatural powers. If they denied the miracles attributed to St. Columba, they must deny the most solemn testimony given, in view of the probability of such denial with an earnestness that should be sufficient evidence of its truth.

Of the miracles in connection with these special relics of the Saint, Adamnan gives those of which he was himself an eye-witness. On the first occasion, he says, we had to draw a number of large boats over land which were made of pine, and others of oak, to bring some building materials to the island of Hy. When they were loaded they needed a favourable wind, and to obtain this they placed some of the books and garments of the Saint upon the altar, fasting and chanting psalms. And their prayers were heard. The wind changed immediately, and the voyage was made safely. The second miracle occurred when some oak trees were cut down at Sule, a site not identified, and the monks having set sail for home, were obliged to take shelter at a neighbouring island. Here Adam-

nan says, with great simplicity, they began to scold St.
Columba, telling him that they expected help from
his powerful intercession, and asking him, did he wish
them to be detained in this place? Soon the Saint
heard their prayers, and the sailors having raised the
sail-yards in the form of a cross, and set the sails
upon them, they put out to sea and reached Hy safely
that morning. The third miraculous occurrence was
during the summer time, after the assembling of a
synod in Ireland, when St. Adamnan and his companions were detained by contrary winds at the island
of Shuma, where the vigil of the Feast of St. Columba
found them sad and desolate, for they wished to celebrate that joyous festival in his own church at Hy.
So again they began to complain and reproach the
Saint, asking him how he liked to have them spend
his festival with strangers, instead of in his own
church, and they told him how easy it was for him to
obtain from God a favourable wind, so that they
might be able to celebrate mass in his own church.
Such faith could hardly fail of its reward. In the
early morning they prepared to set out on the home
voyage, and such a favourable wind sprang up that
they reached Hy after the third hour, Tierce, and having prepared themselves, they were able to celebrate
the mass of the Feast of St. Columba and St. Baithen
at noon.

And so some thousand years ago the faithful Irish
did what the faithful Irish do to-day, for, to them at

least, their God and their faith is the same yesterday, to-day, and for ever.

At the conclusion of the narrative Adamnan adds : Of the miracles recorded in this chapter, there are yet living not merely one or two witnesses, as the law requires, but hundreds who can bear testimony to their truth.

And yet with all this mass of undisputed evidence before them, there are persons found so pitiably foolish as to assert that the Irish were once Protestants. Let it be again noted that the most learned Protestants of the present day admit the authenticity of this life of St. Columba, believe that it was written by Adamnan, and yet are illogical enough to suppose that he deliberately sat down and wrote a tissue of falsehoods.

Certainly it requires a much heavier weight of unbelief to doubt than of faith to believe.

St. Baithen was the first cousin of St. Columba, and his immediate successor in the office of Abbot at Hy. He died in 599.

> They went into the eternal kingdom,
> Into that life of brightest splendour,
> Baithen the noble, the angelical ;
> Columb-cille the resplendent.

The acts of this Saint are still preserved. We are told that on the third *feria*, as the Saint was praying at the altar of God, the stupor of death came over him. As the brethren were weeping around him, Diarmiad, who had been St. Columba's special attendant, said :

"There will be but little interval between the solemnities of your two great seniors."

Then Baithen said : "If I have found favour in the sight of the Lord, and if my way has been perfect before Him unto this day, I trust in Him that I shall not die until the birthday of my great master, which will be in six days from this." He died, as he had desired, on the same day as St. Columba, and hence their festivals are kept together.

It may, perhaps, be well to record here some other miracles of the Saint which Adamnan has given on personal testimony. In our own time, he says, the plague twice desolated the world. This was the terrible yellow-plague mentioned by Tighernach and Bede in 550, and again in 664 : the devastation was terrible, and was, indeed, dreaded by the people. According to Adamnan it visited and devastated all the countries of Europe, the only place that escaped being the districts in Scotland under the spiritual protection of St. Columba. Then he deplores the ingratitude of many in both countries who do not acknowledge their indebtedness to the Saint for their escape from this terrible malady, and says how he often returned thanks to God for having preserved him from it through the intercession of St. Columba. On two occasions he went with some of his companions to visit King Aldfrid, who had honoured him with his friendship ; on each occasion the pestilence was raging, but he and his companions escaped.

It may be observed here that this was a Saxon prince, but Irish on his mother's side. Having taken refuge in Ireland on account of family troubles, he became warmly attached to that country. A poem which he composed is still preserved, and as it shows the ardent attachments which frequently follow English intercourse with the Irish at this period, we give it here.

We have preferred the metrical translation of Mangon, as it adheres very closely to the original :—

> " I found in Innisfail the fair,
> In Ireland, while in exile there,
> Women of worth, both grave and gay men,
> Many clerics and many laymen.

> " I travelled its fruitful provinces round,
> And in every one of the five I found,
> Alike in church and in palace hall,
> Abundant apparel, and food for all.

> " Gold and silver I found, and money,
> Plenty of wheat and plenty of honey ;
> I found God's people rich in pity,
> Found many a feast and many a city.

> " I also found in Armagh the splendid,
> Meekness, wisdom, and prudence blended,
> Fasting, as Christ hath recommended,
> And noble councillors untranscended.

> " I found in each great church moreo'er,
> Whether on island or on shore,
> Piety, learning, fond affection,
> Holy welcome and kind protection.

> " I found the good lay monks and brothers
> Ever beseeching help for others,
> And in their keeping the holy word,
> Pure as it came from Jesus the Lord.

"I found in Munster, unfettered of any,
Kings and queens and poets a many—
Poets well skilled in music and measure—
Prosperous doings, mirth and pleasure.

"I found in Connaught the just redundance
Of riches, milk in lavish abundance,
Hospitality, vigour, fame,
In Cruachan's land of heroic name.

"I found in the country of Connall the glorious,
Bravest heroes, ever victorious,
Fair-complexioned men and warlike,
Ireland's lights, the high, the starlike!

"I found in Ulster, from hill to glen,
Hardy warriors, resolute men,
Beauty that bloomed when youth was gone,
And strength transmitted from sire to son.

"I found in the noble district of Boyle,
          (MS. here illegible)
Brehons, Frenachs, weapons bright,
And horsemen bold and sudden fight.

"I found in Leinster the smooth and sleek,
From Dublin to Slewmargy's peak ;
Flourishing pastures, valour, health,
Long-living worthies, commerce, wealth.

"I found besides, from Ara to Glea,
In the broad rich country of Ossorie,
Sweet fruits, good laws for all and each,
Great chess-players, men of truthful speech.

"I found in Meath's fair principality,
Virtue, vigour, and hospitality ;
Candour, joyfulness, bravery, purity,
Ireland's bulwark and security.

"I found strict morals in age and youth,
I found historians recording truth ;
The things I sing of in verse unsmooth,
I found them all—I have written sooth."

Swords was another famous Columbanian Monastery. It is situated about seven miles from Dublin. St. Finian Lobhar, son of Cean, who gave his name to the territory, is said to have been placed over the church by the Saint. A round tower still remains to show the site of the ancient oratory.

Of the other Irish foundations of St. Columba we can do little more than give the names.

Tory, so called from the *torrs* or pinnacle-shaped rocks by which the island is characterised. This island is situated off the coast of Donegal, and is of considerable antiquarian interest. It has a round tower also.

Drumcliff, in Sligo, where also there are the remains of a round tower.

Raphoe, of which St. Adamnan is the patron, though the foundation is attributed to St. Columba. There was also a round tower here, mentioned by Sir James Ware, but destroyed before his time.

Moone, in the county Kildare, where there is still an ancient sculptured cross called St. Columbkille's cross.

Kilmacreenan, or *Doire Eithne*, to which tribute was payable by the Abbot of Hy and Gaston when St. Columba was born, and where the O'Nahans had the privilege of carrying "Columbkille's reed stone."

Skreen, in the county Meath, where St. Columba's well is still shown, and where his relics were once kept.

Amongst the many poetical remains attributed to St. Columba, there is a poem preserved by Colgan, in which he expresses, as he so often expressed, his dear love for Ireland. Three objects he says he has left dear to him " on this world," Durrow, and Derry, and Tir Luighdech, the district where he was born.

We conclude the history of St. Columba's life in Ireland, with this poem :—

COLUMCILLE CECINIT.

It were delightful, O Son of my God, with a moving train,
To glide o'er the waves of the deluge fountain to the land of Erin;
O'er Moy-n Eolarg, past Ben-Eigny, o'er Loch Feval,
Where we should hear pleasing music from the swans.
The host of gulls would make joyful with eager singing,
Should it reach the port of stern rejoicers, the Dewy Red.
I am filled with wealth, without Erin, did I think it sufficient,
In the unknown land of my sojourn, of sadness and distress.
Alas, the voyage that was enjoined me, O king of secrets,
For having gone myself to the battle of Cuil.
How happy the son of Dima, of the devout church,
When he hears in Durrow the desire of his mind.
The sound of the wind against the elms, when 'tis played,
The blackbird's joyous note when he claps his wings:
To listen at early dawn in Ros-Grencha, to the cattle ;
The cooing of the cuckoo from the tree, on the brink of summer.
Three objects I have left, the dearest to me, on this peopled world,
Durrow, Derry, the noble angelic land, and Tir Luighdech.
I have loved Erin's land of cascades, all but its government.
My visit to Comgall and feast with Cainnech was indeed delightful.

CHAPTER VI.

IN THE LAND OF EXILE.

T was out of the depth of his heart's sorrow that Columba cried :—

"Death is better in reproachless Erin
Than perpetual life in Alba."

We have already touched on the subjects connected with St. Columba's banishment from his native land. They have been warmly canvassed, probably on the very false assumption that a Saint could not do a grievous wrong. Even Protestants appear to have been happily infected with the desire that no discredit should be done to his memory, but in truth there is no discredit in a repented fault. And when times and circumstances are considered, it may be that the fault seemed only so great, because the Saint was so glorious. Certainly the penance was severe, and was undertaken generously, and the result proved that God can glorify Himself and His Saints by their very defects.

The battle of Cooldrevny was fought in the year 561. We have already related the circumstance connected with it. But Columba is said to have instigated, and to have been accessary to other combats. A hymn composed by St. Columba which we shall give later, is said to have been composed in reparation for the three battles which he had caused in Erin. The *Leabhar Breac* thus records the circumstance :—

"Causa quare voluit Deum laudare, *i.e.*, to beseech forgiveness for the three battles which he had caused in Erin, viz., the battle of Cul-Rathain, between him and Comgall contending for a church, viz., Ross Torathair; and the battle of Bealachfheda of the weir of Clonard; and the battle of Cul-Dremhne iu Connacht; and it was against Diarmait MacCerball he fought them both."

The battle of Cul-Rathain or Coleraine is not recorded in the annals. The battle of Cul-Dremhne and that of Cul-fedha were fought between the Northern and Southern Hy Nials. Loghemal has this record—Aedh, son of Aimmine, was victor here, it is said :—

"Broken was, as has been told,
For Colum's sake in the famous battle,
The bestower of jewels by liberal distribution,
By the Conallians and Eugenians."

The greatest of these battles was certainly the only one for which Columba was seriously responsible—the two others occurred after he had passed some years of exile in Hy.

A synod was convened at Teltown, in the county Meath, to excommunicate St. Columba for being the cause of so much bloodshed. It is probable that it was convened by the very king who had acted so justly towards the Saint, and who been guilty of sacrilege himself in not respecting the rights of clerics.

St. Brendan of Birr was present on this occasion, and when he saw St. Columba in the distance, he arose from his seat to salute him, and embraced him affectionately. The other members of the synod ex-postulated with him for this, and inquired how he could thus receive and salute a person who was excommunicated.

But St. Brendan replied, "If you could see what the Lord has been pleased to manifest to me regarding His chosen one, you would never have excommunicated one whom God so honours." Then they inquired how Brendan knew this, and how God had honoured this man whom they had condemned? The Saint replied that he saw a pillar of light preceding this man of God, and that the holy angels had accompanied him on his journey along the plain.

This was sufficient for them, and St. Columba was received with due honour.

But the Saint felt the need of some special repara-tion for the bloodshed which he had caused, whether the side which he took was the one of justice or not.

It is said that **St. Molaisi** of Deirnick or Innishmurry inflicted the **terrible penance of exile.**

The Saint was in the **forty-second year of his age** [A.D. 563], when he accepted his voluntary exile in company with twelve **companions.**

Adamnan gives us some idea of the Saint's personal appearance. That he was angelic in appearance might be expected, since we find that the holy angels were so frequently his companions. His natural gifts were undoubtedly great, and were all sanctified to the service of God, for the idle and useless monk could never be a Saint, and indeed such a being exists only in the imagination of those who are ignorant of Catholic truth and practice. It is related of him, as of other Saints, that a heavenly light was seen to shine upon his countenance, and we cannot doubt that the inward beauty left exterior tokens at all times. Every moment of his time was well and carefully occupied. Either he prayed, or wrote, or studied, or worked, and now well indeed may he reap the reward of his long life of toil, austerity, and mortification.

His tenderness toward others appears to have been a very special character of his mental condition, and such tenderness could only be increased and intensified by his monastic life. Perhaps on all this earth of ours there are no ties so dear and close as the ties of the cloister. We have already given some instances of this affection of the Saint for his spiritual children, another incident may well be noted here.

One severely cold day in winter the Saint was observed weeping bitterly. His own faithful attendant, Diarmiad, inquired the cause. St. Columba replied, "My child, I have reason to grieve, for I see that my poor monks although wearied with their heavy labours are engaged by Laisran in erecting a large building." Laisran was the Superior of the monastery of Durrow, and, as it appeared, exercised more zeal than discretion in his government. But at the moment, touched in some way by the sympathy and desire of Columba, he gave the order to cease work, provided some refreshment for the famished monks, and relieved them from this labour while severe weather lasted.

The island of Hy or Iona is at no great distance from the northern point of Ireland. We do not know from what port the Saint set sail on his penitential voyage, but we can well picture to ourselves the sorrowing last look which he gave towards the Irish shore, consoled in exile only by his longing heart's desire to evangelise other lands where evangelists were more needed.

The island of Hy (I.), properly I. Colum-Kille,— Saint Columb's isle,—now corruptly called Iona, was destined to have a world-wide fame. It is but a small spot in extent, and of no importance except from its connection with the Saint. Its length is three miles, and its breadth a mile and a half. The land, of which but little is now under cultivation, is mostly rock and morass. No doubt when first visited by St. Columba it was an uncultivated waste, with little to reward the toil of monks, who have so often made the wilderness blossom as the rose. The oldest structure at present on the island dates only so far back as the close of the eleventh century, but there is scarce a spot of land which does not bear the sacred impress of Catholic and holy tradition.

The Reformation, the embodiment of the genius of destruction, did evil work even in the eyes of the half infidel antiquaries of modern days. The religion which could not be destroyed because it was Divine was outraged in those assailable points where it was human, because it was destined for humanity. The love of the Cross could not be burned, or scourged, or starved out of the faithful heart; but the visible emblem of the Cross could be destroyed by ungrateful wretches, who professed thus to honour Him who had died thereon. The combined piety and affection of the monks of old had noted all the special sites connected with the great founder; but all, or nearly all, the crosses they erected were ruthlessly destroyed.

Here was one where angels were seen to come and go to him who lived even on earth in their blessed company. Here was another where some prophecy had been uttered, some prediction fulfilled. Here was a memorial of the Saint's last visit to the places endeared to him by a thousand holy recollections. Happily, however, the natural features of the little isle are unchangeable, and many sites can be easily identified.

In the time of St. Columba, Hy was situated between the territories of the Picts and Scots. The Scots were more or less Christianised. The Picts offered a great field to an evangelist. It was necessary, however, that the monks should secure permanent possession of the island, and for this purpose St. Columba crossed the Grampian hills, and visited King Brude near Lake Ness. The site has been identified with *Craig Phad-rick*. It is about two miles south-west of Inverness, and is an eminence of considerable height.

Brude was by no means prepared to receive the Saint cordially, and it is doubtful whether he had received the Christian religion. But a miracle was not wanted for his conversion or conviction. To nations yet unchristianised the power of God's word is often manifested by exterior signs, when after a knowledge of the holy faith its power is best shown by the lives of true Christians. Brude refused to admit the messenger of the heavenly King. His palace was almost impregnable. In his seemingly great altitude he defied all who might climb the almost inaccessible heights on which it was situated. But at the word of the Saint, and the sign of the Cross, the bolts and bars of his massive doors flew back, and Columba with his companions entered the presence of the amazed chieftain. Such a miracle was well calculated to overawe the king and his followers.

It was a defeat and victory such as they had never witnessed before; and the Saint was received with reverence and respect.

It would appear from Adamnan's narrative that he remained for some time in this neighbourhood; for several incidents are related in connection with his visit—or possibly he returned again at an early period to continue the work he had so well begun.

The Saint not having the gift of tongues was obliged to employ the services of an interpreter. A poor man having learned the faith through this person was baptized with all his family. But a few days after one of his sons became dangerously ill, and the Druids did not fail to use this circumstance as a powerful argument against Christianity. Columba soon heard what had happened, and hastened to the afflicted parent. But the child was already dead, and the obsequies had commenced. Columba desired the unhappy father to take him to the place where the corpse was laid out, and here the prayer of faith prevailed, and he raised the dead to life. The multitude were loud in their praises and thanksgiving, "Sorrow was turned into joy, and the God of the Christians glorified."

"Thus," says the faithful and admiring Adamnan —"Thus had our Columba the gift of prophecy like Elias and Eliseus, the power of raising the dead to life, like the Apostles Peter, Paul, and John, and now in the heavenly country, with prophets and apostles,

he is enthroned eternally with Christ, who reigns with
the Father in the unity of the Holy Ghost for ever
and ever."[1]

[1] The simple narrative of this miracle appears to have been too much
for the Protestant editor of St. Adamnan. He tells his readers in a
note that the "story" is evidently told in imitation of a passage in S‧.
Matthew's Gospel. He admits, however (elsewhere), that a good many
similar stories are told by other writers of other saints. He accepts
with perfect confidence all the historical details of this writer, and does
his best to corroborate them ; but the very moment a miracle is
related, he brands him liar. One can only say what a number of
liars there must have been in the world, and what deliberate liars,
for these writers again and again assert what care they have taken to
be correct and accurate, and to give faithfully the facts they narrate.
But that goes for nothing. Dr. Reeves does not believe in miracles,
and therefore miracle scould not have happened, which is pretty
much the same mode of reasoning as if a man said he did not believe
there was such a thing as electricity, and therefore there could
be no telegrams. Miracles are happening almost daily, and not
believing them would give certain persons the doubtful satisfaction of
bringing their intellects to the aid of wilful ignorance ; but that does
not alter facts. Indeed, if he did believe them, he might find himself
in an unpleasant position, for as true miracles only occur in the holy
Catholic Church, it is evident that the power of God is manifested in
it alone. But there is another dilemma which does not seem to have
occurred to Dr. Reeves, or to any Protestant objector to miracles. It
is true indeed that Protestantism is ending where Catholics predicted
long since that it must surely end. The miracles of our Divine Lord
are being denied—as a necessary and logical consequence of denying
the miracles of His saints. But there are happily some good Protestants who shrink with horror from this teaching. They at least
believe the miracles recorded in Scripture. They believe in the
miracles worked by our Divine Lord, and by *His apostles*. But when
they grant that it was possible for mere men like the apostles to work
miracles, they must admit in common fairness that God could equally
give the power to any other man to work miracles—or will they place
the apostles above other men, and make them deny God's? The Catholic
Church does not do this. We believe that the apostles or any other
saint who may work a miracle does so solely by the power granted to
them by God, and not from any power of their own. Hence what
power God can give to one man He can give another.

From the earliest ages the Church has been the
defender of the oppressed, and the Saints have been
distinguished by their desire to alleviate even the
temporal sufferings of the afflicted. Slavery was
generally practised at this period, and Columba found
that a poor Irish girl was kept in captivity by the
Druid Brochan. The Saint urgently requested that
she might be released, but his request was rudely refused. St. Columba threatened him with death and
the judgments of God, but in vain. Having done
this he departed, and at the river Nesa he took a
white pebble from the shore, and told his companions
that it should be used by the permission of God for
the cure of many diseases. Then he added that the
Druid was even at that moment punished by God for
his wickedness, and that an angel had struck him
while he was in the act of drinking, breaking the glass
cup which he held in his hand, and leaving him half
dead.

"Let us wait a little," said the Saint, "for the king
has sent messengers after us in all haste. He wishes
us to relieve Brochan, who has consented to release
his captive." Even as he spoke, two horsemen arrived
and told all that had happened, and begged the Saint,
in the name of the king, to cure his foster father,
Brochan.

St. Columba then sent two of his companions to the
king with the pebble which he had blessed, and desired
them to put it in water and give the water to Brochan

to drink if he promised to release the girl, but if he refused that he should die that moment.

Brochan was thoroughly alarmed, and agreed to all that was asked of him. The captive was handed over to the messenger of the Saint; and when the stone was placed in the water it floated on it, contrary to the laws of nature, and the Druid Brochan drank and was healed immediately.

The miraculous pebble was long kept by the king, and, through the mercy of God, the water in which it was placed cured many diseases. But when any person who desired this means of cure had arrived at the divinely-appointed term of his natural life, the pebble could not be found, and this was the case on the very day on which King Brude died. The pebble was sought for with the greatest care, but it had disappeared from the place where it was kept.[1]

But the Druid was not yet converted—a proof that fear may compel submission when it does not effect conversion; that miracles may be seen and recognised, and yet have no saving effect on the hardened soul. Indeed, when the miracles of our Divine Lord failed to convert some who witnessed them, the miracles of His disciples could not be more efficacious. Man's free will to believe or disbelieve is a mighty citadel, which the great Creator respects. He may press in

---

[1] A similar miracle is related by St. Basil, who says that St. Thecla appeared to Alypius and gave him a round stone, by the touch of which he was cured of a long and dangerous sickness.

love or in fear for an entrance to the human heart, but we are free to open or close the door.

There is no doubt that pagan priests had astounding powers, and that the conversion of a nation was fought out on other than earthly battle-grounds. As the magi of the Egyptians opposed Moses, so, for the most part, have the false prophets of all pagan peoples opposed the entrance of the Gospel of light.

The demoniacal arts which the powers of darkness were permitted to exercise were often of a surprising character, and were ever used for man's temporal or spiritual hurt.

From what Adamnan tells us, it is evident that the true miracles which the druid Brochan witnessed, and of which, indeed, he had personal experience, had not touched his heart.

When the Saint was about to sail he inquired the exact time at which he proposed doing so, and then he boldly announced his intention of frustrating his design by the exercise of magical arts. He raised a storm and procured some degree of darkness, but only to his own confusion; for Columba ordered his sailors to raise their sails against the wind, and the vessel ran against it with a great speed for a little while, then it changed to the opposite point, and enabled Columba to reach his destination the same evening.

The donation of the island of Hy—if indeed it is not a pleonasm to use this expression, since Hy or I signifies an island—is mentioned in the preface to a hymn which is said to have been composed by the Saint, and which is of undeniable antiquity.

In the year 565 after the birth of Christ, Columcille came to Hi, as Bede says : " In the year of our Lord's Incarnation, 565, at which time Justinus Minar, after Justinian, received the government of the Roman Empire, there came to Britain, from Ireland, a presbyter and abbot illustrious by the habit and life of a monk, by name Columbus, to preach the Word of God to the provinces of the Northern Picts. Now, Brudi, son of Melcho, was then king of the Picts, and he it was that granted Hi to Columbus, where Columbus was buried, after he had been there seventy-six years, and thirty-three after he had gone to Britain to preach."

Although the hymn is of considerable length, we give a metrical translation (on page 868), as there is little doubt that the greater part of it, if not the whole, was composed by the Saint.

The preface commences in the usual manner by giving the place of composition, the time of composition, the persons who composed, and the cause of composition.

Indeed the Irish writers were remarkable for their exactness in all their records. " The place of the hymn was Hi." That is, the hymn was composed in the island of Hy, now Iona. The time " was during the reigns of Aedan, king of Alba, and of Aed, son of

Ainnine, king of Erin. "The person (composer) was Columcille, of the noble race of the Scots (Irish). He is called Columba, from the text, *Estole pendantis secent serpentes, et simplices sicut Columba.* The cause was because he was desirous of praising God"—a good cause truly, and the motive power of the holy existence of endless Irish saints.

The writer then goes on to say that the hymn was composed on the following occasion : Columba was assisting Baithen to prepare for illustrious guests whom he was expecting that day, and they had no food except a sieve full of oats. The Saint desired his companions to go and attend to the guests while he went to the mill, and as he waited for the corn to be ground he composed the hymn.

The messenger of Pope Gregory had brought presents to St. Columba, "the Cross, *i.e.,* the Morgemm [great gem] was its name, and the Hymns of the Week." The Cross would appear to have been in existence as late as 1552. The hymns were probably a copy of the *Antiphonary* of St. Gregory.

The hymn composed by Columba was brought to St. Gregory, and it is said that as he stood up to listen to it, he saw the angels of God also stand, and that when a certain monk introduced some verses which had not been written by St. Columba, the angels sat down, and he thus detected the fraud.

St. Gregory applauded the composition, but said that there was not sufficient praise of the Blessed

Trinity; the meaning of this is probably the absence of the usual conclusion. When St. Columba heard this he composed the hymn, *In te Christe*, of which we have already given a translation.

There are many graces upon this hymn: "Angels shall be present whilst it is sung. The devil shall not know the path of him who sings it every day. The singer shall be hidden from his enemies — no slight boon to hope for in those troublesome times — and there shall be no strife in the house where it is frequently sung. It shall preserve from all death," except "death on the pillow," an eloquent Celtic poetism to express "natural death." [1]

The same ancient manuscript has the following quatrain :—

> "Sing the Altus seven times;
> Yield not thy right to the hardy demon.
> There is no disease in the world,
> No difficulty that it will not banish."

A very curious and very interesting historical tale still remains, which refers to the religious recital of the Altus, as it also shows the fervent faith, the impassioned charity, and the unswerving mortification of our people in the early ages of Christianity; we give it here in full, *Maelsuthain Ua Cearbhaill* (O'Carroll) became a monk in the Abbey of Inisfallen, county Kerry, late in life, and died in the year

---

[1] Another account in the "Leabhar Breac" says that Columba composed this hymn while doing seven years penance at Derry; but the above account is for many reasons the more probable.

1010. He was a distinguished chieftain, and a man of great learning, and he was the "soul friend" and adviser of Brian Boru. The story of the Altus is as follows, and has been translated from the original Irish, by the late Eugene O'Curry :—

"There came three students at one time from *Cuinnire* to receive education from the Anamchara [soul friend] of Brian MacCeinneidigh, that is Maelsuthain Ua Cearbhaill, of the Eoganacht of Loch Lein, because he was the best man of his time. These three students resembled each other in figure, in features, and in their name, which was Domnall. They remained three years learning with him. At the end of three years, they said to their preceptor : 'It is our desire,' said they, 'to go to Jerusalem, in the land of Judea, in order that our feet may tread every path which the Saviour trod on earth.' The tutor answered, 'You shall not go until you have left with me the reward of my labour.' The pupils said, 'We have not,' said they, 'anything that we could give thee, but we will remain three years more, to serve thee humbly, if you desire it.' 'I do not wish that,' said he, 'but you shall grant me my own demand, or I will lay my curse upon you.' 'We will grant thee that,' said they, 'if we can.' He then bound them by an oath on the Gospel of the Lord. 'You shall go in the path that you desire,' said he, 'and you shall die all at the same time together, on the pilgrimage, and the demand I require from you is, that you go not to heaven after your deaths, until you have first visited me, to tell me the length of my life, and until you tell me whether I shall obtain the peace of the Lord.' 'We promise thee this,' said they, 'for the sake of the Lord ;' and then they departed, and they took a blessing with them from their tutor, and they left him their blessing also. They walked in every path in which they had heard the Saviour had walked. They came at last to Jerusalem, and there they found their joint death, and were buried with great honour in Jerusalem. Then Michael the Archangel came from God for them. But they said, 'We will not go until we fulfil the promise we made to our preceptor on the Gospel of Christ.' 'Go,' said the angel, 'and tell him that he has still three years and a half to live, and that he goes to hell for ever, after the sentence is passed upon him on the day of judgment.'"

They then inquire of the angel why this terrible sentence is pronounced on him, and he replies that he had interpolated the canon, that he had not observed chastity, and that he had abandoned the Altus.

The reason why was this : He had a good son whose name was Maelpatrick. This son was seized with a mortal sickness, and the *Altus* was sung seven times around him that the son should not die. This was, however, of no avail for him, as the son died forthwith. Maelsuthain then said that he would not again sing the Altus, as he did not see that God honoured it. But it was not in dishonour of the *Altus* that God did not restore his son to health, but because He chose that the youth should be among the family of heaven, rather than among the people of earth. Maelsuthain had then been seven years without singing the Altus. After this his three pupils came to talk to Maelsuthain, in the form of three white doves, and he bade them welcome.

"Tell me" [said he] "what shall be the length of my life, and if I shall receive the heavenly reward." "Thou hast," said they, "three years to live, and thou goest to hell for ever then." "What shall I go to hell for ?" said he. "For three causes," said they ; and they related to him the three causes that we have already mentioned. "It is not true that I shall go to

hell," said he, "for those three vices that are mine
this day, shall not be mine even this day, nor shall
they be mine from this time forth, and I will abandon
these vices, and God will forgive me for them, as
He himself hath promised, when He said, ' Impietas
impii in quacumque hora conversus fuerit non noce-
bit ei' [Ezek. xxxiii. 12]. I will put no sense of my
own into the canon, but such as I shall find in the
Divine books. I will perform an hundred genu-
flexions every day. Seven years have I been without
singing the Altus, and now I will sing the Altus seven
time every night while I live, and I will keep a three
days' fast every week. Go you now to heaven," said
he, "and come on the day of my death to tell me
the result." "We will come," said they; and the
three of them departed as they came, first leaving a
blessing with him, and receiving a blessing from him.
On the day of his death, the three came in the same
forms, and they saluted him, and he returned their
salutation, and said to them, "Is my life the same
before God, that it was on the former day that ye
came to talk to me?" "It is not, indeed, the same,"
said they, "for we were shown thy place in heaven,
and we are satisfied with its goodness. We have
come, as we promised, for thee, and come now with us
to the place that is prepared for thee in the presence
of God, and in the unity of the Trinity, and of the
hosts of heaven, until the judgment of judgments."

There then assembled about him many priests and

ecclesiastics, and he was anointed, and his pupils parted not from him until they all went to heaven together. And it is this good man's writings ["Scripta"] that are in Inisfallen, in the church, still.

Two Antiphons follow this remarkable composition, the more ancient being the first, as given below :—

> Quis potest deo placere novissimo in tempore,
> Variatis insignibus veritatis ordinibus
> Exceptis contemptoribus mundi presentis ipsius.

> Who now to please God sets his mind,
> When all around him change we find,
> Save he who casts the world behind.

> Deum patrem ingenitum, celi ac terræ dominum,
> Ab eodemque filium secula ante primogenitum,
> Deumque spiritum sanctum verum unum altissimum,
> Invoco ut auxilium mihi oportunissimum
> Minimo prestet omnium sibi deseruientium,
> Quem angelorum milibus consociabit dominus.

> God the Father unbegotten,
>   And begotten of Him the Son,
> With the Holy Spirit, true God,
>   I invoke these Three in One;
> May He give me aid and help,
>   Though the least of all I stand,
> Yet His grace shall make me one
>   With the bright angelic band.

The many miraculous incidents in the Saint's life at Iona are recorded with affectionate fidelity by his great biographer Adamnan. Monastic life then was just what monastic life has ever been,—the sanctification of the individual, the good of all mankind; these were the two great ends for which the monk lived and wept and laboured. When he prayed in the

K

church or cell, it was first that he might glorify God, by giving the honour due to His holy name as Creator and Redeemer. To say matins he rose at midnight, while the world slept, careless or, perhaps, reckless, heedless or scornful, little thinking of the ills to be atoned for in the past, of the good which might be done in the future. He thought of that midnight hour when Jesus his master, betrayed and forsaken, sweated blood for his forgetful, sinful creatures. He did penance that others might have peace ; he laboured for the salvation of the whole world, helping the salvation of many.

And long ere morning dawned he was at prayer again. There was the laud of praise, and the prime of supplication, and the tierce of sweet and sorrowful memory of the crowning with thorns. And then the Mass was said, the great central point of all Christian worship. On Calvary the sacrifice was celebrated by Him who was at once priest and victim. Now, the priest needs not to be a victim, though in spirit he is ever such ; but the victim is still the same, for none but God can atone for mortal sin.

There was the office of Sext and None, the hours when they commemorated, the nailing to the Cross, and the dying thereupon ; and these men also had their nailing and their crucifixion through their vows, and how strictly they were kept we have ample evidence. They deprived themselves of all pleasure of time and sense, choosing to forego a little here of even

that which was lawful, that they might enjoy hereafter an eternal abundance of joy without fear of sin
or loss. Nailed in truth they were by their vow of
obedience to their superior and to their monastery, to
their work and labour; but other Hands had been
pierced for them, and for them had laboured also in
obedience, to sanctify and lighten theirs.

The routine of daily work was scarcely less a source
of sanctification than the hours of prayer, for work is
also prayer; and the magnificent and unmistakeable
freedom of the human will leaves us the power of
making what we desire, of every movement, of every
purpose, of every thought, of every word.

The sign of the Cross was everywhere the exterior
sanctification of the interior act. In our earthly life
we have to do with body and soul, with matter and
spirit. Our bodily organs convey to our spiritual
senses what they need to know, and since our body is
soiled by the fall of man, too often they convey much
evil. Hence the need of the sanctification of the
interior by the exterior, of ascending by steps to the
tabernacle of God in our heart. And since God is
the maker of our physical as well as of our spiritual
being, we need to worship Him with each, and only
ignorance could excuse the refusal to do Him homage
both with soul and sense.

There is no doubt also, that the use of exterior signs
helps interior recollection. Earthly monarchs claim
especial and often humiliating exterior deference from

their subjects. We all know that we may help our recollection of certain mental acts which we desire to make by exterior acts; and the wise monks of old, whose first business was to serve God, took care to leave no means unused to remind them how frequent and how fervent this service should be.

The sign of the Cross was from the earliest ages the sign of Christianity. The sign of the Cross was from the earliest ages the visible token of invisible power, and as such was used as a God-sanctioned means of working miracles. Thus, as we have already seen in the Life of St. Columba, a miracle was permitted to show how the power of this holy sign could subdue demons and sanctify common food to our use, how unsafe, indeed, it is to use any earthly sustenance without sanctifying it. The tools used in work were thus, as it were, consecrated and set apart to do the Divine service. The bread was blessed, the water was blessed, the going out and the coming in were consecrated. The sour was turned to sweet, the doors of fortresses were opened. Holiness to the Lord was the motive of every action, the object of every life.

Even in the masts of the frail vessels, in which so much time was necessarily spent, they saw the saving sign, and looked from the Calvary of earth to the bright clear sky of heaven, by land and sea still travelling homeward by the holy way of the Cross.

And it should be well and carefully observed in these days, when the mists of heresy have risen up so thick and foul, and shut out so much of the sunlight of faith, that the miracles or miraculous occurrences mentioned in the Life of St. Columba, as in the lives of other saints, had one and all a deep practical teaching.

If sanctification is the great end of life,—and what other end is worth a moment's care? what other end will be worth having sought when this poor world is burned up as a parched scroll?—then all that helps or contributes to sanctification is more worth having than all the wealth of nations, than all the gifts of the most gifted, than all the pleasures of the most happy.

We take, not by special selection, but as they come to hand, two of the Saint's miraculous favours as evidences of this.

The Bishop of *Cuil-raithen* (Coleraine) had made a great festival for St. Columba on his return from Drumceat. Many and rich presents were brought in by the faithful people, ever ready to honour their ecclesiastical superiors; but God, who saw the heart of the poor widow, and how great a gift her mite was, knows, as no human being can know, the worth of every gift or action. But from time to time He has permitted His saints to have a supernatural knowledge of the hearts of others. On this occasion Columba pointed out two gifts. The blessing of God, he said, should be on one of the donors for his charity to the poor, and of the liberality of the other, whom he called a "wise man," he said, "I cannot

partake of his offering until he has repented of
his sins." The latter was a namesake of the Saint—
Columba, the son of Aedh. He heard what had been
said, and proved that he was indeed truly wise by
owning his fault, and admitting that he had been full
of avarice, and by becoming generous and charitable
for all time to come. The rich man had also the
reward of his great benevolence for coming to the
Saint when he heard the commendation that had
been passed on his charity ; he asked his prayers, and
declared his firm purpose to avoid all the faults for
which the Saint reproved him.

Then we see that what seems almost a trivial
matter to those who do not consider the perfection of
a soul as the greatest gain, was in reality a subject of
very high importance. And thus we see also that
God gives supernatural knowledge to His saints for
the sanctification of the souls of others, and for their
help on their heavenward journey.

If even the hairs of our heads are numbered, if we
shall be rewarded for a cup of cold water, or punished
for a thought of sin, we can never consider any
matter trifling which will help our future gain or
loss.

And sometimes, also, it may happen that these
favours will help most even those who have not
witnessed them. We sometimes find in the lives of
the Saints that those with whom they associated were
the last to recognise their sanctity, or to be impressed

by the Divine favours granted to them, while others
yet unborn may be helped and comforted by what
they have passed by with indifference or perhaps
contempt.

On another occasion we find the Saint revealing
his knowledge of the state of a holy soul to a religious
who was walking with him. One of his monks
named Brito was at the point of death; the Saint
went to visit and comfort him, but could not bear to
see him die.

Even as he left the house the happy soul passed to
his reward; and as the Saint walked in the little path
before the monastery, he seemed for a time as one lost
in wonder and adoration.

Then Aedh, the brother who walked with him,
fell upon his knees, and asked the Saint to tell him
what this abstraction meant. The Saint replied that
he had seen the holy angels contending with the
demons, and carrying off the soul of the good monk
to the joy of the heavenly city.

On another occasion the Saint saw the soul of an
ecclesiastic carried to heaven, but he did not know
his name, but afterwards found it was a "soldier of
Christ," called Diarmiad, who had built a monastery
near Armagh.

Thus, indeed, would the brethren be encouraged to
persevere in their life of austerity, since even here
below the rewards prepared for them were so wonderfully made known.

Every moment of time was fully and wisely occupied—was occupied as it should be, by men who knew that a great and eternal reward awaited every action, no matter how trivial, if it was done for the Master's service and glory.

Prayer, manual labour, reading, and writing were the occupations which came round in regular and harmonious rotation.

Scripture was the first great object of study, and especially the Psalms, as a great portion of their office was said from them. But they had also the lives of Saints, and of the Fathers of the Church. We know they had the Life of St. Martin of Tours, the near relative of St. Patrick, for Adamnan quotes from it, and from the Life of St. Germanun also. The acts of St. Patrick were also put on record, and, no doubt, would be in the monastic library. As there was no printing then, copying manuscript was a necessary and holy work, and composing new works was also encouraged in all to whom the ability to do so had been given. The Book of Kells and Durrow yet remain to attest the care and labour bestowed on their manuscripts by holy hands. Nor was art despised, rather was it encouraged and cultivated, and the cloister became the source of a refinement which helped to civilise the world. Severe penitential bodily exercise by no means lessened mental powers, for the spirit soared higher in art, as well as in grace, when the flesh was kept in servitude.

Annals of remarkable events, and of the migrations of the monks from the toils of earth to the rest of heaven, were carefully recorded.

Agriculture and fishing were both necessary occupations, and as straight a road to heaven as the employment of the Scriptorium. It was not what was done, but the manner of doing it, which made the Saint. And in the Catholic Church are practised that grand equality and fraternity which the devil has tried to instate in the world ; men were honoured, not for their rank in human opinion, but for their virtue. The poor lay brethren toiling in the field, the sailor monk seeking necessary sustenance for his brethren on the treacherous sea, was as likely to be enrolled in the calendar of Saints as the abbot or the scribe.

Everything was regulated by obedience. The food, the clothing, the rest, the labour of the monks, were all subject to law. Bread made of barley, with milk and fish, were the principal fare ; but fasts were many, and even on ordinary days the one first and principal meal was not taken till after noon. During Lent the fast was not broken until evening.

The clothing of the monks was coarse and poor ; they had but two garments—a tunic and an outer garment. Sometimes they wore sandals ; and it is said, in an ancient manuscript, that St. Columba used to take the sandals from his monks after they had been engaged in labour, and wash their feet. The monks slept in their habits on straw pallets, and thus were able to present themselves in choir at the sound of the bell for matins.

St. Brendan of Birr, who is specially mentioned in the annals of the Columbian order, died in 573, and St. Columba had a festival kept in honour of his happy departure.

This was made known miraculously to the Saint. One morning he called his faithful attendant Diarmiat, and desired them to prepare quickly for the celebration of the Holy Sacrifice; "for this," he said, "is the birthday of blessed Brendan." The monk asked, "Could this be known, for no messenger had arrived from Ireland to tell of his departure?" But the Saint replied, "Go, and do as I desire, for last night I saw the heavens opening, and choir of angels descending to meet the blessed Brendan, and the light and brightness illuminated the whole world."

On another occasion a somewhat similar revelation was given to the Saint, and the Holy Mass was celebrated in honour of a soul which had gone up to heaven during the night—"beyond the stars, borne up by choirs of angels, this was the soul of St. Colman." [1]

As the Mass was being said, when the priest came to the commemoration of the faithful departed, the

[1] His festival is May 15. He is commemorated in the Calendar of Donegal. The old graveyard where his church once stood is situated in the parish of Stradbally, Queen's County. He was very intimate with St. Columba in early life.

Saint desired the name of St. Colman to be added after the name of St. Martin, and then they knew who it was who had passed to his eternal reward.

We find many records of angelic apparitions in his holy life; and as they occurred principally during the Saint's residence at Iona, we shall mention some of them here.

One day the brethren heard the bell ring loudly which was used to call them together. It was the Saint who had rung it, and he appeared much excited. "Now," he said, "let us assist by our prayers the monks of the Abbot Comgall, for they are in danger of drowning in Lake Vitulus (Belfast Lough), for they are fighting against evil spirits who infest the air, and are trying to seize the soul of a stranger who is dying." Then after some time he arose, with a peaceful countenance, and told them that their prayers were granted, and that the soul was safe.

One day as the father sat in his cell writing, he cried out suddenly, "Help, help!" One of the brethren who were with him inquired the cause of this exclamation. He replied, "I have asked the angel of the Lord who was here, to go to the assistance of one of the monks who fell from the top of a great building which is now being erected in Durrow." [1]

[1] It will be remembered that the name of St. Columba's angel was Help. We cannot but note here with sorrow, how eagerly any antiquarian

Then the Saint spoke of the wonders of the angelic beings, of their rapid movements, and how marvellous it was that the angel who left Iona when the monk began to fall, should have reached him "in the twinkling of an eye," and saved him before he could fall to the ground.

It will be remembered that the Saint was familiar with the angels from his early childhood. We may be well assured that their holy companionship would become still more frequent as, with advancing years, he advanced in sanctity.

One day he told the brethren that he wished to go to the western plain of the island, and strictly forbade any of them to follow him.

Happily all the sites connected with the wonderful incident which followed have been identified past dispute.

point is seized on by Protestant writers ; how the least word that will help to support any theory of their own will be weighed and credited. When a passage comes which supports a favourite idea of these writers, it is held up and insisted upon as the most authentic statement possible. Dr. O'Donovan having a round-tower theory of his own to support, seizes eagerly on this miracle, brings it forward as his best proof that round-towers were bell-towers, and is warmly backed up by Dr. Reeves. It does not appear to have occurred to these learned gentlemen that if Adamnan invented the miracle, he must also have invented the tower. To such inconsistency are men driven who will not believe the words of the very Scriptures which they profess to receive, wherein it is plainly stated that miracles shall be a distinctive mark of the one true Church. So would an infidel writer quote the Acts of the Apostles for the historical fact that St. Peter had been in prison, if he had any archæological theory to support thereby, while he would deny that an angel had delivered him, because he did not chose to believe in angelic apparitions.

The Saint set out on his journey, but a young brother followed at a distance, and sat down on a little hill which overlooked the plain.

This was the eminence now called *Cnoc orain.* The Saint continued his prayer until he came to a little mound on the plain which he ascended, and here he began to pray with his arms extended in the form of a Cross. Then the brother saw a multitude of angels descending from heaven and flying up thither again.

But the Saint knew that this vision had been seen; and on his return to the monastery he called all the brethren together, and inquired who had disobeyed his command. At last the brother who had witnessed the vision came forward in fear and trembling, acknowledged his fault, and prayed for pardon. The Saint took him aside, and charged him in the most solemn manner never to speak of the angelic apparition during his lifetime. The brother obeyed, but after the death of St. Columba, he was no longer bound to silence; and the place where the Saint had prayed was henceforth called the Hill of the Angels.

Adamnan adds that no doubt many other similar favours were granted to the Saint which can never be known here, and that he frequently passed his nights in some lonely spot in prayer. In another life of the Saint it is said, that he recited the Psalms every night standing in cold water. This was a favourite penitential exercise with the early Irish Saints.

Many visitors were attracted to Iona by the fame of St. Columba's miracles and sanctity. On one occasion "four holy founders of monasteries" came to visit him. These were St. Comgall, St. Caimnech, St. Brendan, and St. Cormac.

St. Comgall was born at Maurne, now Maghermorne, near Larne, County Antrim. He was born in 517, and founded the Church of Bangor in 558.

His history is far too full of interest to touch on here, for to touch would be to yield to the fascination of narrating the life of one "whom Christ loved."

His monastery and his monastic work is fully noticed by the Great St. Bernard. St. Caimnech was a relative of St. Comgall's. He is mentioned in the *Feilire* of Angus on the 11th of October. St. Brendan of Clonfert, whose life we hope will occupy the next volume of this series, a Kerry Saint, around whose memory a halo of exquisitely poetical tradition has been cast and well preserved; alas! that it can be said, not in Ireland, but on the Continent.

And lastly, St. Cormac, who is mentioned as Abbot of Durrow, bishop and anchorite, but the monastery founded by him is not on record. A very curious poem, however, remains in the form of a dialogue between him and St. Columba.

The original is, undoubtedly, of very great antiquity.

St. Columba is represented as welcoming him after his arrival "from over the all-teeming sea." Then the

Saint predicts that his "resurrection shall be in Durrow," no matter where he may travel, for in these beautiful words the Irish Saints and saintly people always described their place of burial. It was on this occasion that Columba uttered the words already quoted:

> "Death is better in reproachless Erin
> Then perpetual life in Alba."

But again we must restrain our desire to touch on subjects so deeply interesting to every child of

> "Reproachless Erin"—

Reproachless, at least, in its unswerving fidelity to the one faith—in the undeniable fact, that of all Christian peoples, it is the only people which has not at some time or other turned traitor to the teaching of the Holy Catholic Church. England apostatised, Scotland denied the faith, France overturned her altars as well as her thrones, Italy has proclaimed an infidel government, Germany scourged itself with the heresy of Luther, Russia revolted and has continued in schism; but the ever-faithful island of the western sea never yet, by word or work or deed, denied or bartered her faith. She has been the scorn of nations for her fidelity; but one day a crown of surpassing glory will more than repay her for all contempt and wrongs. Surely the early Saints of Erin must have no little power in the heavenly courts; and surely we do well not to forget or neglect their memories.

But we have left the four Saints all too long. May they intercede for us, and their host Columba. When these Saints met, what was their first occupation? It was the celebration of the adorable Sacrifice of the Mass which they entrusted St. Columba to offer for them; and even as he said the same solemn words, that are said to-day all over the Christian world when the priest offers the sacrifice of the altar, St. Brendan told his companions that he saw a globe of fire over the head of St. Columba, the Dove of the Church.

But again we must turn from details of singular interest, which would occupy more space than we can give.

The Saint visited Ireland more than once before his death, but it is said he never allowed himself the pleasure of looking upon Irish soil.

He paid a second visit, as we have recorded, to the chief or petty king who had donated Hy to him. In the year 574, Conall, chief of Dalriada, died. His cousin Aedan assumed the sovereignty, and was inaugurated by St. Columba in the monastery of Iona.

Some circumstances of special interest connected with this matter are related by Adamnan.

On a certain night, when St. Columba was wrapt in ecstasy, an angel appeared to him from heaven with a " book of glass," containing the rite for the consecration of kings. The Saint was commanded to read it, but " he loved Eoghan better than his brother Aedan," and he refused to inaugurate him, though he was commanded to do so in the book. The angel then scourged the Saint for his disobedience, so severely that the wounds of the discipline remained until his death. This occurred for three successive nights, and then the Saint resolved to sail to the island of Hy. He was then at Hinba. Aedan (or Aedh) arrived at the same time as Columba, and was then consecrated king. At the ceremony the Saint prophesied that none of the adversaries of Aedh should be able to resist him unless he did some injury to the monks, and that if he ever did so, the scourge he had suffered for him should be turned against his family.

Adamnan relates that even in his time the prophecy was fulfilled, and to his great grief the grandson of Aedh suffered the punishment.

The convention of Drumceat was held in the year 575. For details of the political and other subjects discussed there we have no space.

It may, however, be observed, that the presence of St. Columba on this occasion, and the important part which he took, is an evidence of the great weight which was given to his opinion, and of the general belief in his extrordinary sanctity.

The Saint returned from Scotland by Coleraine, but he visited Ireland again in the year 585, going from Durrow to Clonmacnoise. The circumstances of this visit have been already related.

His holy life was drawing to its close, and he was soon to join the company of the angels in heaven,

L

who had been so often his companions when on earth.

His love of Ireland was as strong as ever. No time, no change, could lessen this passion of his heart. Can we doubt that he loves it still, but with an intenser, purer love? Can we doubt that he will hear every cry that comes to him from his guiltless Erin? In the swift flight of the endless ages of eternity, it is as if he had left us but yesterday; how, then, can he have ceased to care for us?

The great love of animals which has been characteristic of so many Saints was, as we have said, the characteristic of the Dove of the Churches.

One day he called a brother to him, and told him that he was to go to the western shore of the island (Iona), on the morning of the third day from that time, and wait for a crane which should come, weary and exhausted from long journey and adverse winds. He was to treat the bird tenderly, and bring it to a house near at hand, where it should be nursed for three days and nights, when "it would be unwilling to stay any longer in that strange land," and would fly back to its beautiful home in Ireland.

With the third day came the crane, and the brother cared for it as he had been desired. In the evening he returned to the monastery, and the Saint, before he had time to explain that he had done all that was desired, began to thank him for his care of the bird, which had come from "his own native place," again predicting that it would not remain long in a "distant country."

And on the third day, as the Saint had said, the crane rose gently on its wings to a great height, and then flew in a direct line to the dear fatherland.

On many occasions the Saint was rapt in ecstasy, but once he remained for three days wholly absorbed in God. During this time he neither ate nor drank; and during the night the rays of heavenly brightness which surrounded him were seen to pour forth from the house in which this wonderful miracle took place.

One night a brother named Virgnous, "burning with the love of God," came to the church to pour out his pure love at his Master's feet. After he had prayed for about an hour, St. Columba came into the church, "and there shone around him a golden light that came from heaven." The brilliancy was so great that the monk could not bear to look at it. On the following day St. Columba sent for him, and told him that he had pleased God very much by keeping his eyes on the ground, and that if he had gazed upon the light he would have lost his sight. But he commanded him, at the same time, not to let this matter be known during his lifetime.

The great care which St. Adamnan took to be accurate in every statement which he made is manifested here again; for he says he obtained his information from Comman, a holy priest, who was nephew of this very Virgnous who had seen the vision, and Comman, who had told him that he heard the account of it from the very lips of his holy uncle.[1]

In the year 593, when the Saint had been settled in Hy for just thirty years, he had a vision of angels in answer to very fervent prayer, that he might pass to that heavenly country which was dearer to him than his dear Ireland. Two of the brothers who were watching him saw that he looked first full of gladness and then very sorrowful. With great entreaties they obtained from him the reason of this change. The gladness was because God had sent His holy angels to take him to heaven in answer to his prayers that he might die that day, but at the request of many of the Churches he had withdrawn the angels; and the sorrow was because he was left in exile. But he foretold his death then, which was to take place in four years, and while he was apparently in perfect health.[2]

---

[1] We do not envy the state of mind of any person who can doubt such testimony. Virgnous, whose name is also sometimes written Ferguous, was fourth abbot of Hy or Iona. Under the year 622, the four masters have his obituary thus: "St. Fergua Bist, abbot of Ja, and a bishop, died on the 2d day of March. He was from Donegal." Comman, his nephew, who related the above to Adamnan, was a bishop, and brother of St. Crimine Fronn, seventh abbot of Hy.

[2] The comments of Protestant writers would be amusing, if it were not sad to see great intellect and natural goodness overcome by prejudice. Dr. Reeves says: "The Saint seems to have been visited by sickness, and brought near death." There is not one word in the whole narrative to give even the slightest ground for such an assertion, but as he would not believe the miraculous narrative, he is forced to invent. Is this the very history that should be written?

In the year 597, St. Columba went to visit some of the monks who were at work on the western part of the island. He travelled in a chariot, for he was now sinking under the weight of years. When he came to them he told them how he had desired to have gone to our Lord during the Paschal solemnities of the precious month (April) ; but as he would not like a joyous festival to be turned into a day of mourning for his children, he had deferred his departure until now.

Then he blessed the island, and from henceforth no venomous beast was seen on it, as we have already related. On Sunday, at Mass, he saw an angel coming to call him home, and the glory of the vision shone on his countenance, so that it was observed by all.

The following Saturday the Saint went to bless the barn where the brethren were winnowing corn, and he congratulated the monks that they had a sufficient supply for the year, "should he be obliged to leave them."

But the faithful Diarmiat could bear these allusions to his father's death no longer. He told the Saint that he grieved his children by his frequent reference to his departure from this world. The Saint replied that he would tell him a little secret, but he must promise not to reveal it till after his death. The promise was solemnly made, and the Saint replied : "This day is called the Sabbath in

Holy Scripture, which means **rest ; to-day** is indeed a Sabbath **to me, for it is the last day of my** weary life in which I shall **begin to keep** eternal Sabbath **after my labours. For even now my Lord Jesus Christ invites me to go to Him, and I shall go in the middle of** the night, as **our Lord has** revealed **it to me."**

The **faithful monk** began **to weep bitterly, as** indeed well he might, **and** the **Saint tried to comfort him ; but what comfort could he give one who** knew **so well that the** prophetic **utterances of his** father **had never failed** of their **fulfilment?**

As they **returned homewards the** Saint stopped **to** rest where, St. Adamnus says, **"a cross** was afterwards **erected, and is still** standing." While here, a white **horse,** which, **no doubt, he had** carressed many **a time, came up to** him, and, putting his **head into his bosom,** began to **utter** plaintive cries, **as if knowing that his** best friend **was** about **to** leave it. The brother tried **to drive it** away, **but St. Columba** would **not** permit **him, and he** blessed the poor animal, **who then** turned away sadly.

Then the **Saint ascended the** hill which overlooked the monastery, and remained **for** some **time on** the summit, and **blessed** the enclosure, saying, **"This** place, though **it is so** small **and** contemptible, shall **be** honoured **not** only **by** Irish **kings** and **people, but also by the** governors **of** distant and barbarous nations **and their** subjects, **and the** saints **of these**

churches will give great honour to it also." Then
he descended the hill, and went to his cell to his
usual occupation of writing—a lesson to us of great
value. He knew it was the last day of his saintly
life, and yet he still occupied himself with his ordinary work and duties. When he came to that verse
of the Thirty-third Psalm, " *They that seek the Lord
shall not want any good thing,*" he said, " Here I must
stop writing, having finished this page, let Baithen
write what follows." And, says Adamnan, " it was
meet that Baithen should write it from ' Come,
children, listen to me : I will teach you the fear of the
Lord,' for he succeeded the Saint not only in writing,
but in teaching also."

Then he went to the church to say the Evening
Office, and having returned to his cell, he lay down
upon his couch, which was a bare flag, with a stone
for a pillow. Here he gave his last instructions to
the faithful Diarmiat, who should restrain his tears as
best he might.

His last advice to his brethren was to preserve
peace and charity with each other, and he promised if
they did this, and imitated the example of the fathers,
that God the Creator of the good would assist them ;
and that he, being with God, would intercede for them,
that He would give them, not only sufficient for the
wants of this mortal life, but that He would bestow on
them the eternal rewards promised to those who keep
His commandments.

Then as the time of his departure drew near, he became silent; and when the midnight bell rang for matins, he hastened to the church, and reached it before the rest. Here he knelt down to pray at the altar.

Diarmiat followed him at a distance; and as he approached the church, he saw that it was filled with light, which fell on the Saint. Some of the brethren also saw this light, but when they approached the door it disappeared suddenly.

Then the dear brother called out in a sorrowful voice, "Where are you, father?" and groped about in the dark, until he found the dying Saint lying before the altar. The monks had now all assembled with lights, and crowded round the beloved Abbot, weeping, while he expired. His head lay on Diarmiat's bosom, and the monk raised his hand to bless the brethren for the last time; the Saint seeing what was requested, of himself raised up his hand, and though he could not speak, gave them his last earthly blessing.

And so he went joyously to his Lord. Adamnan says he was told by some who were present, that the Saint looked up at the last moment with wonderful joy, as if he saw, as no doubt he did see, the holy angels coming to meet him.

And so the dove was at rest, no longer weeping in exile for an earthly fatherland, for he was at home; no longer grieving for his "faultless Erin," for he was surrounded with the "faultless" sons of Erin who had gone before; no longer in pain, and weeping, and weariness, and tears. It was all over. The dove had taken its flight to the land of doves, to wait the Day when all the little birds who have built their nests in the clefts of the Rock shall be welcomed to the Summer Land.

But those who were left wept for him as men must weep even for the blessed dead. Yet he looked not like one who had died, but rather like one who had passed from death to life.

As his soul soared up to his eternal home, many holy persons were permitted to know of his departure. Only one of those incidents can be recorded here. An aged servant of Christ called Ernene, a holy monk, told St. Adamnan himself that he was engaged with others fishing in the valley of the Finn,[1] on the night on which St. Columba died, and that they saw the atmosphere illuminated suddenly. Amazed by the miraculous light they looked towards the east, and saw a pillar of fire ascending up to heaven, which illuminated the whole earth as if it had been day, and that this light was also seen by several other persons who were fishing at different places on the same night.

This incident is related on the best authority—that is to say, Adamnan, who has placed this fact on record,

---

[1] A river which passes through the barony of Raphoe, County Donegal.

had it from the lips of the very person who witnessed it.

The fame of Hy or Iona became very great after the death of the Saint. It is said, but on very insufficient authority, that St. Columba travelled on the Continent, and even that he visited Rome. His character has been strangely misrepresented. Even Montalembert has written of him as "vindictive," a character he certainly never deserved. Except that he is said to have instigated the battle of Cooldrevny, for which he did long and bitter penance, and that he excommunicated several persons who richly deserved it, there is not one single circumstance in his long and well-known career to show that he had any such disposition. Such words as "rude," "irritable," "ironical," "imperious," and "revengeful," are utterly inapplicable to one who ever showed himself overflowing with tenderness even to the very brute creation. But he was Irish, and Irishmen, whether saints or soldiers, are well accustomed to scant justice, and even if a little meed of praise is doled out, it must be carefully qualified lest the writer should injure his own religion or literary character by approving what has been for so many centuries condemned.

The history of Hy, and the various persecutions to which its faithful monks were subject, cannot be noted here. For centuries the place was looked on as holy ground, and Scottish kings for many ages thought themselves happy to be laid near the bones of the Saints.[1] But the Danes had small respect for relics, and their depredations were so frequent that the monks at last resolved to remove the remains of St. Columba to Ireland, and here his body rests beneath the stone under which are Patrick and Brigit.[2]

---

[1] Even Shakespeare notes this when he makes Macduff say that Duncan's body is

> " Carried to Colme-kill;
> The sacred storehouse of his predecessors,
> And guardian of their bones."—*Macbeth.*

[2] We defer further details on this subject until we come to treat of it in connection with the burial-place of St. Brigit.

HYMN OF ST. COLUMBA.

"ALTUS PROSATOR."

A ltus prosator vetustus dierum et ingenitus
Erat absque origine primordi et crepidine
Est et erit in secula seculorum infinita
Cui est unigenitus Christus et Sanctus Spiritus
Coeternus in gloria deitatis perpetua
Non treis Deos depromimus sed unum Deum dicimus
Salva fide in personis tribus gloriosissimis.

B onos creavit angelos ordines et archangelos
Principatuum ac sedium potestatum virtutum.
Uti non esset bonitas otiosa ac majestas
Trinitatis in omnibus largitatis muneribus
Sed haberet celestia in quibus previgilia
Ostenderet magnopere possibili fatimino.

C eli de regni apice stationis angelicæ
Claritate præfulgoris venustate speciminis
Superbiendo ruerat Lucifer quem formaverat
Apostatæque angeli eodem lapsu lugubri
Auctoris cenodoxiæ pervicacis invidiæ
Ceteris remanentibus in suis principatibus.

HYMN OF ST. COLUMBA.

"ALTUS PROSATOR."

A ncient of days,
    Father most high,
    Who art, and shall be,
    As the ages go by,
    With Christ and the Spirit,
    In glory supernal,
    Who art God evermore,
    Unbegotten, eternal.
    We preach not three Gods,
    But the unity, One,
    The Father, the Spirit,
    And co-equal Son.

B right Angel-thrones,
    And virtues, and powers,
    By good angels and seraphs
    His mercies He showers ;
    That the Godhead most blessed,
    By His goodness and grace,
    With celestial expression
    Might all things embrace.

C ast down from high Heaven,
    Apostate ranks fell,
    And the Son of the Morning
    Was dashed down to hell ;
    By the foul stain of pride
    All his glory was lost,
    While the lowly remained
    The angelical host.

D raco magnus deterrimus terribilis et antiquus

Qui fuit serpens lubricus sapientior omnibus

Bestiis et animantibus terræ feracioribus

Tertiam partem siderum traxit secum in barathrum

Locorum infernalium diversorumque carcerum

Refuga veri luminis parasito præcipites.

E xcelsus mundi machinam previdens et armoniam

Cœlum et terram fecerat mare et aquas condidit

Herbarum quoque germina virgultorum arbuscula

Solem lunam ac sidera ignem ac necessaria

Aves pisces et pecora bestias et animalia

Hominem demum regere protoplastum præsagmine.

F actis simul sideribus etheris luminaribus

Collaudaverunt angeli factura præmirabili

Immensæ molis dominum apificem celestium

Preconio laudabile debito et immobile

Concentuque egregio grates egerunt domino

Amore et arbitrio non naturæ donario.

G rassatis primis duobus seductisque parentibus

Secundo ruit zabulus cum suis satilitibus

Quorum horrore vultuum sonoque volitantium

Consternarentur homines metu territi fragiles

Non valentes carnalibus hæc intueri visibus

Qui nunc ligantur fascibus ergastolorum nexibus.

D emon most fearful,
  Once mighty, once wise,
Fell, and with him he drew
  A third part of the skies,
Forsaking the true light
  In pit most profound,
Was flung this deceiver,
  And for evermore bound.

E xcelling and perfect
  The great world was made,
The earth and the ocean
  Came forth as He said,
The herb and the grasses,
  The fish and the fire,
And lastly came man,
  Created yet higher.

F air the structure was built,
  And the angels their lays
Came to offer to God,
  And loudly gave praise.
The stars thus created
  Sang loud to His name;
The universe rang
  With the great Maker's fame.

G reat the horror and trembling,
  The dread and affright,
That our first parents felt
  At this vision of night,
At the traitorous angels
  In prison house kept,
While they in atonement
  Their first sin had wept.

H ic sublatus e medio dejectus est a domino
　　Cujus æris spatium constipatur satilitum
　　Globo invisibilium turbido perduellium
　　Ne malis exemplaribus imbuti ac sceleribus
　　Nullis unquam tegentibus septis ac parietibus
　　Fornicarentur homines palam omnium oculis.

I nvehunt nubes pontias ex fontibus brumalias
　　Tribus profundioribus occiani dodrantibus
　　Maris celi climatibus ceruleis turbinibus
　　Profuturas segitibus viniis et germinibus
　　Agitatæ flaminibus tesauris emergentibus
　　Quique paludes marinas evacuant reciprocas.

K aduca ac tirannica mundique momentania
　　Regum presenti gloria nutu dei depossita
　　Ecce gigantes gemere sub aquis magno ulcere
　　Comprobantur incendio aduri ac suplicio
　　Cocitique carubdibus strangulati turgentibus
　　Scillis obtecti fluctibus eliduntur et scropibus.

L igatas aquas nubibus frequenter crebrat **dominus**
　　Ut ne erumpant protinus simul ruptis objicibus
　　Quarum uberioribus venis velut uberibus
　　Pedetemtim natantibus telli pertractus **istius**
　　Gellidis ac ferventibus diversis in **temporibus**
　　Usquam influunt flumina nunquam deficientia.

H id from sight of all mortals,
 Lest their crime should defile,
While crowds of rank demons,
 An atmosphere vile ;
Concealed from men only,
 But known to the Lord,
These legends of devils
 Condemned by His word.

I n whirlwinds of azure,
 The clouds deeply blue
Are uplifted to Heaven,
 God's great work to do ;
At His bidding they pour forth
 On vineyard and field,
The streams which fertility
 Everywhere yield.

K ings and tyrants once famed,
 Of old world renown,
Are dashed deep in ocean,
 Remorselessly down ;
The floods and the rock-stones,
 The fire and the flame,
Are the torment eternal
 Of these men of great fame.

L o, gently the waters,
 Held fast by God's word,
In soft drops do the bidding
 Of their Maker and Lord.
Now with warm breath or cold,
 As the seasons come round,
God's rivers make fruitful,
 And flow on the ground.

M agni dei virtutibus appenditur dialibus
　　Globus terræ **et circulus** abyssi magnæ inditus
　　Suffulta dei iduma omnipotentis **valida**
　　Columnis velut vectibus eundem sustentantibus
　　Promontoriis et rupibus soli[di]s fundaminibus
　　Velut quibusdam bassibus firmatis immobilibus.

N ulli **videtur** dubium in imis esse infernum
　　Ubi habentur tenebræ vermes ac diræ bestiæ
　　Ubi ignis solphorius ardens flammis edacibus
　　Ubi rugitus hominum fletus ac stridor dentium
　　Ubi gehennæ gemitus terribilis et antiquus
　　Ubi ardor flammaticus sitis famisque **horridus.**

O rbem infra, ut legimus, incolas esse novimus,
　　Quorum genu præcario frequenter flectit Domino,
　　Quibusque impossibile librum scriptum **revolvere**
　　Obsignatum signaculis . . . . . . monitis
　　Quem idem resignaverat, per quem victor extiterat,
　　Explens sui præsagmena adventus prophetalia.

P lantatum a prohemio paradisum a Domino
　　Legimus in Primordio genesis nobilissimo.
　　Cujus ex fonte flumina quatuor sunt manantia,
　　Cujus et situm florido lignum vitæ est medio
　　Cujus non cadunt folia gentibus salutifera
　　Cujus inenarrabiles deliciæ ac fertiles.

M ost mighty foundations
   Support the great earth,
     On pillar and beam,
   Sustained since its birth
     By the power of God ;
   Made for ever secure,
     It rests on foundations
   Eternally sure.

N one doubts that hell lieth
     Where worm and foul beast
   On corruption, and in darkness,
     For ever shall feast ;
   Where sulphuric fires
     The lost souls assail,
   Where for ever resoundeth
     The shriek and the wail.

O f the dwellers below earth,
     Who live in the deep,
   Yet pray to the Lord,
     As in mystical sleep,
   Know not of th' unrolling
     Of what prophet reveals,
   Nor the mysteries writ
     In the book with seven seals.

P raise, health, and abundance
     In Paradise dwelt,
   Where no sorrow nor sickness
     Nor grief could be felt ;
   Where the tree of life flowered,
     Where four rivers ran,
   Where the leaves all unfading
     Gave healing to man.

Q uis ad condictum Domini montem conscendit Sinai,
Quis audivit tonitrua supra modum sonantia?
Quis clangorem perstreperæ enormitatis buccinæ?
Quis quoque vidit fulgura in gyro coruscantia?
Quis lampades et jacula, saxaque collidentia?
Præter Israelitici Moysen judicem populi?

R egis regum rectissimi, prope est dies Domini;
Dies iræ et vindictæ, tenebrarum et nebulæ;
Diesque mirabilium tonitruorum fortium;
Dies quoque angustiæ, mœroris ac tristitiæ;
In quo cessabit mulierum amor et desiderium,
Hominumque contentio, mundi hujus et cupido.

S tantes erimus pavidi ante tribunal Domini;
Reddemusque de omnibus rationem effectibus;
Videntes quoque posita ante obtutus crimina,
Librosque conscientiæ patefactos in facie,
In fletus amarissimos ac singultus erumpemus
Subtracta necessaria operandi materia.

T uba primi Archangeli strepente admirabilia,
Erumpent munitissima claustra ac poliandria,
Mundi præsentis frigora hominum liquescentia,
Undique conglobantibus ad Compagines ossibus
Animabus ætherialibus, eisdem obeuntibus,
Rursumque redeuntibus debitis in mansionibus.

Q uivered the mountains,
   Shouted the thunder,
Loud roared the tempest,
   Lightning flashed under,
On the mountain of Sinai,
   In terror and awe,
When Moses ascended,
   When God gave the law.

R un and hide, for the day
   Of the Lord is at hand ;
The King of all kingdoms
   In judgment will stand.
Wrath, vengeance, and darkness,
   And sadness and fear,
Take the place of all pleasure
   Which man has had here.

S ore stricken in terror
   At God's judgment-seat,
The deeds we have done here
   Receive what is meet.
No more time for repentance,
   No more time to do well ;
Our doom is eternal
   For heaven or hell.

T he trump of the angels
   Shall sound wondrous things ;
All bonds dash asunder
   With flash of their wings,
And souls meeting bodies
   Shall for ever unite,
Some descending to hell,
   Some ascending to light.

V agatur ex climatico orion cœli cardine,

Derelicto Virgilio astrorum splendissimo,

Per methas Tithis ignoti orientalis circuli

Girans certis ambagibus redit priscis reditibus,

Oriens post biennium, vesperugo in vesperum,

Sumpta in proplasmatibus tropicis intellectibus.

X **to** de cœlis Domino descendente altissimo,

Præfulgebit clarissimum signum crucis et **vexillum**

Tactisque luminaribus duobus principalibus

Cadent in terram sydera, **ut** fructus de **ficulnea,**

Eritque mundi spatium, ut fornacis incendium,

Tunc in montium specubus abscondent se exercitus.

Y morum cantionibus sedulo tinnientibus

Tropodis sanctis milibus angelorum vernantibus

Quatuorque plenissimis animalibus oculis

Cum viginti felicibus quatuor senioribus

Coronas admittentibus agni dei sub pedibus

Laudatur Tribus vicibus trinitas eternalibus.

Z elus ignis furibundus consumet adversarios

Nolentes Christum credere deo a patre **venisse**

Nos vero evolabimus obviam ei protimus

Et sic cum ipso erimus in diversis ordinibus

Dignitatum pro meritis premiorum perpetuis

Permansuri in gloria a seculis in gloria.

W ildly north and to south
    Wanders each star,
  Driven hither and thither
    By tempest afar ;
  And the light of the sun
    Shall cease from the skies,
  And the moon quenched in darkness,
    Shall never more rise.

X t descending from heaven,
    His banner the Cross,
  Then indeed shall men know
    That all else is but loss.
  To the earth the stars falling,
    The Cross all shall hide,
  For the terrors of judgment
    No man can abide.

Y et the chanting of hymns
    From the heights shall resound,
  And music angelic
    Shall be heard all around.
  By the four living creatures
    In sanctus threefold,
  Casting crowns at His feet,
    God's praise shall be told.

Z eal-kindled fire
    The unjust shall destroy,
  Who deny the Lord Jesus,
    Our hope and our joy.
  And the good shall be raised
    In the heavenly choir,
  As our merit and glory
    Have made each one higher.

THE
LIFE OF ST. BRIGIT

OF KILDARE.

" Brigit, the spotless of highest fame,
Chaste head of the Nuns of Erin."

LIFE OF BRIGIT OF KILDARE.

———⊹———

CHAPTER I.

HER PARENTAGE AND EARLY LIFE.

T. ÆNGUS, in his Felire or Collection of Rhymes, in which he commemorates the Saints of God, has noted St. Brigit as—

"The chaste head of the Nuns of Erin."

And it is a point of view, from which we may consider her life with special interest. We have in her a threefold history—the history of her own sanctification, the foundation of everything else, for without personal sanctity, work for others is simply waste of time; the history of her religious foundations; and the history of her public life.

Another Saint (we are indeed rich in them), St. Cuimin of Conor, who has written in quatrain verse the special characteristics and virtues of our old Saints, has this verse on St. Brigit :—

> " Brigit of the benedictions, loved
> Perpetual mortifications beyond all womanhood,
> Watching and early rising ;
> Hospitality to saintly men." [1]

We have in these few lines the key-note of a perfect religious character—mortification, the only solid ground of sanctity, not capricious, intermittent, or uncertain, but perpetual ; and how difficult perpetual mortification is, let those tell who have laboured to attain it — mortification not only perpetual but beyond all womanhood, so that in her great love for God she surpassed the feebleness of her sex. Watching and early rising ; in her great love for her Lord how could she choose but watch and wait on Him, in prayer or work, for the life of the spouse has ever been a life of labour. Hospitality to saintly men ; she could scarcely be Irish and not hospitable, but as a Saint "like to like" and "kind to kind," she chose the saintly for her guests and the recipients of her hospitality.

There is a poem still extant which St. Brigit composed. In it she expressed the desires of her

---

[1] Ængus composed his Festology in the reign of *Aedh Oirduidhe,* who was monarch of Ireland, from the year 793 to the year 817. He founded the church of *Disert Aengusa,* near Ballingarry, county Limerick, the ruins of which still exist. St. Cuimin lived in the middle of the seventh century.

heart. It is said to have been written on the occasion of a synod held in Munster, under Bishop Ibar, when "three thousand father confessors" were assembled, and when Brigit made a feast for Jesus in her heart. In this poem her desire to do temporal service to God's dear ones is told in the quaint language of the times.

She would have food for them in great abundance, the "viands of belief and pure piety;" she would have "vessels of charity for distribution;" she would have Jesus to be there, and the three Marys, and the people of heaven "from all parts;" and she would like to suffer "distress" for her Lord, and to be a "rent payer" to Him, for "He would bestow on her a good blessing."

There was more than common charity in this great Saint towards God and man. She would be munificent in her giving, in her doing, in her suffering; and now she is the guest, and she who when on earth entertained her Lord so well, and made a perpetual feast for Jesus in her heart, is for evermore enjoying the feast which He has prepared for souls like hers.

Well might St. Bernard say—

> "Oh blessed retribution,
> Short toil, eternal rest."

A little fast here, and a long feast there; a little pain here, and an eternity of joy there; a little denial of our own will here, and the satisfaction of all the desires of our hearts for endless ages.

Well, indeed, may Brigit be called

" The head of the Nuns of Erin."

How many thousands of Irish nuns have passed, year after year, to the same beatitude since Brigit lived and loved and migrated to the heavenly country.

Walking in her footsteps with mortification and work and burning charity, they may well look up to her as their patron, and invoke that Thaumaturgus in their needs. Her power is not less to-day than it was a thousand years ago—nor will she care less for her "spotless Erin."

Truly, with such faithful and loving intercessors in heaven as Brigit and Patrick and Columba, it is little wonder that Ireland has preserved her faith undefiled, and that her children have, even to this very day, been increasing the ranks of the noble army of martyrs.[1]

Wherever the Irish missionary has gone to evangelise, there the Irish nun has gone to teach. With her heart full of love to her country and her people, she has left them, not, indeed, without tears, for sacrifice means pain, but with a willing heart. Love of Christ has triumphed over love of Erin, and a desire for the better country has proved stronger than

---

[1] It is not long since an Irish nun was martyred in China. In the Rule of St. Columba there is mention of *red martyrdom* and *white martyrdom*. Dorman went to St. Columba and asked him to be his " soul friend " [confessor], but the Saint refused out of humility, as he did not consider himself worthy to be a soul friend to an " heir " to red martyrdom.

love of fatherland. And we have also the history of the Saint's public life. It was a life of public charity, a life for God and Ireland, a life which proves that the retirement of the cloister is no selfish hiding from duty ; but on this subject the following pages will give ample details.

The material for the Life of St. Brigit is abundant, and well authenticated.

Father Colgan, the great Franciscan hagiologist, collected and published all or nearly all these documents in his rare and costly work, " The Trias Thaumaturgus." The first of these lives is metrical. He gives the original Irish printed in such fashion as could then be done, and he adds a Latin translation.

This hymn, which is of considerable length, is attributed to St. Brogan Cloen, and was probably composed in the early part of the sixth century.

The second " Life of St. Brigit " was written by Cogitosus ; from internal evidence it was probably compiled in the eighth century.

The authorship of the third life has been much disputed. Colgan attributed it to St. Ultan, bishop of Ardbraccan, in Meath, who died at a great age, A.D. 656. It is also conjectured to have been written by St. Ninnidh of the " undefiled hand," and by St. Fiacc, who composed the metrical " Life of St. Patrick." The fourth " Life of St. Brigit " is attributed to " Animosus." He has not been satisfactorily identified, but there was a Bishop of Kildare,

Anmchadh, who died A.D. 980. From internal evidence it is clear that the writer of this life was a monk or bishop of Kildare.

The fifth "Life of St. Brigit" is notable as having been written by an Englishman. The writer, besides stating his nationality, says that he composed this life after the Norman invasion of England, and before the Norman invasion of Ireland. This gives a clue to the person and the date. It is known that Lawrence of Durham wrote a Life of St. Brigit, and that he lived at this period; there is, therefore, little doubt that this is the very Life of St. Brigit. The sixth life is also metrical, and is attributed by Colgan to St. Colean, a monk of Inis-Keltran Abbey on the Shannon; the codex was preserved in the library of the world-famed Benedictine Abbey of Monte Cassino, and was collated with another copy in the Vatican Library. If the authorship be justly attributed to St. Colean, the work is one of great antiquity, as he lived in the eighth century. A prologue is prefixed to the life, which was written by St. Donat, bishop of Fiesole, in the ninth century. Besides these more important works, a very large number of manuscript lives of the Saint are extant. There is, therefore, abundant and authoritative material for the life of this great Irish nun.

Opposition has been raised as usual to the narrative of her miracles, and to the miraculous occurrences recorded in her acts. We have already said so much

on this subject, that we do not enter upon it again.
The same argument applies equally in all cases. If
miracles are possible, and if they are recorded on
sufficient evidence, we can ask no more.[1]

St. Brigit was of noble birth. Ireland, indeed,
would seem to have been the only exception to the
rule that the gospel of Christ would be embraced by
the poor. In other countries we find a few of the
great, and noble, and wealthy listening to the gospel of
the evangelist, but in Ireland the noble and wealthy
were quite as forward to receive it as the poor and
unlearned.

Eochaidh Finn was the progenitor of the numerous
Saints, and from him St. Brigit was descended. We
find St. Gall, the evangelist of Switzerland, and his

---

[1] While these pages are passing through the press we have read a
sketch of the " Life of St. Walburge," an English Saint. It is written
by the Rev. W. H. Anderdon, S.J., in the happy style which is so exclusively his own, and which combines the highest intellectual culture
with the most fervent and simple piety. It is a style which makes his
works equally acceptable to the learned and the unlearned, a rare gift,
indeed, as well as the piety which is not ashamed to openly express
belief in the supernatural. St. Walburge lived in the latter part of the
eighth century. Now, it is a simple matter of fact, that at the present
day, on her feast-day, and on several other days in the year, a miraculous
oil oozes through the solid stone in which her relics were placed in the
year 893. This oil frequently works miracles. And what is still, if
possible, more wonderful, at the present day, Father Anderdon says,
that "when any sin is committed by those who carry or keep this oil
in their possession, especially of cursing, swearing, or vicious acts, it
vanishes away, and leaves the phial empty." God has His own ways
of honouring His saints. We have our choice, either to honour them
with Him, or to despise and reject, and what is perhaps quite as
dangerous, to disregard these favours.

N

brother Deicolus, St. Aidan of Clontarf, St. Berchan of Glasnevin, of whom we have already given some account.

St. Finan, St. Declan of Ardmore, and many others, were of his descendants also. Fiedhinidh Rechtmar, or the lawgiver, father of Eochaidh Finn, flourished in the second century of the Christian era, and from him Brigit was the eleventh in descent. Her mother, Broeseach, was an O'Connor, and was of noble birth ; both her parents were Christians.[1]

There has been no question as to the birthplace of the Saint. The village where she was born was called Fochart Muirthemme, and was situated in the district of Conaille Muirthemme in Ulster. Faughart is now in the diocese of Armagh, and is no way remarkable except as the birthplace of the Saint. It is in the present province of Leinster, and near the town of Dundalk. The ruins of St. Brigit's old church are still here. The situation is very picturesque, looking out on the Bay of Dundalk, the scene of many a notable event in Irish history.[2]

---

[1] In some of the early lives of St. Brigit it is said that her mother was a slave, and that she was not the lawful wife of Brigit's father. The subject is one which has been discussed with some acrimony, and no very useful result. There is no question as to the parentage of the Saint, and it seems unlikely that her mother, who was of good birth, should have been a slave, but slavery, or rather servitude in bondage, was then common. The tradition at least shows that Irish hagiographers were not anxious to extol the parentage of this Saint at the expense of truth.

[2] St. Bernard mentions this place in his " Life of St. Malachy," as the birthplace of St. Brigit. When the sixth life of the Saint was written,

A dun is still to be seen, which it is conjectured may have been the dwelling of the Saint's father. It commands a magnificent view, and is just such a site as an Irish chief would have chosen. St. Brigit's well has been carefully enclosed by an arch of masonry.

The date of St. Brigit's birth has also been a subject of lively discussion, though there has been no question as to the century in which she lived. One of the principal difficulties has arisen, from the fact that while her biographers wrote of her constant intercourse with St. Patrick, the historians of his life do not mention her name except in one instance.[1]

On this occasion it is said that she fell asleep, presumedly a mystical sleep, during the preaching of St. Patrick, and that she had a vision in which she saw the state of the Irish Church and its future troubles. The Saint hearing she had this heavenly communication, desired her to tell what she had seen. Brigit replied that she saw first a herd of white oxen, then spotted ones, and then dark. These were followed by sheep, and swine, and wolves, and dogs, who quarrelled with each other. It is mentioned in nearly all the lives of St. Brigit that she wove the shroud in which St. Patrick was buried, and that she did this at his

there was a church and burial-place there dedicated to the Saint, and situated on the very site of the house where she was born. A stone is shown on which the infant was said to have been laid at her birth.

[1] By the writer of the tripartite Life of St. Patrick, the translation of which is now published in the illustrated quarto edition of our work—the "Trias Thaumaturgus."

special request. **It is quite clear, that** if St. Patrick **met** her on any one occasion, he would have discovered her special virtue **and** character, and he was not the man to lose sight of **her.**

Of her early life many incidents are recorded which resemble those which have been related of more modern Saints. It is said that when she was **a child** the angels were her constant companions, and even assisted her **in** setting up a little altar with which she **amused** herself. A column of fire was seen ascending from the house where **she lived ;** and, when a growing **girl, whatever she touched or** had charge of in the way **of** food, multiplied under her hand.[1] Her occupations **were** the simple ones **of** the simple state of life which obtained at that period even amongst the noble. She looked after her father's flocks **and** herds, and fed the poor ones of her Lord. Even in childhood she commenced the practice **of** severe abstinence, often remaining a considerable time without food. Her nurse was afflicted at one time **with a** burning fever, and the young Saint relieved her by making the sign of the Cross on some water which was turned to mead, the common drink of the country at that time.

We have already related **the** anecdote of what passed **during the preaching of St.** Patrick. It was

---

[1] The power to increase food has been given to many Saints. The "Life of Blessed Lucy of Narni," published by Burns & Co. **some years** since, relates many miraculous favours granted to her when a **very** young child, especially in the companionship of angels.

in the territory of Lemaine, in Tyrone. The great apostle is said to have discoursed for three days and three nights to an enraptured people, who never thought during all this time of food or rest.

A great deal of unnecessary explanation and apology has been written on the subject of the comparison made by early Irish writers between the Blessed Virgin and St. Brigit. After all has been said they amount simply to this, that the early Irish, in their high veneration for their Saint, used very strong expressions and very poetical ones ; but throughout all, there is not one trace of putting her on a level with the one Immaculate Virgin. The Irish writers of those ages had common sense, and gave others credit for it. The comparison used, that Brigit was "the Mary of the Irish," was simply a poetical way of expressing that she of all Irish maidens most resembled in her life and character the Mother of Jesus.

The first and metrical life of the Saint is too long for insertion here, but we give a few of the concluding verses.

CONCLUSION OF THE METRICAL IRISH "LIFE OF ST. BRIGIT."

Pro Nobis Precetur Brigida.

For us may holy Brigit pray,
  And keep us safe from harm ;
Until we see God's Spirit blest,
  Where fears no more alarm.

Against the demons may she be
  A fiery sword and strong,
Until her prayers shall bring us safe
  To join the angel throng.

To praise God in His Holy Church,
  Be still our constant task ;
Like holy Brigit, let us not
  For earthly pleasures ask.

With all Kildare's holy ones,
  To Brigit I will pray,
That she may save from pain and loss
  On the great judgment-day.

O holy Saint ! who Currah's plains
  Hast in thy lifetime trod ;
There's none but Mary ever blessed
  Has come so near to God.

In Brigit, then, oh let us trust,
  She will protect us all ;
For not in vain shall Erin's hosts
  On holy Brigit call.

To praise Christ is a glorious work—
  Then louder be our lays,
And special grace be given to all
  Who thus St. Brigit praise.

And they who praise God and His Saints
  From God and Brigit too,
In heaven above shall have reward,
  And honour as is due.

Two virgins are in heaven above,
  Their client I would be ;
Mary and Brigit I invoke,
  Protection give to me

There is an alphabetical hymn in honour of St. Brigit, but only a part of this composition remains, unless indeed, as has been conjectured, the hymn consisted of only three verses. This hymn, or what remains of it, is both quoted and referred to in very ancient manuscripts at present extant in Continental libraries.

There is as usual an historical preface to this hymn, in which the authors are given, and the plan of composition, as we have already mentioned.

ALPHABETICAL HYMN.

CHRISTUS IN NOSTRA INSULA.

Christ in our isle was shown to men,
    By Brigit's saintly life;
Excelling all who came before,
    She conquered in the strife.

Like her no other Saint was found,
    But Jesu's mother blest;
Her virtues and her wondrous fame
    Can never be expressed.

With holy fervour girdled round,
    The victor's palm she gains;
And like the glorious sun above,
    In heaven refulgent reigns.

Then listen to this virgin's praise:
    To Christ she gave her vow,
Faithful she kept it; her reward
    Is reigning with Him now.

O queen, enthroned in heaven above,
  Look on thy children dear ;
An l help them to eternal life,
  In God's most holy fear.

Christ Jesus, author of all good,
  Have mercy upon me ;
That with Thy angels up in heaven,
  I may Thy mercy see.[1]

Colgan gives another poem on the Saint, which he
found in manuscript in the Monastery of St. Cuthbert
at Cambray, and which is attributed to the author of
the former composition. The style is, we had almost
said, more classical ; it is perhaps more correct to say
that it is less rude.

HYMN IN HONOUR OF ST. BRIGIT.

BRIGIDA NOMEN HABET.

Resplendent is great Brigit's name
  Like flash of diamond bright !
Resplendent is great Brigit's name,
  Shining in heavenly light !

A virgin of the Lord is she—
  A virgin crucified ;
A virgin of the Lord is she,
  To His Cross closely tied.

---

[1] Objections have been made to some of the expressions in the
original of this hymn by Protestants, and even by some Catholics, who
were not familiar with the language of mystical theology. If the Saint
is spoken of as *Veri Dei Regina*, it means no more or no less than what
Scripture tells us that the just shall reign hereafter with Him, and
that He will even delegate to them authority and power in His kingdom. The more saintly the soul the nearer to Him, and the nearer
to Him the greater power and honour in His kingdom.

With exaltation see she scorns
    The world, and all its joys !
With exaltation see she scorns
    Earth's passing shows and toys !

She dreaded earthly pomp and state,
    Its riches she despised ;
She dreaded earthly pomp and state,
    For God alone she prized.

She looked for everlasting joys,
    She sought a great reward ;
She looked for everlasting joys
    With Christ, her love and Lord.

She heard the echoing shouts of heaven,
    The triumph of the blest !
She heard the echoing shouts of heaven—
    Of those with Christ at rest !

Oh ! pray for us ; kind virgin, pray
    That we may joy with thee.
Oh ! pray for us ; kind virgin, pray
    That Christ we too may see.[1]

---

[1] The repetition of the first line is in the original.

CHAPTER II.

HERE is, perhaps, no better proof of the great devotion to learning which obtained amongst the early Irish than the intimate knowledge shown in their writings of the authors of preceding ages, both Pagan and Christian. Nor were they mere copiers or mechanical readers. They studied and pondered, digested and mused. Hence, with a special aptitude for comparison, the result of a poetical imagination, they liked to find out resemblances between their own saints and the saints of preceding centuries.

St. Patrick they compared to the Apostle Peter and to Moses, St. Columba to St. Andrew, St. Adamnan to Pope Silvester, but to their thinking there was no female Saint to whom Brigit was equal, and so they compared her to Mary, the Mother of Jesus. It was a keen and just appreciation of the dignity of woman. To be like the one perfect woman was to be as near perfection as possible.

The history of the early life of the Saint has been so mixed up with wild legends that it is impossible to separate truth from error. It is more than probable that a solid substratum of truth underlies this vast mass of tradition, but it would be a difficult and a dangerous task to attempt any division, and there is quite sufficient authentic history recorded as to her later life.

After many difficulties, and much opposition from her relations, she wished to consecrate her virginity to Christ. It is said that her father and mother were converted to her desires by a miracle. Her rare beauty had attracted attention, and she obtained from God the grace of a temporary disfigurement, the miraculous character of which was fully proved by its disappearance when her request was granted. Seven holy virgins prepared to join her in making a religious foundation, and they went to a Bishop called Maccelle, that he might consecrate them to Christ, but the Bishop hesitated to grant her request. Brigit was young and beautiful, and he well knew that for such the world had its temptations and attractions, and he did not yet know the extraordinary sanctity of the postulant.

The Saint betook herself to the never-failing

resource of prayer. She desired to be the spouse of
Jesus; but Jesus must first have desired to take her
for His spouse. It was from Him the blessed inspira-
tion came; her part was to obey, and to suffer, if
need be, in her obedience. The work was His, so she
could rest confident; but she was none the less bound
to use her own efforts for its accomplishment—to
will and to work.

As she prayed a column of fire was seen over her
head, and the Bishop, who heard of the miracle, sent
to make special inquiries about her. With the holy
instinct of true sanctity, he did not turn from what
was out of the ordinary course of the spiritual life,
for, happily, he lived in an age of faith. With true
prudence, not less a mark of sanctity, he made careful
inquiries as to the previous life of this young maiden,
knowing that though miracles might be granted to
sanctity, there could be no true supernatural grace
given where there had not been a supernatural corres-
pondence with grace. What he heard was sufficient;
her life had been more than ordinarily holy, and
marked by extraordinary favours. These miracles
were granted, no doubt, to confirm the faith and
enkindle the zeal of a faithful people so recently
converted to Christ.

As the Bishop blessed the virgins, and accepted
the holocaust of their young lives to the Lord, St.
Brigit touched some wood which supported the altar,
and which had been long dried and in use. But it at

once became green, as if newly cut, and when the church was destroyed by fire at a later period, this portion alone escaped.

It is said that the Saint was born, veiled, and died on a Wednesday, and that she was in the eighteenth year of her age when she was consecrated to the service of Christ. Bishop Mel, St. Patrick's nephew and disciple, had also some share in the ceremony.

An ancient Irish life says that she began to practise the Beatitudes in her eighth year, and that she used to call them the "food of mercy." They are indeed a food on which saintly souls have been nourished for long ages since, and on which they will be fed for ages yet to come. The church in which St. Brigit made her religious profession was called *Cruachan Brigh-eile.* Cogitosus mentions that it was renowned for pilgrimages and miracles in his day; but the site has not been satisfactorily identified.[1]

A distinctive dress was used by religious at this period, and a veil; but many who were consecrated to Christ still remained with their families. White appears to have been the colour then worn by nuns, and for some centuries the rule of St. Brigit was the only one known in Ireland.

It is by no means certain where St. Brigit's first foundation was established. Local tradition points to several places in different counties.

---

[1] It is conjectured to have been on the eastern side of the Hill of Croghan, near Tyrrell's Pass, in the King's County.

According to one tradition **she** and her sisters established themselves at **Foughart, in** the county Louth. **This place** has already **been described.**

Another tradition points to Usneach near **Castletown County,** Westmeath. There was a Brigidstown (*Rathbridghe*) in ancient Meath, **now** Ballycown, King's **County.** The district of *Teathbna* is frequently mentioned in the Saint's **life, and** Ardagh **holds the** Saint as the principal patron **with St.** Mel. There is at present a **well dedicated to her near the town of** Ardagh. **In one of the early lives of the** Saint the parents **of those maidens who** were consecrated with **her** are represented as entreating **her** to **make her** foundation where they were.

It is very interesting **to find that the little** devotional practices which **are in** use **at the** present day, in so many religious **houses, were** in use also in the **first** convent **of Irish** nuns. **We have our** special devotions for Christmas and Lent, for the sorrows **of the** Passion **and the** joys of Easter, and what **helps us now** heavenward, helped our ancient mothers **also.**

On one occasion **the holy** Bishop Maccelle invited St. Brigit **and her nuns to a** banquet, **which** he had prepared for them. Before the **food** was distributed **the** Saint begged him to give her religious some spiritual instructions. He complied with her **request,** and spoke on the eight Beatitudes, **the steps to the** heavenly kingdom.

When he had concluded his discourse, St. Brigit turned to her sisters and said :—

" We are eight virgins, and eight virtues are offered to us as a means of sanctification. It is true that whoever practises one virtue perfectly must possess every other ; yet let us each choose a virtue now for special devotion." [1]

The sisters, already prepared to show deference and respect to their superior, requested her to take the first choice. Without a moment's hesitation she took the beatitude of " mercy " as the virtue to which she especially desired to devote herself. A happy choice, consecrating the lives and life work of thousands of religious women who should follow her.

The Saint soon became the Superior of a large and fervent community. The fame of her miracles and of her life, which in truth like the life of every nun was in itself a miracle, brought many to her house. But she did not allow increase of work to cause decrease of fervour, and she accomplished the most difficult task of guiding a multitude of souls to the highest perfection with all her public work. [2]

---

[1] In a little book, which we wrote some years since, called "The Flowers of Mary," we wrote devotional practices for each month in the year, to be drawn by lot. The eight Beatitudes were chosen for the month of February ; when writing this work we knew but little of Irish Saints, and never suspected that "the head of all the Nuns of Erin " had already introduced the same practices.

[2] A most extraordinary statement has been put forward in a Life of St. Brigit by a recent Catholic writer. He says, " Moral goodness does not usually abound in a very exalted degree, except in large reli-

The miracles of this Saint are related in the usual way, without any regard to chronological sequence. They are just such miracles as we find in the lives of all God's Saints, for though the conditions of human life may be different at different times, and in different ages, the substance remains the same.

It will be remembered that Ireland was but just emerging from the darkness of paganism at this period. Hence we find, as we might expect, that miracles were more frequent and more striking in character than at other periods of our history.

The primitive customs and history of the times show in all these narratives.

The cow was the great source of wealth and barter, and hence, as we might expect, there are many mira-

gious communities; yet virtue consists not in having many together so much as in a store of merit."

It is something new to learn that virtue is cumulative in this fashion. This certainly is not the doctrine taught by St. Teresa, and the founders of religious orders. Their great desire was rather to have small communities, as likely to be far more perfect and fervent than those where a number were assembled together. How the mere fact of "having many together" could be in itself virtue is incomprehensible. We regret also that the same writer has frequently quoted a Protestant clergyman as authority for the lives of Saints. On archæology and kindred subjects the opinion of such persons may be well worth having, but in matters of faith and practice the less said of them the better. This author is quoted in such a way as might lead many persons to suppose him a Catholic. We have before us now a series of articles written by this very same Protestant clergyman in Fraser's Magazine, in which he has written on the Saints of the early Roman Church with ridicule and bitterness. If it has suited his purpose to write differently at another time, what has been written remains and shows the animus of heresy, which, however it may be concealed for a time, is ever ready to come to the surface again.

culous occurrences related in connection with this animal.

The Celt, always generous, would not be behind hand in supporting the priest or nun, in giving them temporal aid in return for their spiritual help. A good woman bethought herself that she would offer a cow and calf for the use of the convent, but as she had to pass through a thick wood the calf was lost, and she sought for it in vain.

The miraculous power of the Saint, however, occurred to her, and she called out in a loud voice for her assistance, and help was given. The cow followed the woman quietly to the Convent, and the Saint told her not to trouble herself about the calf as it would soon come after its mother.

St. Brigit's hospitality was often taxed to the uttermost. On one occasion, when a number of ecclesiastics were her guests, she had only one cow to supply the needs of the whole house.

But with a Saint such little deficiencies were soon remedied. The one cow gave as much milk as three cows had given formerly, and all necessary wants were satisfied.

At another time, when her herds were more numerous, a band of robbers came and stole some of her oxen. But their ill-gotten booty did not profit them. As they were making their escape with their prey, the river which they crossed had become so swollen that the men were all drowned, and their bodies swept down the stream ; but the oxen escaped and returned safely to their pastures.

The fearful disease of leprosy appears to have been prevalent, or at least not unfrequent, in Ireland at this period. Lepers came for milk many times to the saintly Abbess, and on one occasion two lepers came to beg an alms. The Saint gave them a cow, and told them to divide the animal between them. But one of these men was of that thankless disposition which is never satisfied : were abundance and satiety the portions of such persons they would even then seek more ; and, unhappily, those who have much to do with the poor not unfrequently find such characters. The thankless leper would have the whole cow or none, and gave insolence when he should have given gratitude. St. Brigit then turned to the thankful and humble leper, and told him to let his discontented companion go with the cow, and that she would give him whatever God would send if he would remain with her. The covetous leper was satisfied ; he had got all he desired and set off on his journey. But the cow could not be driven ; and, at last, the man wearied out, returned to give fresh insolence to his generous benefactor. It was her fault that the cow proved so stubborn. The Saint tried to satisfy him with kind words, but he would not be silenced, and the time had come for just and holy anger. She turned to the wretched man and told him plainly that he was a " son of perdition," and that he should obtain no profit from her gift though the cow would become perfectly docile. A present of another cow having been offered to the Saint in the meantime, she gave it to the good leper, and both departed with their presents.

As they crossed a river, the thankless leper was drowned, but the good and grateful sufferer passed over safely.

While St. Brigit was living in her great foundation at Kildare (the Cell of the Oak), the poor people who lived in the surrounding districts were generous in such offerings as their poverty could afford. On the eve of a great festival, a young girl came with some little gift to the nuns, and in giving it remembered that she should hasten home to take charge of her flocks, as her father and mother desired to come to Kildare for the festival ; but the Saint desired her to remain with her, assuring her that God would protect her property, and that her parents would soon follow her.

All happened as the Saint had said ; but in the night some thieves took advantage of the unguarded state of the little flocks, and stole what they could. They drove the animals towards the Liffey, but the river had risen during the night, and they could not drive the terrified cattle through it.

Confused and not knowing what they did in their guilty experiences, they turned the cattle in the wrong direction, and when morning dawned they found

themselves close to the Cell of the Oak, just the very
last place where they would have wished to be. The
result was a happy one for all parties concerned. The
men were amazed at what had happened. They confessed their sin, and drove the cattle home to the
owners, and all who heard of the miraculous occurrence
glorified God for the power He manifests in His saints.

On the vigil of another festival, alms were brought
to the Saint by a young girl, who also was obliged,
she said, to return home to care for her foster father
and his cows. But the holy Abbess desired her to
remain all night, so that she might receive the most
holy sacrament in the morning. She did as she was
desired, and her foster father, on her return, told her
that the time of her absence seemed only as if it had
been one hour, and that the cattle had not suffered in
any way from the want of the usual care, while the
sun seemed not to have set during her absence. Well
may the writer of the metrical life exclaim :

"O memoranda Dei virtus ! O magna potestas !"

The wonderful gift of bilocation which has been
granted to different Saints is also attributed to St.
Brigit. It need not be said here that God bestows
His gifts where and as He wills, and that it is worse
than shortsighted folly to discuss the wherefore of what
we cannot understand. Why certain gifts are given
to some Saints and not to others, we do not know ;
why some are distinguished for miraculous gifts, while

in the lives of others we scarcely hear of a miracle,[1] are amongst the secrets of God. That the divine reasons are divine is sufficient for us to know, that they are full of mercy is a grace beyond our deserts. Indeed, it is only pride and self-love which directs such criticism, and a poor faith which doubts where sufficient proof is given.

Even in our time Saints have been seen in ecstasy and so absorbed in God as to be utterly unconscious of all created things. And this favour was constantly granted to St. Brigit. It is, in truth, but a little anticipation of that blessed time when the things of time and sense shall cease to be, an anticipation of the bliss prepared in degree and measure for every child of earth who shall be admitted to the enjoyment of the beatific vision of God.

It would indeed appear from the biography of St. Brigit that she was always absorbed in God. Her charity to others was but the overflow of her charity to God. It was love in action; the blessed fruit of love is contemplation—the fruit whereby the contemplation was proved to be divine, and not the mere impulse of a pious feeling or fancy.

A young man came once to the Saint and wished to speak with her; but she was absorbed in God, and so utterly lost in contemplation, as to be unconscious of his presence. An unusual disturbance was going on around her, and men and women were shouting

[1] *E.g.* St., Vincent of Paul.

and herding cattle, but the Saint was past all knowledge of human sight or sound. The young man went away, finding he could not engage her attention, and returned in about an hour. The Saint in the meantime had become conscious of earthly things, and he inquired, had she not heard the noise and cries of the people? She replied that she had not heard them. He then asked, what had become of her hearing? "As God is my witness," she replied, "I heard mass at that very time in Rome, at the tombs of St. Peter and St. Paul." Then she added her desire to have copies of the Roman ritual, so that she might use the ceremonies approved there, and as soon as she could do so she sent messengers to Rome to procure them.[1]

St. Brogan Cloen, in his metrical life, celebrates the assistance she gave to her labourers in harvest times, but takes care to add that her doing so was not to be considered wrong in a religious person, *i.e.*, that it was not wrong for her to assist her own people, while others were allowed to suffer. The rain poured down in torrents, and the rivers were flooded all over the country, but the Saint's labourers and harvest escaped all harm.

A good mother once brought her child to see the Saint. The girl was about twelve years of age, but she had been born dumb. St. Brigit was not aware

---

[1] In one of the ancient lives of St. Brigit, a miraculous cure is attributed to her shadow. It is said that a "layman" came to the Saint carrying his mother, who was paralysed. When he came to where St. Brigit was, he placed his mother on the grass in the Saint's shadow, and she was cured immediately.

of her infirmity, and began to speak to the child, and caress her, asking if she intended to be a nun. The little girl did not reply, and the mother told the Saint why she could not do so. But the holy wonder-worker said she could not let go the child's hand until she received an answer ; and on her asking the question a second time, the child replied, "I desire to do whatever you wish." The girl thus miraculously cured remained with the Saint until her death.

An anecdote is related of her conventual discipline which shows that the spirit of the religious life has not changed with changing ages. Indeed, such changes would not be possible. The Christian perfection of the first ages of Christianity is the same as the Christian perfection of to-day. The one Church knows no change in its teaching, or in the practices of its faithful followers.

Obedience has ever been the key note of sanctity, since He who was all holy gave the high example of this virtue by being obedient even unto death.

But the enemy who rages round the most saintly, and who rejoices in seeing even a shade of evil in those who are earnestly desirous of good, is unceasing in his temptations. He cannot entice such souls to open violation of Christian principles or of evangelical precepts; but he can, and unhappily he does too often, mar the perfection of their sacrifice by inducing them to take up wrong principles and to act on them.

The device is cunning, subtle, and admirably

suited to its end.   They fix on some ideal of perfection, which, indeed, might be perfection in others,
or under other circumstances, and they cling to that
in defiance of obedience; sometimes, even, in a bold
open defiance, which they justify to themselves under
a pretext of virtue ; and yet if such persons are
charged with pride and self-will, or disobedience, they
will indignantly deny being guided by such motives,
so utterly are they blinded by the temptation to
which they have yielded.

At one time when there was a great scarcity of
corn, the Saint went with some of her nuns to beg
for help from St. Ibar.[1]   It was in Lent, and the Saint
had nothing to give his visitors but some inferior
bread and bacon.   At that time perpetual abstinence
was observed at that holy season, but necessity and
the impossibility of procuring proper food would then,
as now, make a dispensation lawful.

The two Saints took the only food to be had with
the simplicity of true sanctity, but two of the nuns
thought themselves wiser, or more perfect, and refused their portion.

St. Brigit was exceedingly displeased, and reproved
them severely before the Bishop, ordering them to
commence a fast as a penance for their self-will.

If we did not know too well the perverseness of
human natures and the deceitfulness of our hearts,
we might marvel that these religious should have dis-

[1] St. Ibar lived then at Maggesille, the plain of the Liffey.

obeyed a Superior whose sanctity was manifested by such wonderful miracles. Even then another miracle was about to happen.

The Saint, with the true instinct of spiritual maternity, could not bear to inflict suffering without sharing it in some way, and she also began a fast. But when St. Ibar heard why the Saint had come to him, he exclaimed that it was impossible to help her, that if she had known how little corn was in his possession, she would not have come to him for a supply. But she replied, " It is not so, for you have twenty-four waggon-loads of grain in your barn," and when search was made it proved to be even so. The grain was divided, Ibar keeping half for his own use, and sending the rest to the convent. After this, the Bishop went to the monastery and celebrated mass there for all the people.

The Saint's tender care of her religious was manifested by another miracle. One of the sisters was very ill, and asked for a little milk, but none was to be had. But Brigit desired a sister to fill a vessel with water and give it to the sufferer. When she received it the water had been changed to milk, which was as warm as if it were just taken from the cow, and the draught cured her of her sickness.

The Saint could not bear to see any want of charity in others. Once when a woman came to her with a present of apples, some lepers came at the same time asking for an alms. St. Brigit told the woman to divide the fruit amongst them, but she replied that she had brought the present for the nuns, and not for the lepers. The Saint was seriously displeased at her want of charity, and told her that her trees should never bear fruit after this.

On her return home she found the prediction verified, for the trees which had been laden with fruit before were now quite bare.

It is related in several of her ancient lives that she visited Tailten (now Telltown), county Meath, while St. Patrick was at this place, which was one of the most famous sites in early Irish history. The great fair of the nation was held here, and our apostle probably took this opportunity to preach to the people. A certain man who had witnessed some of the miracles wrought by St. Brigit asked her to stop at his house, with the sisters who accompanied her.

He showed all possible desire to entertain them well and hospitably, but when meat was set before them St. Brigit refused to partake of it, saying that our Lord had at that moment revealed to her that the man had refused to be baptized. One of her religious replied that this was certainly true, for she had heard that he had resisted St. Patrick's preaching, and refused holy baptism. But when St. Brigit told this man that she could not eat in his house until he was baptized, his heart was so touched that he was at once converted, and was baptized with his whole family.

Possibly if there was a little more straightforward

dealing with heresy in the present day, a little less so-called courtesy, and a little more truth, there might be more conversions.

When St. Patrick heard of this conversion, he desired that a priest should always accompany St. Brigit, as even in later times a priest accompanied St. Catherine of Sienna, to administer the sacraments to those who were converted by her preaching. A priest named Nadfeaich was the person appointed to attend St. Brigit, and he performed this duty faithfully till the end of her life.

Like all religious the Saint devoted herself specially to the promotion of union in families, and to assist those who lived in the world to observe a Christian life. If the virgin consecrates her virginity to Christ, it is not because she despises marriage, but because she chooses a more excellent way. But she is the last to forget that there are canonised saints who have been wives and mothers, and she remembers that she must be a faithful spouse, and procure for her Lord an abundant harvest of souls. By leaving the world the nun becomes the benefactor of the world. In living apart from the world she takes in it a new and better interest, because such interest is altogether heavenly. In leaving the ties of human affection, she binds herself to the whole human race with the cords of Divine love, and she pours forth upon all around her a stream of vivifying charity. When her interest in earth seems to cease, it has actually intensified.

She no longer looks on its concerns as a matter of indifference, but rather, seeing them in the light of eternity, she knows all the momentous import of the least human act.

It would appear that St. Brigit frequently travelled in different parts of the country, and thus extended her religious foundations far and wide. On one of these occasions she went to visit St. Lasrea, who is said to have been a direct descendant of King Leoghaires. There are many similar names in the calendar of Irish Saints, so that her identification has not been satisfactorily established. St. Lasrea had already founded a small community of nuns, and here St. Patrick came at the same time, to the dismay of the sisters, for there was not food enough for all. The nuns told their troubles at once to St. Brigit, who "desired the Scriptures to be read," and then the little which they had so multiplied as to be quite sufficient for all. St. Lasrea then put herself and her community under the special care of St. Brigit.

While the Saint was staying at this place, a good man came to her to tell his domestic troubles. His wife would not live happily with him, having taken an unaccountable aversion to him. St. Brigit then gave the man some water, desiring him to sprinkle his house with it during his wife's absence. He did as he was desired, and when his wife returned home her dislike was turned to the tenderest affection, which continued during the lifetime of the now happy couple.

The holy bishop, Erc, of whom we have already written in our Life of St. Patrick, was a contemporary of St. Brigit's. He was descended from a royal line, but he preferred heavenly to earthly honours. He had returned to Slane, on the banks of the Boyne, where at the present day the ruins of a Franciscan monastery marks the site of his cell. This Saint was specially intimate with St. Brigit, and accompanied her on several of her journeys. On one occasion, about the year 484, they travelled together into Munster. As they passed on, the Saint asked the Bishop to point out the direction in which his native place lay. He did so, and she immediately exclaimed that war was raging there between his people and another clan. He replied that there were two tribes at variance when he left home. Then the Saint cried out, "O Father, your people are defeated!" But the Saints had an incredulous companion in their company, who would not believe that what he did not see could be seen by others, and expressed his opinion very plainly. The Bishop reproved him for his want of faith, and "for not believing in the gifts of the Holy Ghost," who could confer even greater powers if He pleased. But he was soon to have a proof which would satisfy even his poor faith.

Erc asked the Saint to "sign their eyes," that they might see what she saw. She did as he desired, and soon the young man cried out that two brothers were killed.

This was subsequently proved to have happened, and established the truth of the vision.

As they passed on, food was miraculously prepared for them by the intercession of St. Brigit.

The tender heart of the Saint was easily moved to compassionate any human grief ; and we are told how she rescued a child whom an eagle had carried off, and obliged the bird to bring it back to the distressed parents.

Like St. Columba, she was always anxious to help those who were in bondage according to the custom of the times. She remained for some time at a place on the plain of Cliach, in the county Limerick, and while here a poor girl fled to her protection to escape the tyranny of a cruel mistress. The mistress came after her to reclaim her, and would not listen to the entreaties of the Saint. She seized the unhappy girl, and tried to drag her with violence from the protection of St. Brigit.

But the holy Abbess knew where to exercise severity, which in saintly hands is another form of mercy. She procured pardon for the maid, and the repentance of the mistress, by obtaining that the hand which held the girl should become withered. The woman, terrified at what had befallen her, and no longer able to hold the girl, gave her the freedom she desired, and immediately her hand was restored. But miracles of mercy were, indeed, worthy of her who had chosen mercy as her special virtue.

While she was remaining for a short time at a place called Labrathi,[1] a poor woman came to her with her daughter, who was afflicted with leprosy, and besought her help. The Saint blessed some water and gave it to her mother, and as soon as the girl was touched with it she was perfectly healed of her terrible disease.

St. Brigit remained for some time in Roscommon, where she built several cells and religious houses.

In Colgan's time he obtained a list of places where her memory still remained, and where local tradition agreed with the written accounts of her foundations. While in this part of Ireland she practised the severe mortification of remaining for some part of the night in a pool of water near the convent, and this she did during the most severe weather.

A sister always accompanied her, and on one occasion, when they went to the same place, they found the water had quite disappeared, and nothing remained but the sand at the bottom of the pool. They returned home, but came next morning to see what had caused the disappearance of the water; but the little lake was found as full as usual. This happened for

---

[1] Identified with Hy-Kinsellach. Labrathia, son of Bressal Belach, was the founder of this family. Colgan says that in his time there was a well in this district dedicated to St. Brigit, where many cures were wrought.

three successive nights, and the Saint then recognised the hand of God, and yielded to the entreaties of her friends to forego this practice of mortification.

The Saint's great foundation at Kildare, which has been ever associated with her name, was undertaken at the urgent request of the people of Leinster. It seemed to them unjust that their own Saint should devote herself so much to other districts and places when they conceived themselves to have the first claim on her.

Having determined to get the Saint back, they bethought themselves how best to secure their object, and resolved to send a deputation to entreat her to return to them, and to make her principal foundation in her own district.

The Saint complied with their request very readily, and set out for Leinster, crossing the Shannon on her way into the present town of Athlone.[1]

Some of the religious requested the ferry men to take them across the river, but they were probably pagans, as they refused to do so without payment. The sisters then said they would walk across, and they begged St. Brigit to make the sign of the Cross on the river, so that it might become sufficiently shallow for this purpose. The Saint did as she was requested, and to the amazement of all who were present,

---

[1] There is a well near this called *Tobar-Breghde.* In Colgan's time it was famous for the miracles worked there.

the nuns passed through the water, which only came up to their knees.

The Saint was warmly welcomed when she arrived in Leinster, and she selected, as the site for her convent, a slight elevation overlooking the "plain of the Liffey," anciently called *Druim Criadh*. A large oak-tree grew here, and is inseparably connected with the memory of Ireland's great nun.

CHAPTER III.

THE CONVENT OF KILDARE.

KILDARE, or the Cell of the Oak, became henceforth a famous place in Irish history. In the great eternity to come the fame of many a site once reverenced on earth will cease to be. But, surely, for evermore the memory of those places where God was specially glorified, where souls were sanctified, where creatures were perfected in the love of the Creator, will abide as a sweet odour of eternal perfume. The Saint is the true hero, the Saint is the perfection of God's creation. We may obtain honour from our fellows for this or that, but only one honour abideth for ever. The undying fame is the only fame worth having.

The customs of the times were sufficiently primitive, and yet, as our antiquities attest, not without a dignity of their own. Most buildings were formed of wattles, and we have in the Lives of one of our Saints a curious poem, describing the construction of such buildings, and the moral lesson to be derived therefrom.

St. Brigit's first convent at Kildare was built in the usual way, and as it was erected under the shelter of the oak, it obtained the name of the Cell of the Oak, or Kildare. The great plain of the Curragh was her pasture ground, donated to her by some famous chief. Bishop Mel assisted her in her arrangements, and Ailill, the king of Leinster, gave her the wood for her building. This establishment was erected some time between the years 480 and 490.[1]

If the monks of old made the wilderness fertile, the nuns were by no means behindhand in their help to human culture and happiness.

The little cell soon became far too small for the number of postulants who came to learn how to love God more and the world less under the rule of St. Brigit, and those who had left the world for their own good, benefited the world even in leaving it. Soon the place became famous; multitudes flocked thither; and peace, cultivation, and abundance prevailed where

[1] As every writer has a theory of his own as to the date of this foundation, it is quite useless to enter into a discussion here on the subject. Each has his own opinion, but opinions are not proof; all are, however, agreed that the correct date lies between the years given above.

barrenness and desolation had reigned supreme. Many persons came to the Abbess of Kildare for advice, many for charity ; all were received and assisted according to their needs. A secular community was soon formed, and a number of families settled in the place, a village became a town, and later a city, and ere long a bishop's see.

Kings looked to her as a "nursing mother," princesses were happy to call her their guide. Those who honoured her in life asked to be near her in death, and Cruitham, king of Leinster, sought the favour of being buried near the humble religious.

In those times men were apt to deal out justice somewhat roughly, and did not always make as careful distinction between intentions and deeds as in modern days. There was probably quite as much justice, if not more than there is now, and quite as much respect for law ; but men were free to act on the defensive or offensive at a moment's notice, and a sanctuary where the innocent might find shelter was indeed a boon, even if it sometimes protected the wicked. The right of sanctuary, as far as the clergy were concerned, was generally acknowledged and regarded. But St. Brigit, having founded a city as well as a monastery, claimed sanctuary for her abode, and placed a line round the town which was respected.

After the Saint had fully established her monastery at Kildare, she proceeded to Armagh, probably at the request of St. Patrick. It has been objected by some of her modern biographers that the Saint is seldom mentioned in the early lives of our apostle, though he is frequently mentioned in her life.

This omission could be very easily accounted for. Though the Saints were contemporary, their work was of a widely, different nature, and there was no marked incident in the life of the holy Abbess which was in any way directly connected with St. Patrick's great mission. An ancient Convent Church in the vicinity of Armagh is pointed out as the probable site of her foundation then ; and our Irish written annals, and our written traditions, agree so closely on every subject connected with our early history, that such coincidences must be received with satisfaction.

During the Saint's residence at Armagh, miracles were as frequent as they had been previously. Indeed this Saint, St. Patrick, and St. Columba, are constantly distinguished by their Irish biographers as the three wonder-workers, *Trias Thaumaturga* of Ireland, as it pleased God to distinguish them in a more extraordinary manner than other Saints by the gift of miracles.

But, while occupied in settling her new foundations, and in journeying from place to place, she never forgot for one moment that the individual perfection of her subjects was the most important work which could occupy her attention. Of little use, indeed, would it be to found many religious houses, if the inmates of these houses were not saints. And she could not forget for one moment that a far different degree of sanctity was required for a nun than for a secular; that from those to whom God gave that grace He expects an abundant return.

Obedience is the very foundation of the religious life; and if St. Brigit's nuns were made to feel its restraints a little sharply at times, it was a pain they might well pay for the privilege of living under the guidance of a Saint.

Her example in the matter is, indeed, a deep lesson to all religious, and especially to religious of our own times, since we may fear lest the licentiousness and self-will of the age should throw its shadow even in the cloister, and dim the lustre and beauty of that sacrifice which God expects from His spouses.

A leper came to the convent and asked to have his clothes washed, but, as he had no change of raiment, it was necessary to provide him with clothing while this act of charity was being accomplished. The Saint desired one of her nuns to give the man a second habit which she did not use. But the nun was unwilling to obey, and as a punishment she was immediately struck with leprosy. At the end of an hour, she repented her disobedience, and was cured by the intercession of the Saint. Another nun, whose perfect spirit of obedience led her to do not only what her superiors desired, but what she knew they wished, had provided the man with clothing; and when his poor rags were washed and returned to him, he was cured of his terrible disease.   Thus was God glorified ; for the miracles of the Saints are not for their own glory, or for their own benefit.   A lesson of charity and obedience was given which, we may be assured, helped not a little to build up a solid foundation of sanctity in many a convent in old Ireland.

A curious story is told of how the Saint's power was used to baffle thieves.

One night during Lent, eight men came and stole four horses belonging to the convent.   A nun, who discovered the theft at the time it was committed, went to inform St. Brigit ; but the Saint took it quietly, and said that others who were more powerful than they were would do justice on the robbers.

When the thieves had secured the horses, they went off to a farm near at hand and took a quantity of corn, when they proceeded home, as they supposed ; but " by the miracle of God and St. Brigit," instead of going home with the horses and the corn, they returned to the nuns' farm where they secured their ill-gotten gains, and went to sleep in the barn.

Next morning the men from whom the corn had been stolen, followed the track of the horses until they came to the convent, and asked an explanation of the matter.

The Saint took them to the barn where the robbers were found fast asleep.   On being awoke they were extremely surprised, and admitted what they could not well deny, saying that they had returned as they thought to their own place on the previous night. The Saint sent for St. Patrick, who obtained pardon for the repenting robbers, and the corn was given to the convent.

On another occasion, the Saint pleaded for the oppressed poor in a way which showed her high sense of justice.

A rich and good man lived on the plain of Macha[1] in great prosperity; but he suffered from a terrible disease which defied all the efforts of his physician. He sent for the wonder-working Brigit, hoping for help from her intercession. The Saint came as requested, but as she approached his *dun*,[2] she said that the wind would bring disease to the master of the house from whatever quarter it might blow.

This certainly was not very encouraging. When the chief heard what she had said, he expressed his surprise, as in his opinion he had never injured any one.

But the mystery was soon solved—one of his attendants said that every one who passed cursed this unfortunate man, because he had closed up a highway from the people to their most serious loss.

St. Brigit declared that this was the cause of his affliction, and it seemed no longer a matter of surprise that it had not been cured by human skill.

Orders were given to open the road again, and the man at once recovered, thanking God and St. Brigit.

---

[1] This plain extended round Armagh.
[2] The Celtic name for a fort or entrenched place of safety.

As some men were passing by where the Saint was, they asked her to bless a large vessel of water which they carried. She complied with their request. As they passed on the vessel fell, but not one drop of the water was spilled.

When St. Patrick heard of this miracle, he desired part of the water to be used in the Holy Sacrifice of the Mass, and the remainder to be sprinkled on the fields to make them fertile.

While St. Patrick was preaching one day in the province of Ulster, and while the "Pearl of Ireland," as the Saint was called, was amongst the listening crowd, a cloud of light was seen to descend from heaven to earth. The light rested for a little space near where the people were assembled, and then passed away towards *Dun da Lethglass*[1] where it disappeared.

The people, amazed at the marvel, desired to know what it meant, but fearing to ask St. Patrick, they appealed to St. Brigit; she referred them to St. Patrick, but he desired her to give the explanation.

The Saint then told them that the luminosity indicated the spirit of St. Patrick which went to visit the place where he should be interred after his death. At the place where the light first rested, she said his body should remain for some days after his

---

[1] This *dun* is still in existence near Downpatrick. It is composed of great earthen ramparts with trenches between each. It was formerly surrounded with the water of Strangford Lough.

death, and **where the light disappeared he should be** buried, and remain there **until the day of judgment.**

It was **on** this occasion that St. Patrick is said **to** have asked her **to make his** shroud, and here **she is** said to have prophesied of **St. Columba, and said** that he with herself and St. Patrick would **arise for** judgment from the same grave.

As the Saint returned home from Armagh, she passed over the plain of *Breagh* in Meath. She remained for a short time in this district, and while here the wife of Fergus, son of **Conall** Cruitham, son of the famous Niall[1] the king of Ireland, came to visit her.

The object of the lady was to obtain children through the intercession of the Saint. The circumstances of the interview are remarkable, as indicating, like a narrative before recorded, that St. Brigit was the faithful friend of the poor people, and ever ready to prefer them to the great and wealthy of this world.

The lady brought a rich silver vessel as an offering, but the holy Abbess did not appear to her, preferring to send one of her nuns. The nun brought the message of the **royal lady** to her Superior, and she **inquired** why she would not go to her, and why **she would not** pray for the favour she so much desired, since she had been frequently asked **to obtain the** same favour

---

[1] Niall had **two** sons, **both** of whom were called Conall, and **were** distinguished as Conall Cruitham and Conall Goulban.

for poor women, and had always granted their request.

The Saint gave an admirable reply. She said that the children of the poor, with few exceptions, were good and virtuous, whereas the offspring of kings and princes were more frequently wicked and licentious.

The family, for whom the favour was asked, were certainly of a most turbulent race, and had but little devotion to religion or virtue.

It is said, however, that the Saint was prevailed on eventually to obtain the desired offspring, and that the descendant of Diarmiad afterwards became the supreme monarch of Ireland.

As we have already said, St. Brigit's prayers were fervent, and every road she travelled was marked by wonders effected through her intercession. The mode of conveyance at that time, for those who could not walk long distances, was a kind of chariot drawn by two or more horses, and it must have been sufficiently fatiguing, since there were but few roads.

On one occasion as she travelled along the public road, she met a poor man, with his wife and family and household goods. These people were worn out with the heat of summer, and could hardly continue their journey. Her tender heart was touched, and she had the horses taken from her own chariot, and given to them. As she sat by the wayside with her nuns, she desired one of them to dig for a well of water, as she said some persons were coming who would need it. A fountain immediately sprang up in the place where the nun dug, and soon after a large party came up with the chief at their head. This man having heard that the Saint had given away her horses, desired that she should be given two of his which were led by his servants. These animals had never been trained, but they became docile at once, under the care of the Saint.

Soon after this, some of St. Patrick's followers came the same way, and said to the Saint, We have suffered a great deal on our journey, for we have had nothing to drink though we had sufficient food.

The sisters then told them of the miracle, and that their need had been provided for by the Abbess, and showed them the spring of running water which she had obtained for them. Then the holy men and women took a repast in common, and rejoiced in the wonders which God had done.

Lepers were constantly attracted to the Saint, having heard the fame of her miraculous cures and of her exceeding great charity. On one occasion when she was followed by an immense crowd of people, two lepers came up to her, but they quarrelled with each other, and even came to blows. But, behold a miracle! The arm of the man who had just raised his hand to strike became bent, so that he could not lift it, and the other man's arm, which was raised, remained in that position until the Saint came and healed them, and then they repented.

At one time the Saint was afflicted with sore eyes, and Bishop Mel, who heard of her suffering, sent her a message to come to him so that he might get a physician to cure her. The Saint had no wish to do this—on the contrary, she was opposed to it, not desiring human help or care ; but she gave an example to all religious superiors for all time to come, by obeying the desire of her ecclesiastical superior.

On her journey she fell from her chariot in passing a river, and her head was sorely hurt and bled profusely.

After this accident, she went to the physician, and he said to her, "A better physician than I am has healed you; He is able to drive away all your diseases : seek His help always." The good bishop, satisfied with her obedience and her miraculous cure, by what might have proved a fatal injury, said that he would not again ask her to have recourse to temporal means of cure.

The miracles of the Saint had the effect which no doubt God desired them to have. Thousands of pagans who witnessed them, or heard of them, were converted to the true faith ; and those who were converted, and who were surrounded with many temptations, were greatly strengthened thereby. In the Saint's metrical Life these wonders are thus chanted—

" Brigit, Saint of highest fame,
　　For Christ the world despised ;
　Like bird on high she sat and sang,
　　And only virtue prized.

" Her only thought was heaven and God,
　　Her only joy was pure ;
　She sought bright mansions in the skies,
　　And life for aye secure.

" And in her waking and her sleep,
　　She pined for Christ, her love ;
　And for His Passion grieved alone,
　　With cry like captive dove.

" O Brigit ! near to Christ my Lord,
　　Of earthly souls the best,
　Pray still for me that I may come
　　To His eternal rest."

After the Saint's miraculous cure she went with
Bishop Mel to Teffia, where he founded a great monastery, in a place now known as Ardagh. While here
a neighbouring chief gave a magnificent banquet. A
servant who was attending the royal guests broke a
most valuable vessel.[1] The chief was furious, and
ordered the man to be bound on the spot, and then
put to death.

Bishop Mel heard of the dreadful sentence, and
hastened to the king to intercede for the unhappy
victim. But his entreaties were all in vain. At last

[1] For an account of the costly and magnificent vessels used by the
ancient Irish, and the high state of art which then existed, we refer
the reader to our recently published " History of the Irish
Nation," in which some rare engravings of these precious objects will
be found.

he gathered up the fragments of the cup and brought them to Brigit, who immediately put them together again, and thus obtained the man's liberty.[1]

On another occasion the Saint obtained a marvellous escape for a poor captive, also sentenced to death. The holy Abbess was at this time in the district of Feara Ross.[2] While here she was urgently requested to visit a chief who lived in the plain of Brugh, the plain in which the royal palace of Tara was situated. This prince had an unhappy captive whom he was determined to kill ; and, indeed, a life, more or less, in those days was of little account.

But the constant pleadings of the Saint were in vain, and the only promise she could obtain was that the man should not be executed until the following night.

The friends of the condemned man and the Saint remained at the place where he was confined, and Brigit was miraculously warned of a clever plot to kill him there and then. The friends of the chief went to him and said that they were quite certain Brigit would find means to release him the next day, that they would go that night and kill the man, and say they had done so contrary to the king's wishes, so as to save his honour.

During the night the captive saw St. Brigit near

---

[1] There are several instances of this kind of miracle in the lives of later canonised Saints.

[2] The men of Ross. This district was situated in the present county Louth and Monaghan, around Carrickmacross.

him as in a vision, and she warned him of what these men had resolved to do, and told him when they dragged him out to death that he should call on her name frequently, and that when the chain was broken off his neck, when they proceeded to kill him, that he was to slip away quietly on the right hand side, and escape to his friends.

The man did exactly as he was desired, and when the moment came he escaped; but the men thought he was killed, and went in triumph to tell the king. Next day they came to seek for his body, but it could not be found, and their amazement was indeed great, until a message arrived from St. Brigit telling how the man had been rescued from their hands.

The king then repented of his desire to murder his captive, and gave him a free pardon in honour of the Saint.

If the Saint obtained royal heirs by her intercession, she certainly had little intercourse with them in their future lives. Conall Cruitham, son of Niall, of the Nine Hostages, came to Brigit one day while she was walking with her nuns, and begged her blessing as a protection against his brother Carbry, who, he said, wished to get the kingdom. The Saint told him to order his soldiers to go before her, and said, "I will bless your followers then." As the troops advanced before Niall, the sister who accompanied St. Brigit cried out in dismay that they saw Carbry approaching, and they feared a collision between the brothers.

Such quarrels in those days were apt to be as sharp as they were sudden.

At that moment Carbry came up to the Saint and asked her to bless him, because he feared to meet his brother Conall. But the Saint obtained a miraculous blindness for both, so that they could not see each other, and they parted, going away in different directions.[1]

One of the most beautiful incidents in the life of St. Brigit is her meeting with the youthful student, Ninnid, or Nenedius. As she was going from her monastery on the plains of the Liffey she met a young student who was running along with all the impetuosity of his age. St. Brigit desired one of her religious to call him to her, but he was in such haste he could scarcely be prevailed to stay a moment.

The Saint inquired whither he was going with such speed. Ninnid replied, that he was "running to heaven."

Brigit said, "Would to God that I were worthy to run with you to that blessed place. Pray for me that I may enter there one day."

Her words seem to have touched the heart of the impetuous youth, for he answered, "O holy Virgin, pray for me that I may persevere in my course towards the kingdom of heaven."

---

[1] The reader will have noted in the preceding "Life of St. Columba," how "a veil of unrecognition" was cast over his guards on the momentous occasion when he escaped from Tara.

And Brigit prayed for him ; for who ever asked the
prayers of a Saint in vain ! Then the Saint prophesied
to him that she should receive the Holy Viaticum from
him on the day of her death ; but, as he wished that
the Saint might live to an extreme old age, he replied,
that he desired that she might, indeed, live until she
should receive the Holy Eucharist from him.

Then St. Ninnid (for he was afterward honoured as
a Saint) determined that he would take a special care
of the hand which was to administer the Holy Sacrament, and he had a gauntlet of brass made for his
hand, with a lock and key, so that he might not touch
anything with that hand which should be unclean.[1]

Ninnid obtained the name of *Ninnidh lamglan*, or
Ninnid of the clean hand, from this circumstance.
His humility was so great that it was long before he
would allow himself to be ordained priest.

He spent many years in pilgrimages, according to
the pious custom of the age, but eventually he returned to Ireland to fulfil the sad office to which he
had been destined.

---

[1] This incident has been made the subject of some comment and
controversy ; but it should be remembered that the age was one in
which peculiar penitential exercises were practised, and when extraordinary penance was common.

CHAPTER IV.

THE LAST DAYS AND THE END.

THE little conventual building in Kildare was soon surrounded by a great city. We have said little, for such it was in its beginnings, but soon it became a vast building, and contained many hundred inmates.

It was then a matter of necessity that a bishop should be at hand to perform the functions belonging to his office which could not be fulfilled by a priest.

The Saint was allowed to choose her own bishop; and she selected a holy man named Cronleath, who was especially suited for the post, as he had long persevered in the hard life of a religious anchorite.

St. Brigit exercised some degree of authority over the Episcopal Church, a circumstance which was not altogether without precedent on the continent of Europe. Such an arrangement would, of course, be exceptional. The hierarchy of Ireland at this period were men of large minds and of most saintly lives; and the devoted attendance which more than one bestowed on the Saint, and their united reverence for her, and respect for her work, were as honourable to them as to the object.

There was happily little jealousy of her work because it was so public, or because it was so prosperous, a more likely cause of jealousy which would in lower minds be concealed under the plausible pretext that a woman should not appear before the world. They saw in Brigit one to whom God had given a great work to do; and they were far too devoted to His service to hinder her by coldness or neglect. They knew that the manner and method of her work was not her choice, to whom the privacy of an entire seclusion would have been infinitely preferable. But the will of God who led women, like St. Catherine of Sienna and St. Catherine of Alexandria, to do public work for His service, was also her will. And so throughout the whole long, and varied, and public life of the Saint we do not hear that one bishop or one priest ever gave her the pain of opposition, or the grief which to a Saint would be, of all others, the most bitter —of condemning her God-given mission.

It is to the eternal honour of Ireland that it should have been so ; for there are few Saints gifted as she was, who have not been the object of more or less persecution from those who should have been their most faithful and affectionate supporters.

St. Brigit was intimately connected with all the leading ecclesiastics of Ireland. She was so well known to St. Brendan, that she told him the very secrets of her heart; probably because she knew he was one who would understand what others less saintly would condemn, or hear with the indifference of less perfect souls.

St. Brendan of Clonfert came to her for advice and instruction. St. Finian of Clonard preached for her nuns ; St. Ailbe, Bishop of Emly, came to her more than once, to have the benefit of her counsel on difficult questions ; St. Fiacc, of Sletty, wrote a hymn in her praise ; St. Tighernach, Bishop of Clogher, was her god-son. These holy and tender friendships must have been a great consolation to her, for the most perfect souls have ever been the tenderest in their affection, the quickest to feel the stings of contempt or indifference, the first to receive or do with pleasure an act of charity. The very nearness of such souls to Christ, the source of love and His merciful designs of sanctification in their regard, leave them a vast field of suffering of which others are but partly conscious ; which the multitude cannot understand, since they have never been called to live a life of supernatural suffering. If, however, she was not to suffer from indif-

ference, or opposition, or contempt, she was yet destined
to suffer in her affections. One by one her nearest
friends passed from her, and, as life closed in, she was
left almost alone. Her great friend St. Mel made his
migration to heaven in the year 485. The Bishop of
Duleek, St. Cianan, followed him. Bishop Maccelle,
who gave her the veil and consecrated her to Christ,
died in the next year. St. Patrick went home in 493.
St. Ibar, of whom so much is related in her life, died
in the early part of the sixth century ; and her dear
friend, Bishop Broon, obtained his crown in 511.

But St. Brigit, with all her work and penance,
found time for literary pursuits. A most interesting
anecdote is related of a scribe whom she employed to
illustrate the manuscripts written in her monastery.
This scribe, being desired by the Saint to copy the
holy gospels according to the version of St. Jerome,
had a vision in which he saw an angel who held a
tablet with an illustrated inscription. The angel
asked him if he could imitate all he saw on the title-
page of his gospels. The poor scribe said it would be
impossible for him to do so. Then the angel desired
him to ask St. Brigit to pray for him, so that he might
be able to do this. The next night the angel appeared
to him again, and showed him other and equally magnificent illustrations ; and through the intercession
of St. Brigit he was enabled, not only to remember
the details of what he had seen in his vision, but also
to copy them with fidelity. And this wonderful book

existed even at the time of the Norman invasion of Ireland, and demanded even then the admiration of the bitterest enemies of our people.[1]

St. Brigit was herself an author. A book of Revelations was attributed to her pen, but this was the result of a confusion of names in later times.[2]

Colgan had several works which he considered authentic, and which, therefore, we may believe to have been written by the Irish Thaumaturgus.

She wrote a poem on the virtues of St. Patrick, and a little work called "The Quiver of Divine Desires."

Four years before her death the Saint had an intimation of her coming end. It is said that she expressed a wish to visit her various religious establishments before her departure, and also to see the shrine of Ireland's great apostle, St. Patrick. All this she accomplished, though at the very advanced age of eighty-seven. She predicted that her successor, Darlagdacha, should survive her only for one year, and that she should die on the same day, so that they would both be remembered together.

In the meantime St. Ninnid was approaching the

---

[1] **Giraldus Cambrensis**, the Froude of his day, who wrote the bitterest calumnies of Ireland and the Irish, could not contain his expressions of admiration on seeing this work.

[2] The book circulated largely at the present day under the title of "Revelations of St. Brigit," was not written by her, but by St. Bridget of Sweden, who lived many centuries later. Many persons have been deceived by the name and title.

Irish shore after his long pilgrimage. He came in time to administer the Sacraments of the Church to the dying Saint.

We have no exact particulars of her last days on earth, save, only, that it is said the angels waited for her around her couch, as, indeed, well they might, since she had, when on earth, so often enjoyed their blessed company.

There is strong concurrent testimony to prove that she died on a Wednesday, and on the 1st of February 523.[1]

St. Brigit's Rule has not survived the persecutions and trials of her country, but we see from her life that it must have been founded on a very strict observance of obedience.

The Saint died at Kildare, where she spent the later years of her pilgrimage. Her relics were enshrined here on one side of the altar in a magnificent monument.[2]

St. Brigit's falcon and St. Brigit's fire are inseparably connected with her name. The falcon is said to have lived from the time of St. Brigit to the twelfth century on the Round Tower of Kildare. It was killed in the reign of King John. St. Brigit's fire was always kept burning by her nuns.

---

[1] The 1st of February fell on a Wednesday in that year.

[2] We have given some engravings of the shrines of Irish Saints in our "History of the Irish Nation" just published. They were masterpieces of art. This new work should not be confounded with the "Illustrated History of Ireland," which we published some years since.

About the year 830 the Danes began to ravish this part of Ireland, and the relics of the Saint were carried for safety to Downpatrick.

It is a most amazing fact that the tradition of the burial-place of these three most marvellous Saints, Patrick, Brigit, and Columba, had faded out of the memory of the most devout people in the world for several centuries.

The reason probably was that the bodies were hidden somewhere by a few ecclesiastics in order to protect them from the desecrations of the Danes, and that when these ecclesiastics died the knowledge was not transmitted to others.

In the year 1185, when Malachy was Bishop of Down, he devoted himself by prayer and fast to obtain from God the knowledge of where their bodies were laid. His desire was granted. He who honours and guards even the earthly remains of His blessed ones sent a ray of light through the church as St. Malachy knelt in prayer, and then the light rested on the graves of the Three.

The saintly Bishop prayed that the light might remain until he had discovered the bodies, which he proceeded to do as soon as he could procure the necessary implements.

He found St. Patrick in the centre, with St. Brigit and Columba on either side.

He afterwards buried the relics again, and revealed what he had discovered to John de Courcy. They agreed to despatch messengers to Rome for the authorisation of a solemn translation of the relics. The reigning Pope, Urban III., entered heartily into the design, and despatched Cardinal Vivian to Ireland to assist at the solemnity. Fifteen bishops and a crowd of ecclesiastics attended on the solemn festival. The day chosen being the 9th of June, 1186, the feast of St. Columba. The tombs of the Saints were discovered and destroyed, at the time of the so-called Reformation.

The head of St. Brigit is said to have been secured by a priest, who carried it to Neustadt, in Austria. It was eventually taken to the church of the Jesuits at Lisbon.

The number of churches and holy wells dedicated to, or honoured in connection with, St. Brigit, in Ireland, are so numerous that it would be impossible to give even a catalogue of their names. The faithful exiled Celt has also consecrated many churches to her memory on the great American continent.

On the continent of Europe her name is honoured and venerated in many places, where votive offerings in her honour may be seen at this very day, showing that her power has not decreased with the lapse of ages.

Especially, as might be expected, was she honoured at St. Martin's monastery of Tours. Her office was said not only in Ireland, but also on the continent. In Cologne and in other places her feast day was observed as a great solemnity.

In the poetical language of her people, she was called "a dove" amongst birds, a vine amongst trees, and a sun amidst stars. May she intercede for us!

But St. Brigit's work in Ireland did not cease with her life. There is no possibility of ascertaining now how long the various houses which she founded survived the vicissitudes of time. They must certainly have flourished for several centuries, and probably some convents continued even after the Norman invasion. But the spirit of her order could not die. The substance of what is called the religious life is ever the same in all ages; interior discipline may differ with changes of time, or place, or circumstances, but everywhere and in all orders the nun is "the maiden dedicated to Christ;" one who devotes herself by prayer, or work, which rightly done is also prayer, to the service of God and her neighbour.

For some centuries, however, there was no order of nuns in Ireland bearing the name of this Saint. Indeed, until the present century, there were very few religious houses of women. The storms of persecution were too frequent, and were too severe to allow women to brave their cruel force. The poor Clares were obliged again and again to resume a secular dress, and to fly their peaceful convent homes; and we believe a Dominican convent shared a similar trial.

In the year 1807, the Right Rev. Dr. Delany, then Bishop of Kildare and Leighlin, founded a congregation of religious women under the invocation of St.

Brigit. It was further protected and assisted by the Right Rev. Dr. Doyle.

This congregation still flourishes in Ireland. One of the great duties of the sisters is the instruction of adults in the parish church on Sundays. Three different hours during the day are thus occupied. The parent house was at Tullow, in the county Carlow. A convent of the order was founded in 1842 at Abbeyleix, by the Very Rev. J. Nolan. This indefatigable priest has built another convent at Ballyroan, which the sisters are to take possession of during the present year. The other houses of the order are in Mountrath, Goresbridge, and Paulstown. The children of the upper classes are also educated by these excellent religious.

It would seem, indeed, as if later ages were to repair any apparent indifference to the memory of our great Saint.

Who has not heard of St. Brigit's Orphanage in Dublin, and of the glorious work done there. The noble energy and self-devotion of one woman accomplished this magnificent work, and happily she found such support, both ecclesiastical and secular, as is rarely given to any undertaking, however meritorious.

It is too well known that Ireland has been for years not only the debatable land of all political strifes, but it has also been the unhappy victim of such a system of bribery and corruption, in the name of religion, as probably is unequalled in the civilised world. It is certainly past all honest comprehension how "converts," who are made such by bribery, can be acceptable to men professing any form of religious belief, or having any spark of conscience. Facts, however, remain to prove that such are welcome; and while some people are found weak enough to deny their faith for gold, it would appear that others are found quite willing to lavish this gold on any one whom they can persuade to take it.

But those who think to turn the people of Ireland from the faith of their fathers have spent their money and their labour in vain. They have not made converts of those who are driven by destitution to profess belief in a creed which they abhor; nor yet of those who have not the excuse of temporal misery for their conversion. Such persons soon prove that their "conversion" is to evil, and if they do not descend lower in the social scale, they descend with fearful rapidity in moral obliquity.

It is to save children from such a miserable fate that this congregation has been founded, and it is well and wisely put under the patronage of the great Irish nun.

OFFICES FOR THE FEAST OF BRIGIT.

(From the Breviary.)

THE holy virgin, Brigit, born in the province of Leinster, in Ireland, of parents of noble blood and of the Christian faith, became the mother in Christ of many consecrated virgins. While she was yet a little child, her father saw in a vision men clothed in white garments, pouring oil upon her head. As she reached the early years of girlhood she chose Christ the Saviour as her Spouse, and clung to Him so ardently, from her inmost heart, as, for His love, to give away all she had to the poor. Her matchless beauty drew around her a multitude of suitors; and fearing that their importunity might render impossible her purpose of devoting her life to God in holy virginity, she prayed that her beauty might be changed into ugliness. Her prayer was at once heard. One of her eyes became quite swollen, and her whole face so altered, that all her suitors retired in disgust, leaving her free to consecrate her virginity to Christ by a solemn vow.

Taking with her three young maidens, she repaired without delay to Bishop Macheas, a disciple of St. Patrick. The good Bishop, seeing a pillar of fire over

her head, clothed her in a fair garment and a white
mantle ; and reciting the Ritual prayers, received her
to holy profession, according to the Canonical form
introduced into Ireland by blessed Patrick.   In the
course of the ceremony, as she bent her head to receive
the sacred veil, she leant her hand on the wooden
altar-step.   At the moment, the dry, seasoned wood
became green and fresh ; on the instant her eye was
cured, and her whole face recovered its former beauty.
In process of time, her example drew young maidens
to embrace the religious life in such numbers as to
cover all Ireland with communities of nuns, of that
order over which Brigit herself presided, and upon
which all the rest were dependent.

The virgin's sanctity is attested by the miracles she
wrought in her life time, as well as after death.   She
frequently cleansed lepers, and by her prayers obtained
cure for people sick of divers diseases ; she gave
sight to one blind from his birth.   An abandoned
woman sought to father her base-born child upon
Bishop Brooney.   The Saint, making the sign of the
cross upon the poor baby's lips, made it declare the
name of its true father, thus vindicating the Bishop's
character.   Filled with the spirit of prophecy, she
foretold things to come as if they were passing before
her eyes.

She enjoyed the most intimate friendship of St.
Patrick, the Apostle of Ireland, and foretold the time
of his departure from this world, and the place of his

burial. She was present at his death, and supplied the winding sheet, which she had long and carefully kept for the purpose, in which his blessed remains were wrapped; and when she came to give back her beautiful soul to Christ, her Spouse, she was laid in the same grave with him.

THE END.

Ballantyne Press
BALLANTYNE, HANSON AND CO.
EDINBURGH AND LONDON

Kenmare Publications.

NEW WORKS AND NEW EDITIONS.

APPROBATION OF THE RIGHT REV. DR. MORIARTY.

"THE PALACE, KILLARNEY, *Oct.* 24, 1876.

"MY DEAR SISTER IN CHRIST,—I learn that you are issuing some new works, and some new editions of those already published : your literary labours reflect honour on your Convent, on your Order, and on this Diocese.

"But I rejoice much more in this, that you are contributing to supply one of our greatest needs—a Catholic Literature. I know, too, that the funds realised by the sale of your works are exclusively devoted to the service of religion.

"Praying God to bless you, and to preserve your health and strength, yours sincerely in Christ, ✠ D. MORIARTY.

"To SISTER M. FRANCES CLARE,
    "Convent of Poor Clares, Kenmare, Co. Kerry."

THE VOICE OF THE HOLY FATHER.

"Providence seems to have given in our day a great mission to the Catholic Press. It is for it to preserve the principles of order and faith where they prevail, and to propagate them where impiety and cold indifference have caused them to be forgotten."—*Letter from* **Pope Pius IX., in 1855.**

"We urgently beseech of you to assist, with all good will and favour, those men who, animated with a Catholic spirit, and possessed with sufficient learning, are labouring in writing and publishing books and journals for the defence and propagation of Catholic doctrine."—*Encyclical Letter of* **Pope Pius** *in* 1853.

Extract from the Apostolic Letter of His Holiness Pope Pius IX. to Sister M. Frances Clare.

"Beloved Daughter in Christ, Health and Apostolic Benediction.— We congratulate you, Beloved Daughter in Christ, on having completed a long and difficult work which seemed to be above woman's strength, with a success that has justly earned the applause of the pious and the learned. We rejoice, not only because you have promoted by this learned and eloquent volume the glory of the illustrious Apostle of Ireland, St. Patrick, but also because you have deserved well of the whole Church ; we impart to you, most lovingly, the Apostolic Benediction, as an earnest of God's favour and a pledge of Our good will.

"Given at Rome, at St. Peter's, the 6th October 1870, the Twenty-Fifth year of Our Pontificate.

"PIUS P.P. IX."

Kenmare Publications.

Now Ready,

Lives of Saints. Kenmare Series.

The Life of St. Patrick, Apostle of Ireland.

Demy 8vo., 360 pp., 6s.

Also,

A magnificently Illustrated Edition of the above, richly gilt edges
and sides, &c., 10s.

Just Ready,

Lives of Saints. Kenmare Series, Vol. 2.

The Life of St. Columba and St. Bridget.

Uniform with the above,

The Life of His Grace the Most Rev.

JOSEPH DIXON, late Archbishop of Armagh, and Primate
of all Ireland. Crown 8vo, 7s. 6d.

This memorial of the sainted prelate has been written at the
request of His Grace the Most Rev. DANIEL M. GETTIGAN, Primate
of all Ireland, and of the clergy of the archdiocese.

POPE PIUS AND THE POOR CLARES.

"In the midst of his troubles Pope Pius has found time to send an Apostolic letter to our countrywoman, Miss Cusack, known in religion as Sister
Mary Frances Clare, author of the 'Life of St. Patrick.' . . . He compli-
ments her on having completed 'a long and difficult work, which seemed
to be above woman's strength, with a success that has justly earned the
applause of the pious and the learned.' We believe this is the first time
the Holy See has congratulated a woman on the success of her literary
labours. And the compliment was never more deserved. . . . His
Holiness does not forget the 'Island of Saints,' which now so keenly sym-
pathises with his sufferings. The letter is a charming summary of the
benefits conferred on Ireland by the Apostle, and a tribute to the learning
and sanctity of his successors, who, in the sixth and seventh centuries, as
Apostles and Missionaries, illumined the darkness of Pagan Europe with the
light of Divine truth. The Poor Clares, in their seclusion in Kerry, must be
delighted at this testimony to the genius and services of one of their community. The rarity of the tribute vastly enhances its value."—*Freeman's
Journal* [Dublin].

Good Reading for Girls.

A Nun's Advice to her Girls. 12mo. 2s. 6d.

Fourth Thousand.

This little book is the first of a series, which has already obtained an immense circulation, especially in the United States, where it has gone through many editions.

"The Nun who gives this book of excellent counsels to the pupils of her convent school is the Nun of Kenmare, whose name has indeed become a household word. It is needless to say that the advice she gives to the good Irish girls at home and abroad is the very best and wisest, and conveyed in a very agreeable and forcible manner. We may add that we are pleased not only with what is said, but with what is left unsaid. Certain warnings that are often given in books of a somewhat similar aim are here more wisely left entirely to sad experience, and God's grace acting through various appointed ministries. No wonder that this book, or one substantially the same as the present, has already had a wide circulation amongst our countrymen at the other side of the Atlantic."—*The Irish Monthly.*

"We venture to say that there is a genius for taking advice, as there is a genius for giving it: with the latter Sister Mary Frances is richly gifted. A Nun's Advice to her Girls was first published in America, where it had a brilliant success. We are very glad that the writer has been induced to republish it for these Isles. It is a charming book; its advice is excellent, thoroughly practical, and conveyed in so attractive a manner that it will be read, as it has been read, with pleasure by the girls to whom it is addressed. We are glad to see how much interest is shown in it for Catholic servant girls, and we hope that it will be largely distributed amongst them, and read by them. It is also pleasing to find that it is the first of a 'Series of Books for Girls and Young Women,' for if they are all as good as this, they will form a valuable series indeed. This volume is deserving of encomium for its excellent large and clear type.

"The Book of the Blessed Ones is a sort of commentary on the Eight Beatitudes. The vigorous, impressive, and eminently practical writing of the 'Nun of Kenmare' is here seen at its best; strictly speaking, we have here a collection of short and thoughtful sermons—very beautiful sermons—on the various texts of Holy Scripture which describe the man who is blessed, and who is to be called 'blessed' by our Lord on the great Accounting Day."—*Catholic Opinion* (London).

"The Book of the Blessed Ones.—This is another volume of the admirable Kenmare Series, by the celebrated Sister Mary Frances Clare. And an exquisite composition it is, by far the most beautiful, we think, of all the many works of piety and devotion which Sister Mary Frances has contributed to the growing Catholic literature of our English tongue. It is most original in its conceptions, high and pure in thought, and wonderfully charming in style and manner of expression. We know of no book of piety in our own, or indeed any other, language better adapted to increase the number of 'The Blessed Ones,' by making piety dear, and sweet, and attractive to Christians. Over every page is diffused an ineffable charm, a halo of mingled poetry and devotion, which cannot fail to inspire in those who read the modest volume, with good dispositions, a tender love for the ways of holiness, and a great desire to walk therein. If Sister Mary Frances had only given this one book to the Catholic world, it would entitle her to a very high place amongst the Catholic authors of the age. We can only hope that THE BOOK OF THE BLESSED ONES will be as extensively circulated amongst the children of the Church as its rare merits deserve."—*The New York Tablet.*

The Life of Father Mathew. Uniform with "Advice to Girls." Beautifully illustrated. 2s. 6d.

"The gifted pen of our devoted 'Nun of Kenmare' records her aspirations that our cause may be blessed. Surely such advocacy would sanctify any cause."—*Catholic Total Abstinence Union,* (New York).

Woman's Work in Modern Society. New Cheap Edition. 4s. 6d.

"In all that concerns the great question of education, training, and study, Miss Cusack's work will furnish many useful hints to its readers. Almost every one of the numerous chapters would have afforded matter for a book as large as the whole series, and we have no doubt Miss Cusack could have written it."—*The Month.*

CONTENTS.

CHAP.
1. Woman's Place in the Economy of Creation.
2. Facts and Opinions.
3. The Moral Education of Girls.
4. The Moral Education of Children.
5. Of the Physical Education of Children.
6. Of the Intellectual Education of Girls.
8. Of the Technical Education of Girls.
9. Of the Religious Education of Women.
10. In what Religious Education should Consist.
11. Of the Conditions of Religious Education.
12. First Principles—Are Women to be Christian or Pagan?
13. The Christian Woman in Society.
14. The Occupation of Women.
15. What is to be Done?
16. Woman's Work in the Household.
18. Woman's Rights.
20. Woman's Work as Wife and Mother, and Woman's Work in Society.
21. Woman's Work in the Cloister.

"A narrow cell extends its cry to the limits of the civilised world, and the world is instructed by the 'inexperiences' of the cloister."—*M. Veuillot, Univers.*

THE GUARD OF HONOUR OF THE SACRED HEART, with Hymns and Devotions. 1d.

THE ASSOCIATION OF OUR LADY OF THE SACRED
HEART, with Litanies, &c. 6d.

HYMNS FOR CHILDREN. Price 6d. New Edition, with
Music, in preparation.

ST. FRANCIS AND THE FRANCISCANS, 4s. 6d. ST.
CLARE AND THE POOR CLARES. 4s. 6d. THE FLOWERS OF
MARY. 2s. 6d. MEDITATIONS FOR LENT. 2s. 6d.

NEW PRAYER-BOOK.

St. Patrick's Manual. New type—clear print.
Has all the Epistles and Gospels. 3s. 6d. Richly gilt sides
and cover.

INSTRUCTIONS AND DEVOTIONS FOR EVERY STATE IN LIFE.

Devotions for Mass—Devotions for Holy Communion—Devotions for Benediction—Instructions for Parents—Instructions for Children—Prayers for the
Old—Prayers for the Young.

INSTRUCTIONS FOR ALTAR BOYS.

Prayers for the Sick—Prayers for the Dead—The Stations of the Cross.

This Prayer-book is honoured with the imprimatur of the Right Rev. Dr.
Moriarty. It has been compiled, at the urgent request of an American
publisher, by Sister Mary Frances Clare, and is now republished here. The
American publisher says :—"This Prayer-book supplies a want which has
been long felt by the Catholic community. It has been compiled by one
whose fame is world-wide, though cloistered in the shades of Kenmare.
Much original matter has been added, and the work is presented as a
devotional manual that will, from its completeness and comprehensiveness,
take the place of the many manuals which, though carefully compiled and
edited, still lack many of the features that at the present day should be
comprised in a complete prayer-book."

This work contains the Epistles and Gospels for each Sunday and Holiday
throughout the year.

*The French, German, and Italian translations of many of the above works
can be obtained through Messrs. Burns & Oates, Portman Square, London.*

Le Pelerinage Celeste.

LE PELERINAGE CELESTE, par MARIE FRANCOISE CLARE,
auteur de plusiurs ouvrages religieux et historiques. Traduit de l'Anglais
par l'Abbé Ouin La Croix, Chanoine Honoraire de Saint Denis, Chevalier
de la Légion d'Honneur, avec une Préface de M. l'Abbé Maigne, Docteur
en Théologie. Paris : O. de La Touche, 1875.

"Ce qui m'a vivement frappé, dans 'Le Pélerinage Céleste,' ce qui j'ai
grandement admiré, c'est la simplicité, la lucidité d'esprit et d'expression de
l'auteur. . . . La clarté est même quelquefois si grande qu'on croirait à une
vérité nouvelle, quoiqu'il s'agisse d'une vérité vielle comme le monde. . . .
Elle m'a fait beaucoup de bien ; puisse-t-elle vous en faire beaucoup aussi,
chers lecteurs."—*Préface de M. l'Abbé Maigne*, p. viii.

APPROBATION DE MGR. L'ARCHEVÊQUE DE RENNES.

"RENNES, *le 4 Juin* 1875.

" CHER ET DIGNE ABBÉ,—Votre ' Pélerinage ' est excellent, et je ne fais point de difficulté de le préférer à tous ceux qui de nos jours excitent d'une manière si édifiante la piété des fidèles.

"✠ GODEFROY, archevêque de Rennes."

APPROBATION DE MGR. MARET, EVÊQUE DE SURA.

" J'ai lu avec attention le volume que vous avez bien voulu me faire remettre : ' Le Pélerinage Céleste.' Cet ouvrage est digne de grand éloge. La doctrine en est forte et sûre : elle est présentée avec ordre et éloquence. La traduction de M. l'Abbé Ouin La Croix ne dépare pas l'œuvre de la vénérable Marie Françoise Clare. Je forme le vœu que ce livre pieux et substantiel obtienne en France le même succès qu'il a mérité en Angleterre.

" Agréez, Monsieur le Chanoine, mes sentiments de parfaite considération.

" Le Primicier de Saint-Denis,

"H. LC., Evêque de Sura."

APPROBATION DE MGR. L'ÉVÊQUE DE NEVERS.

"NEVERS, *le 27 Novembre* 1875.

" L'auteur de ce pieux opuscule est une humble religieuse clarisse, renfermée derrière les grilles d'un monastère d'Irlande. Que l'on ne s'imagine pas qu'une pauvre fille du cloître, vouée à la vie contemplative, soit peu apte à diriger les hommes, ses frères, à travers les sentiers divers de la vie active ! Dans la solitude l'œil est pur et éclairé ; il connaît et discerne mieux les besoins des âmes et les remèdes qui leur conviennent. N'est-ce pas du cloître qu'est sorti ce guide merveilleux, ' L'Imitation de Jésus Christ,' où chacun trouve les règles et les avis le mieux appropriés à sa situation ? Le livre de la religieuse irlandaise est de la famille de ' L'Imitation,' on y trouve la même simplicité droite et ferme, la même doctrine spirituelle, sans exagération et sans faiblesse, la même onction de piété et, chose plus singulière ! la même connaissance intime des besoins des âmes. Il n'y a pas de personne à qui ce livre ne convienne et ne puisse faire beaucoup de bien. Nous le recommandons en pleine confiance. Nous désirerions seulement qu'il fût fait une autre édition en format plus portatif, de manière que l'on pût le porter et toujours l'avoir avec soi comme un vrai *Vade mecum*.

"✠ TH. CAS., Evêque de Nevers."

All the works for children have been translated by M. la Vicomtesse de Saint Seine.

Just published, Third Edition, Fourth Thousand,

THE LIFE AND REVELATIONS OF ST. GERTRUDE.

7s. 6d.

THE SPIRIT OF ST. GERTRUDE. 2s. 6d.

"Twelve years ago F. Faber directed the attention of persons desiring to lead lives of perfection in the world to St. Gertrude. We have now to thank the Religious of Kenmare for this labour of love, a worthy offering to the Order of St. Benedict."—*Dublin Review.*

"This work has a literary character of no small worth."—*Evening Post.*

"The pains which have been taken by the translator deserve every praise, and the notes which stud the work from one end to the other are a valuable illumination of the text. The author has shown great discrimination, great patience, great love of the Saint, great appreciation of Benedictine life, no small acquaintance with liturgy, and no common power of research. May St. Benedict bless what St. Frances has begun."—*The Tablet.*

CHEAP LIVES OF SAINTS.

THE LIFE OF ST. JOSEPH. 6d.—THE LIFE OF ST. PATRICK. 6d.—THE LIFE OF ST. ALOYSIUS. 6d.

INSTRUCTIONS AND DEVOTIONS FOR MASS AND HOLY COMMUNION. Cloth, 2s. 6d.

A RETREAT FOR THE THREE LAST DAYS OF THE YEAR. 1s.

CHRISTMAS BOOKS.

VISITS TO THE CRIB. 6d.—THE LIVING CRIB. 2d.

THE CHILD'S MONTH OF MARY. 6d.—VISITS TO THE ALTAR OF MARY.

The Spouse of Christ: Her Privileges and Her Duties. Vol. I. Uniform with the "Life and Revelations of St. Gertrude." 7s. 6d.

This work will be completed in Three Volumes, of which the first only has been issued, but which is complete in itself. Each volume will be sold separately.

"This is another work by the indefatigable Nun of Kenmare, and shows her to be no less a proficient in ascetic science than she is in archæology and history. Every page is full of thought, showing wide reading and practical knowledge of the spirit of religious life."—*Catholic Opinion* [London].

"There is hardly anything in this volume which may not be read with benefit by seculars. One of the special characteristics of the work is the practical common sense by which it is distinguished. Fervent and earnest as she is, and thoroughly appreciating the blessings of the life she has chosen, she does not attempt to conceal from herself or others its trials and difficulties. We cannot bring to a close this admirable addition to the Kenmare publications, without citing a few passages which are as beautiful in thought as they are in expression."—*The Tablet* [London].

In Preparation,

The Spouse of Christ: Her Duties and Her
Privileges.

VOLUME II.

CHAP.   CONTENTS.

1. On the Vows in general.
2. On the Vow of Poverty, with examples of the Practice of this Vow from the Lives of the Saints.
3. On the Vow of Chastity and on Purity of Intention, with examples from the Lives of the Saints.
4. On the Vow of Obedience, with examples of its Obligations and perfect Observance from the Lives of the Saints.
5. On Spiritual Reading, Prayer, and other helps to Perfection.
6. On the Office and Assisting at the Holy Sacrifice of the Mass.
7. On the Domestic Duties of the Convent and of the Spirit in which they should be performed, with examples from the Lives of the Saints.
8. The Refectory and Recreation.
9. On Exterior Duties—Teaching in the Schools, Visiting the Sick, &c.
10. On Inclosure, and of our Intercourse with Seculars.
11. On the Sanctification of a Day in the Cloister, and Suggestions for little practices of Devotion.
12. On Sickness—the Love of the Cross—the Interior Life—and of general and particular Temptations.
13. Of Imperfect Religious—of Fervour and Tepidity—of True and False Piety—and of True and False Detachment.
14. Of Confession and Manifestation of Conscience.
15. Of the Chapter of Faults, and of the practice of Exterior and Interior Penance.
16. Of Peace, the fruit of Mortification.

It is hoped that this volume will soon be ready for publication.

The Memorare Mass. 2d.

The object of this little work is to offer a form of hearing Mass in honour of Our Lady, in which each prayer concludes with the *Memorare.*

Historical Works and General Literature.

Now Publishing,

A NEW HISTORY OF IRELAND.

THE

HISTORY OF THE IRISH NATION,

Social, Ecclesiastical, Biographical, Industrial, and Antiquarian,

WITH FORTY FULL-PAGE ENGRAVINGS OF NATIONAL EVENTS OR CELEBRATED ANTIQUITIES,

AND MORE THAN

THREE HUNDRED ILLLUSTRATIONS

OF IRISH ANTIQUITIES, ROUND TOWERS, RUINED ABBEYS, ANTIQUARIAN
REMAINS, ANCIENT URNS AND DRINKING VESSELS, &c., &c.

This work is the first Irish History ever published dealing in detail with every subject of Irish history and Irish art.

An English writer has said lately, " Politicians may have in future to take into account not merely the Irish vote in Parliament, but the Anglo-Irish vote in the constituencies of Great Britain."— *Graphic*, August 1876. Let Irishmen, then, learn to know the history of their nation, its claims to antiquity, to early culture, and its unflinching devotion to the faith. In the present work they have the fruit of years of patient study, and, at a comparatively trifling expense, the information to be obtained only from rare and costly volumes, to which few indeed have access, and which enables the reader to have the full value for a few shillings of what would cost hundreds of pounds.

To Englishmen, whatever their political or religious opinions may be, the study of Irish history is as much a duty to themselves as to Ireland.

Conditions of Publication.—This work will be issued in Forty 1s. Numbers, or Eight 5s. Parts. A large and magnificent illustration will be given gratuitously with the last number.

The principal object of the writer of this work has been to supply a History which should take the place of one written by an English Protestant, and published in a more expensive form. Though the writer ill conceals his bitterness against the Catholic clergy, denies the antiquity of our most authentic MS. and historical remains, and invariably speaks of the Irish as rebels and heretics, the work has had a large circulation, principally, we believe, because there was no Catholic or national work to offer as a substitute for it.

Now Publishing, uniform with the above,

The Trias Thaumaturga; or, The Lives of St. Patrick, St. Bridget, and St. Columba.

This work will be issued also in **Forty Shilling Numbers,** and **Eight Monthly Parts at 5s. each,** richly illustrated with scenes from the lives of these Saints.

Every Irishman should secure this most valuable and important work. It is based upon rare and authentic manuscripts, on costly works of which there are not half-a-dozen copies in the United Kingdom, and the use of which can only be obtained with great difficulty. The *Hymn of St. Patrick going to Tara,* and other most interesting and ancient pieces, will be contained in this volume. Also the *Hymn of St. Bridget,* which tells of miracles, her goodness to the poor, and her great sanctity.

The value and importance of this work to antiquarians and hagiographers can scarcely be over-estimated. It will contain well-authenticated and important documents of the fourth, fifth, and sixth centuries, which throw a flood of light, not only upon the histories of the Saints of that age, but also upon liturgical uses and ecclesiastical customs.

HISTORICAL WORKS

ALREADY PUBLISHED.

O'CONNELL'S PARLIAMENTARY AND PUBLIC SPEECHES.

HIS LETTERS TO THE PEOPLE OF IRELAND.

HIS LETTER TO THE LATE RIGHT REV. DR. BLAKE, ON THE SECESSION OF THE YOUNG IRELAND PARTY.

HIS FAMOUS LETTER TO LORD SHREWSBURY.

HIS FAMOUS CONTROVERSIAL LETTER TO DR. DALY.

In 2 Vols. Demy 8vo, 1200 pp. Price 12s. each Vol.

O'CONNELL'S SPEECHES.

O'CONNELL'S PARLIAMENTARY SPEECHES.

O'CONNELL'S LETTERS TO THE PEOPLE OF IRELAND.

O'CONNELL'S FAMOUS CONTROVERSIAL LETTERS TO DR. DALY.

O'CONNELL'S LETTER TO THE RIGHT REV. DR. BLAKE, ON THE SECESSION OF THE YOUNG IRELAND PARTY—A STARTLING AND MOST IMPORTANT DOCUMENT.

O'CONNELL'S LETTERS ON INDEPENDENT PARLIAMENTARY OPPOSITION.

O'CONNELL'S DEFENCE OF THE EDUCATION AND INTELLECTUAL STATUS OF THE CATHOLIC PRIESTHOOD.

O'CONNELL ON REPEAL OF THE UNION.

☞ The public are cautioned against purchasing Works which are offered as a cheap substitute for these Volumes, and which do not contain even one of these valuable Speeches or Letters.

The Letters, having been obtained from private sources, are copyright.

The Liberator, his Life and Times : Political, Social, and Religious. New Library Edition, Seventh Thousand. Two Vols. ; 12s. each Vol.

OPINIONS OF THE PRESS.

"It is appropriate, according to our thinking, that this Liberator of the Altars of God should have his utterances and his writings at last collected together and systematically arranged by the hands of a nun. And it is in accordance with the fitness of things, in the instance of the good and gifted Nun of Kenmare, that one of the crowning labours of her intellectual and industrious life should be the production of these noble volumes."—*Weekly Register* (London).

"A more energetic Pamphlet (O'Connell's Letter to Lord Shrewsbury, contained in these volumes) never was written. An extract from this celebrated letter must conclude our notice of Miss Cusack's volumes. They are the last and not the least of her valuable labours, and they help to make her remarkable as combining in a very unusual degree the qualities suited to a religious life and literary career."—*Tablet* (London).

The Illustrated History of Ireland. Tenth Thousand, demy 8vo, 700 pages, 10s. cloth ; gilt, 12s.

"We have already introduced Miss Cusack, in a late number, to our readers as eminently the literary nun of the age ; and we told them that her cell in the Convent of Poor Clares, at Kenmare, is no place of indolent repose, but a genuine place of study, a literary workshop of no common merit, as proved by her 'Life of St. Patrick.' To-day we have to bring before their notice the same lady, not as a biographer, but as an historian. Miss Cusack has devoted herself heart and soul to works of charity and mercy, and who has been able to combine with those works a devotion to the Muse of History, and which we do not often see realised, except in such persons as Miss Strickland, Miss Everett Green, and Mrs. Cowden Clarke. Miss Cusack is not overstating her case when she claims for herself the credit of having written the first life of the great 'Apostle of Ireland' which has 'given full details of his acts and missionary labours,' as it is certainly the first in which a real practical use has been made of the materials at hand."—*Illustrated Review* (London).

A HISTORY OF THE KINGDOM OF KERRY. 8vo. Illustrated with wood engravings of remarkable sites and antiquities. On toned paper. Price 20s., cloth lettered. Now price 30s., as few copies remain on hands.

A HISTORY OF THE COUNTY AND CITY OF CORK. Demy 8vo, magnificently illustrated. 25s.

This work contains a Chapter on Geology, by the Rev R. Close, M.R.I.A., and on the Flora and Fauna, by Dr. Harvey and Mr. Isaac Carroll. It also contains histories and genealogies of all the Southern Septs—the MacCarthys, O'Sullivans, Murphys, O'Driscolls, Donovans, &c., &c.

"This magnificent volume forms one of the most remarkable and comprehensive of the many valuable works for which we are indebted to the indefatigable pen of the gifted 'Nun of Kenmare.'"—*Weekly Register.*

OPINIONS OF THE PRESS ON MISS CUSACK'S HISTORICAL WORKS.

"Much of the nonsense which has been spoken and written regarding Ireland for the last two years has arisen from ignorance of Irish History. Miss Cusack's volume will help to remove this, as well as for educational purposes."—*London Examiner.*

"Miss Cusack's work will repay a perusal."—*Evening Standard.*

"A great many points in a small compass. The narrative, though condensed, is not reduced to dryness."—*Daily News.*

"Moderate, clear, and purposeful."—*Daily Telegraph.*

"A very valuable book."—*Catholic Opinion.*

"The research, the care, the intelligence necessary to the production of such a work as that before us are remarkable, and Miss Cusack has demonstrated that she possesses the highest capacity for works of this kind. We are sure that amongst the many student's histories now published, Miss Cusack's History of Ireland will deservedly occupy a high place."—*Civil Service Gazette.*

"A very useful and desirable work."—*Literary World.*

"This lady has contributed more than one book of note to our libraries, one of which, a 'Life of St. Patrick,' we lately reviewed at length. The present volume is one which will not lower her literary character. As a compilation it is terse and well constructed, and in that part of the history which deals with the actions of William of Orange in Ireland, she is far more generous in her tone than could have been expected."—*Church Times.*

"The purchaser of this large and handsome volume will find (firstly) that he has it cheaper than he would obtain Froude's Falsehoods for ; (secondly) that it has illustrations, some of which, like the 'Crowning of O'Connell,' are of real beauty.

"We have taken occasion, before this, to call attention to the public service which Sister Mary Frances Cusack has been doing to her country in this way. By her energy and enterprise, as well as by her literary abilities, she has been infusing home life and spirit into these classes, and insisting on their helping to clear off some of their own dishonour. The very worthy gentlemen who conduct the various publishing establishments are all put to shame by one lady. If at Limerick 'the women fought before the men,' as Davis says, at least they had the comfort of knowing that 'each man became a match for ten'—which is not yet the case in the publishing trade, though we hope it may be. The various ladies who talk so eloquently concerning Woman's Rights may learn a lesson from seeing how this woman achieves her Right—by writing herself !

"There was no market open to her, any more than to others who, in Ireland, produced books—yet she, a cloistered nun, in a remote convent, has laboured so wisely and so perseveringly as to make for her works a market. She deserves success, for she has conquered it.

"Her works have a good wholesome Irish spirit in them. Whether it be a Romance, a contribution to Hagiology, a History, or a Biography—an Irish heart inspires all, an Irish pulse beats through all, an Irish spirit quickens all."—*The Irishman* [Dublin].

www.ingramcontent.com/pod-product-compliance
Lightning Source LLC
Chambersburg PA
CBHW021056030726
47496CB00006B/1860